Romance
in My
RAMBLER

Romance in My RAMBLER

DAVID A. BOURBON

authorHOUSE®

AuthorHouse™
1663 Liberty Drive
Bloomington, IN 47403
www.authorhouse.com
Phone: 1 (800) 839-8640

Romance in My Rambler is the first book in The Class President Series (www.theclasspresidentseries.com). The series follows David A. Bourbon's life to the end. It is a book of fiction inspired by true events. Names, characters, and events are creations of the author's imagination. Any resemblance to actual events, locales, or people, living or dead, is entirely coincidental.

Published by AuthorHouse 05/14/2015

ISBN: 978-1-5049-0360-8 (sc)
ISBN: 978-1-5049-0361-5 (hc)
ISBN: 978-1-5049-0362-2 (e)

Library of Congress Control Number: 2015904688

Print information available on the last page.

Any people depicted in stock imagery provided by Thinkstock are models, and such images are being used for illustrative purposes only. Certain stock imagery © Thinkstock.

This book is printed on acid-free paper.

Because of the dynamic nature of the Internet, any web addresses or links contained in this book may have changed since publication and may no longer be valid. The views expressed in this work are solely those of the author and do not necessarily reflect the views of the publisher, and the publisher hereby disclaims any responsibility for them.

To all the 1965 high school graduating classes

To the baby boomers

If you meet a jolly fellow with a twinkle in his eye,
Do not think he's always happy and has no cause to cry.
He has faced some grief and sorrows just as you and I have done,
But he's learned life has its problems, and
he's fought them one by one.
He has met a disappointment as he went along his way,
And like us, he too has witnessed a dark night as well as day.
So if you should meet a fellow who is cheerful all the while,
Be assured there could be teardrops he
could shed instead of a smile.

CONTENTS

CHAPTER 1

The Devil's Pit

"Davey, take the end of the fork and press it around the edges of the pie crust," Mom said as she held my wrist. Her caress was strong but gentle, and I felt safe. Only mothers know how to do that. I was standing on a stool next to the white porcelain kitchen sink. I was five years old, and Mom was twenty-eight. *The Howdy Doody Show* was playing in the background on our radio.

Dorothy Bourbon had dark-brown, curly hair that fell slightly off her shoulders. She wore a white scarf tied in a knot on the back of her head to keep her hair out of her face. Mom's red apron with a small white-flower print and two big pockets with bows fit tightly around her slim waist. The apron fit over her shoulders and around her slender neck like an evening gown. Even at five years old, I knew Mom was beautiful.

The smell of flour and sliced apples permeated our small duplex. Mom's dress and kitchen spoke of strength and order. Heavy iron or steel pots and pans all had their places. Mom knew exactly how to cook an apple pie. There was no uncertainty. As the conductor of our kitchen, Mom reassured me that all was well: whatever awaited me outside would not dare venture into our kitchen.

All appliances in those days were durable. Our fifties kitchen included a white gas stove, a Norge refrigerator, and an ugly white-and-brown checkered linoleum floor. The light-green Formica top on our kitchen table could take the abuse of a five-year-old boy, and of course, it didn't match the kitchen decor. Our black metal oscillating fan made the kitchen habitable as it hummed away on this hot August day. We had neither plastic fans nor air-conditioning in those days.

My dad, Ham Bourbon, was an electrical contractor. Dad had returned from World War II, and Mom had left her job at the Veterans Administration Hospital to raise a family. The men were at work. It was Saturday morning, and the men worked on Saturdays. Only Sunday was a day off in small-town America.

After diligently working my way around the pie crust, I moved out of Mom's way as she carefully placed the filling into the pan and began lacing the pie with strips of dough. I poured Kellogg's Frosted Flakes of "Tony the Tiger" fame into a bowl. I pulled out a quart bottle of whole milk from the refrigerator and poured it into my cereal bowl. The milkman delivered our Borden milk in round, reusable glass bottles every Monday, Wednesday, and Friday. I returned the milk to the refrigerator. Then I sat down, ate my cereal, and listened to *The Howdy Doody Show* as Mom finished the pie.

After eating every flake of my cereal, I said, "Mom, I'm going to Mary's house to play."

"Okay, Davey, be careful. I'll be down after I get the pie in the oven and clean up some," Mom replied.

I left my house wearing a plaid yellow-and-green shirt and tan shorts with my Daniel Boone belt. I stepped over my toy rifle and a riding stick with a stuffed horse head on the end. Toys were scattered all over my neighborhood. My red Western Flyer tricycle with a bent front fender became the next obstacle to dodge. I had made this three-hundred-foot journey to Mary's house many times, so I knew every neighbor, tree, and toy along the way.

Mom and Dad rented half of a duplex on Hickory Avenue in Hopewell, Kentucky. Hopewell was a small town of eight thousand people in the middle of thoroughbred country, and it was outlined by rolling hills, curvy roads, and majestic limestone fences. Its people were descendants of hardy pioneers, and my determined parents and grandparents had endured with their neighbors the Roaring Twenties, Prohibition (1920–1933), the Wall Street crash of 1929, World War I, and World War II. Our single-story home had three big rooms: a living room, a bedroom, and a kitchen. It also had a bathroom with a heavy porcelain tub. I slept in a single bed in the same room as my mom and dad.

As I briskly walked down my street, I passed one- and two-story white-clapboard duplexes and Victorian-style single houses. Neighbors were often sitting on their porches to combat the summer heat, but no one was out that day. The structure of the houses and Hickory Avenue itself provided the stage for friendly interactions among the neighbors. In the summer, doors and windows were always open, and the sounds of radios and people talking filled my street. I was proud of my street; it was alive and friendly. And at five years old, I was beginning to master it.

My street was lined with big oak and maple trees. I played around those trees daily. I climbed them and inspected their bark and leaves. I liked the clever design of trees. They were flexible and strong. The intricate veins in the leaves revealed the system that gave them life. I relished the sound of the trees embraced by the gentle breezes. They also changed colors so gracefully. The trees on my street had endured the seasons and watched history—including proud Indian tribes and Model T Fords—and witnessed triumph and tragedy as the people of the neighborhood, including me, lived out their lives. Trees were our cousins, and I subconsciously knew it even at five years old.

As I approached Mary's two-story house, I looked for my playmates, Mary Hallman and Henry Peterson, but they were not outside yet. Mary was five years old, and Henry was six. I stood in the driveway and gazed at Mary's house, which overwhelmed my street. I thought Mary's parents were rich because they owned their house while most people on the street rented. Her house had a steep, black roof. The many gables over the second story windows made the house look ominous. A side porch off the kitchen wrapped around to the front porch and overlooked the gravel driveway. Mary's house had been built in the twenties and had been painted white many times, probably with lead-based paint. Her Victorian-style house was made of robust timber, much like the hardiness of local people.

The old cistern next to Mary's kitchen porch had not been used for decades. A rusty steel top covered the cistern except for a small center hole that was covered by wood. The wood had big cracks and gashes that documented its fight against decades of harsh weather, people, and animals. Before the days of the municipal water supply, buckets used to pass through this smaller opening.

My playmates and I were curious about the cistern. We would bang on the steel covering and hear the hollow echoes. We wondered how deep this well went into the earth. I thought the cistern might be a gateway to hell. We called the cistern the "devil's pit," and it was the biggest demon we faced in our young lives. It was one door we couldn't open. *What nightmarish creatures live there? Could these creatures get out at night and get us?*

My moments of reflection were interrupted by Henry running toward me, yelling, "Hey, Bourbon, where's Mary?" He skidded to a stop in front of me.

I replied, "Let's go get her."

Henry was a tall, skinny kid with brown hair and blue eyes, like me. He wore a plain green T-shirt and brown shorts. We knocked on Mary's front door, and immediately a cute five-year-old girl opened the door and walked out. Mary had very short, red hair and faint freckles. She was wearing a yellow T-shirt and black shorts, and Mary looked exactly like a boy. All of our clothes were from the local J. C. Penney and Sears stores on Main Street, and we seldom cared if they matched.

"What do you want to do today?" I asked as we stood on Mary's front porch.

"Let's go down to the school playground," Mary said.

"No. It's too far to walk, and we'll have to ask our parents," I replied.

"Why don't we see who can jump over the well from the porch," Henry suggested.

"Okay, that sounds like fun," I replied.

The three of us walked around the porch to see our launching pad as Mary trailed behind us. The kitchen porch area was about five feet high. The devil's pit looked benign with its locked steel cover and the wood covering the small hole in the middle. We had played on top of and around the cistern many times, but we had never thought to jump over it from the side porch.

"Henry, you go first," Mary said.

Henry walked up the steps with his lanky legs to the edge of the porch. He stopped and pulled out a bubble-gum package from his pocket as he pondered this challenge. The kitchen door was closed, so Mary's mom could not see or hear us. Henry opened the bubble gum and popped it into his mouth.

"Mark my spot when I hit the ground," Henry declared with a brave smile. With arms swinging and all the power his body could muster, he jumped over the cistern. With a thud, Henry hit the gravel driveway about one foot beyond the cistern. I marked the spot as a line in the gravel with the heel of my black-and-white Converse gym shoes.

"Mary, it's your turn," Henry said in a rushed voice as he tried to calm down from the adrenaline surge and his leap of faith.

"I'm not going to jump. If I fall in, I'm afraid the devil will get me," Mary responded.

Henry and I shrugged; we knew it might be too demanding a feat for "a girl." Of course, we had no fear or experience. From the five-foot-high porch, the steel well cover could definitely hurt someone if you hit it in the wrong way.

"Okay, David. It's your turn," Henry said. I stood at the base of the steps. I wasn't so sure about today's adventure, but I didn't want to be viewed as a coward by my playmates. I didn't want to twist my knee or scrape my arms. But Henry had overcome today's challenge, so I could too.

I climbed the steps and approached the edge of the porch with the caution of an Olympic diver. Swinging my arms in a rhythmic manner to build momentum, I ascended into the air and then began to fall. My two feet crashed squarely through the middle of the small rickety cistern cover. The ancient wood shattered into many pieces with a splintering sound. My legs, arms, and head plunged through the hole as if the devil had planned it. I was gone. I had vanished into the devil's pit.

The story of what happened next is the cumulative wisdom of people who were there. I remember nothing after I fell in.

Mary and Henry stood in stunned silence for a few seconds, hoping they had imagined my fall into the well. I was gone, and not one word came from the selfish cistern. I did not scream. They only heard a faint splash that echoed once within the cistern. The devil's pit had taken me for its own.

"David? David, can you hear us?" Mary and Henry yelled as they approached the edge of the cistern's steel cover. They dared not walk on the steel cistern cover or peer down the small black hole that had been covered in wood for fear it would collapse.

A horrified Mary screamed to her mother, "Mommy, Mommy! David fell in the well!"

Henry ran to get his mom.

Mary's mom burst out of the kitchen door. Some shards of wood lay on the steel cistern in a random pattern. She knelt on the steel cistern cover, peeked into the well, and yelled, "David, David, are you all right? Talk to me! Talk to me!" But there were no sounds coming from hell's entryway. Mary's mom could not see the bottom of the well, so she ran to call the Hopewell Fire Department. She frantically thumbed through the yellow-and-black phone book to find the telephone number.

"Hopewell Fire Department."

"I'm Betty Hallman at 104 Hickory Avenue. David Bourbon has fallen into the well outside our house," she said, sobbing all the while.

"Betty, can you see into the well? Can you hear anything?" asked the fireman.

"No! He must be unconscious and drowning! Hurry!"

"We'll be there in less than ten minutes." Betty and the fireman hung up the telephone.

Betty ran onto the porch and down the steps. She grabbed Mary by both arms and said, "Go get Mrs. Bourbon now! Tell her David fell in the cistern!" Betty knelt by the cistern again and called, "David, David, honey, please say something!"

Mary started running down the street, dodging tricycles and toys. Mary burst through the open front door of my duplex and blurted, "David fell in the well. Hurry!"

Mom, who was washing dishes, dropped a glass on that ugly linoleum floor. She ran down the street, throwing her apron and headscarf to the ground as she ran. By the time Mom reached the cistern, she was gasping for air. Tears rolled down her face. Mom knelt down on the rickety cistern top and looked down into it. She yelled down into the black abyss, "David, oh, my son! Where are you?"

Dorothy looked up at the sky with torrents of tears streaming down her face and said, "Oh, dear God. Please, please save my son! You can take him later. Please!"

Helpless, my mom knelt next to the small, dark hole, shrieking into the devil's pit. But there was only silence. Then Mom stood up and tried to put her body down the hole, but she couldn't fit. She cut both her thighs and tore the bottom of her polka-dot dress. Next she tried to break the rusted steel hinges and lock, but she cut her hands. She was oblivious to the crowd around her. The neighbors watched as the situation intensified, and Mom's blood dripped on the cistern's steel top. The devil's pit would not let her in.

Betty stood to the side of the well, wringing her hands and trying to keep her weight off the cistern top as she talked to Dorothy.

"Dorothy, I've called the fire department." Betty was crying, but with all the confidence she could gather, she added, "They're coming. They can get him. You should get off the top of that well. It could collapse."

Neighbors began to come out of their houses—women, kids, and a few elderly folk. Their windows and doors were open on that hot summer day to let in the cool morning air, and they heard the commotion.

Henry and his mom had returned and stood nearby, holding each other.

Mothers hugged their kids, and grandmothers hugged their daughters. A black beetle about two inches long meandered across the cistern cover. The beetle, and nature itself, ignored the tragedy around it.

A small crowd of neighbors and kids surrounded Mom on the cistern, but none were able to pry her away. Mom knelt on the cistern top like an angel outside the gates to hell. Mom was crying and calling my name down the small black hole. Her blood was smeared over her and the cistern top. Mom's blood mixed with cistern rust to create a thick ooze, an ominous sign of the battle taking place between life and death.

None of the neighbors were brave enough, athletic enough, or small enough to squeeze through that small hole. People were weeping and hugging one another. One elderly neighbor lit a Chesterfield cigarette. Minutes were passing, and so was my chance for life. The neighbor smoked her cigarette, put it out, and lit another. No fire department yet.

A neighbor saw Tommy Holmes, a fourteen-year-old lifeguard at the YMCA pool, walking down the street. "Tommy, come here! Help! We need your help."

Tommy ran over to the cistern and quickly understood the situation. Immediately, Tommy tried to force his body through the hole, but the hole was too small. Only a child's little body would fit through. Tommy scraped his hips. Blood from Mom and Tommy covered the steel cistern top.

A neighbor ran to get a hammer from her car and handed it to Tommy. He banged at the rusted lock, but it would not break. The banging brought more neighbors to the cistern.

The devil was winning.

A bell clanged in the distance. The Hopewell fire truck was coming. Thinking that it might help him squeeze through the hole, Tommy was taking off his clothes—except for his shorts—as the fire truck arrived.

"Get me a sledgehammer and the big crowbar," one of the firemen yelled.

The crowd backed away because my rescue depended on the abilities of these three firemen.

A potbellied fireman hugged Mom as he lifted her off the cistern top. Another hit the lock with all his might. Bang! Bang! The sound echoed up and down the devil's pit like a wailing animal. The small crowd backed farther away. Some held their hands to their ears to muffle the banging sound. The cistern prison would not yield its prey. But on the fifth try, the fireman broke the lock. "Get the crowbar. Let's raise the lid. Get the ladder!"

Two firemen lifted the steel cover and laid it on the ground, its hinges squeaking like the devil's guardians. The third fireman ran to the truck to get a ladder.

The ugly nature of the devil's pit was now revealed. Ragged walls and slimy moss bricks jutted out here and there. The well was about seven feet in diameter. The well water was silent, motionless, and black. It entombed my body. The ladder reached the water's surface about ten feet down. The fireman anchored the ladder to the ground with two big hooks and ropes tied to the fire truck.

Tommy climbed down the ladder to a few feet above the top of the water.

"We forgot to put a rope on Tommy," one of the firemen shouted. It was too late. Tommy jumped into the water, which was later estimated to be twelve feet deep. He dived down into the black water without knowing its depth or what was below.

A minute passed, and Tommy was still down there. Then two minutes passed. "I can't find him," Tommy yelled as he resurfaced after his first dive. His hands and arms were covered in slime.

But on the second dive, Tommy found my feet on the bottom. He grasped my muddy foot and pulled me to the surface. Tommy swam to the ladder and began to bring me up feet first. The fireman grabbed Tommy's shoulders and arms and began to pull him up while Tommy held on to me. As soon as they got me on the ground, the firemen began to resuscitate me.

My lifeless five-year-old body was a dull blue and covered in slime. My clothes were still on, including my Converse gym shoes. The cistern water was cold.

Tommy stood nearby with goose bumps on his body and a towel wrapped around him as the morning sun rose in the sky.

A sturdy woman who lived nearby whispered to the chain-smoking neighbor, "He's dead."

"I cain't find a pulse on this kid," one fireman said as two of them continued to work on me.

Mom stood over me in shock. She had unexpectedly stopped sobbing. Betty hugged her and gave her a towel to help stop her bleeding. The neighbors kept their distance as the tragedy played out.

After several minutes of using a resuscitator on me, I lurched forward slightly, raising my head from the ground. With a huge belch, I spit out black well water mixed with green slime and began breathing at a very feeble rate. I remained unconscious, and my eyes did not open. I was rushed to the hospital by the ambulance that had arrived after the fire truck. Mom went with me in the ambulance. They gave me oxygen on the way to the hospital.

A neighbor had called my dad at work. They told him to go to the hospital. When he arrived at the hospital, he was still wearing his electrician's work belt with pliers and screwdriver. He met Mom in the emergency room. They hugged and watched as the doctor and nurses worked on me. My wet clothes and shoes were in a pile on the floor. The frailty of my young body was revealed.

"Mr. and Mrs. Bourbon, your son is breathing better now. But he was not awake when he arrived at the hospital, and we gave him medication to make sure he sleeps. We'll keep him in the oxygen tent," the doctor said. He was doing his residency at our hospital. Small towns didn't get doctors who specialized in drowning. "And your son's jaw is locked shut. I need to get this tube down his throat. If I can't, I'll have to break his teeth—and maybe his jaw."

"Okay, do what you have to do," Dad replied as he held Mom within five feet of my motionless body. The doctor carefully forced the tube down my throat through a small opening between my upper and lower teeth. After a few hours in the emergency room, I was moved to an intensive care bed. Nurses and doctors watched me constantly, and Mom and Dad hovered around my bedside.

"The doctor would like to speak to you," the intensive care nurse said. "He's waiting for you outside in the hallway lounge." Holding hands and in a state of shock, they met him in the hallway lounge.

"Your son could have permanent brain damage," the doctor said. He glanced into Dad's eyes and then looked down at his shoes. "David was under water for over ten minutes, and his brain was not getting oxygen."

Mom cried, and Dad tried not to. Their little Davey might never be the same. They tried not to imagine what bodily functions or capabilities their son might lose.

"We understand, Doctor. How long will you keep him sedated?" Dad asked.

Mom raised her hands to cover the anguish in her face.

"We'll reduce the medication tomorrow and see if he regains consciousness. You're welcome to stay the night in the hospital," the doctor replied. "Mrs. Bourbon, we need to clean your cuts and get some iodine and bandages on them. I'll have the nurse come by and do this for you now. I don't think you need stitches."

Mom nodded and sat back in the hospital lounge sofa.

"Who was watching them play?" Dad asked with a frown.

"Betty," Mom replied.

"Dammit, you can't leave kids unsupervised," Dad yelled.

Mom and Dad did not leave the hospital. Dad called a neighbor and asked her to go into the duplex, clean up the kitchen, close the windows, and lock the doors. She brought my parents each a change of clothes and other items for their overnight hospital stay. The fire department welded a steel plate over the cistern. No more accidents would happen there. The gateway to the devil's pit was closed.

On Sunday morning, about twenty-four hours after the accident, the doctors reduced my medicine. The intensive care hospital bed and room was functional and stark; it had witnessed many similar scenes. Late that afternoon, I began to wake up. The nurse ran down to the lounge to get Mom and Dad.

Mom, Dad, my doctor, and the nurse watched as I began to move my legs and arms.

"Arbles the waken," I mumbled as my head moved from side to side. "Berk-eh-sock, yelp!" It soon became obvious I was fighting the water and having a nightmare.

"Nurse, let's put him back to sleep," the doctor quickly ordered.

Mom and Dad were both upset. The possibility of brain damage seemed more real than ever.

"We need to wake him again in twenty-four hours," the doctor said. "It's hard to tell if this is a good sign or bad sign for David's recovery." He tried not to look Mom and Dad in the eyes. The doctor kept me asleep for another day while everyone in Hopewell waited and prayed.

Mom and Dad took turns going home for a few hours while the other stayed by my bedside. Flowers and cards arrived in my room.

Relatives and friends visited the hospital but were not allowed in the intensive care area.

Mary and Henry and their parents were allowed a special visit to my room. "Dot, I'm so sorry. I was cooking and had the kitchen door closed. Otherwise, I would have seen what they were going to do and stopped it," Mrs. Hallman said in a defeated voice. "I'm sorry, and I pray every day for David's full recovery." She hugged my mom.

Mom was silent, and Dad left the room.

The story was front-page news in the *Hopewell Enterprise*. Dad closed his business for a week. The minister came by and led Mom and Dad in prayers beside my bed. Our church, the Hopewell First Christian Church, held a special prayer session for me during their Sunday morning service. Only this small town knew, for now, what was happening; the rest of the world hummed along, not knowing or caring about one five-year-old's life in small-town America.

Early Monday morning, the doctors in the hospital decided to reduce my sleeping medication again. "It will take a few hours—or even days—to see if your son suffered brain damage," the doctor said. "So if he wakes up and wants to talk, please don't show extreme emotion or do anything to upset him. David may have lost his ability to speak or hear. I know you will hug him and love him, and that is all you need to do. Give him time."

At nine o'clock that evening, the hospital nurse said, "Mrs. Bourbon, David's arms moved." For the next hour, they watched me begin to stir. Sometimes my body moved in small jerks, and sometimes my legs would slowly drag across the heavily starched hospital sheets.

About an hour later, my eyes opened. I moved my head slowly from left to right and found the faces of Mom and Dad standing at my bedside. "Mom, Dad," I whispered.

"Hi, sweetie. We love you!" Mom said.

I gave them a blank stare.

After a long pause, Dad finally said, "How do you feel?"

"Fine, Dad."

All three of us hugged. Mom and Dad were crying, and I was still trying to figure out what the fuss was about. The doctor entered the room and said, "Is everything all right? David, are you okay?"

"Yes, Doctor. I'm okay, but I'm thirsty," I said.

The doctor gave me a cup of water. He smiled at Mom and Dad. "I'll come back later to check him out." He told the nurses to give us some time before he examined me.

"Mom, what happened?"

"You had an accident. You fell in Mary's cistern. You're in the hospital."

I said nothing. Mom could see I was trying to rethink my whereabouts.

"Do you remember the accident?" Dad asked as he held my hand.

"No." I frowned, trying to recall what actually happened. My parents were silent but smiling all the time. I took another big drink of water and pushed the sheets down to my waist.

A few minutes later, my dad said, "When we get home, I'm going to cover you in newspapers." Dad would often wrestle with me on the floor at home. I played dead, and he would cover me in newspapers. This activity had become a Sunday morning ritual.

"Yeah? I'll punch you in the nose!" I said in a defiant voice. And then Mom and Dad started crying. They knew their little David was okay.

Later, the doctor came in, checked my vital signs and reflexes, and talked with me for a while. I did not remember anything about that dreadful day. My mind was locked shut—just like the steel cover on the cistern. It would not let anyone back into the devil's pit, including me.

The next morning, the doctor checked me out one last time. "Mr. and Mrs. Bourbon, David's recovery is a miracle. I think the water being cold and his jaw being locked shut helped him survive much longer than normal," the doctor said as he signed the discharge papers.

That afternoon, we went home to the cheers of the hospital staff. People outside the isolated world of Hopewell, Kentucky, began to learn of this drama. First, Mom and Dad had the *Hopewell Enterprise* publish a thank-you note to the people involved in saving me. The newspaper began a campaign to gain special recognition for fourteen-year-old Tommy Holmes. They appealed to the Carnegie Foundation to award a medal to Tommy for his role in saving my life. Established in 1904, the Carnegie Hero Fund Commission of Pittsburgh, Pennsylvania, awarded medals for acts of heroism. To qualify for the medal, a person must risk his or her own life to an extraordinary degree to save another. The Hopewell Chamber of Commerce, the newspaper, and numerous residents wrote letters to the commission in support of awarding a medal to Mr. Holmes. Tommy was awarded the Carnegie Hero Medal on Friday, October 31, 1952.

Mom wrote to a national television show about how Tommy saved my life. She wrote, "Tommy had absolutely no way of knowing his fate at the bottom of that well. He didn't know if the water was two or twenty feet deep. He went after my son anyway—with no hesitation. He found David's little feet at the bottom of that well and did the smart thing by pulling him out feet first. He saved my son's life."

Tommy was invited to appear on a coast-to-coast TV show, *Kids and Company*. Tommy and his mother got an all-expenses-paid trip to New York to appear on the show. The show awarded Tommy a bicycle, a watch, a cocker spaniel puppy, and a case of dog food. His mom received pearls and earrings. The US Junior Chamber of Commerce gave him a special citation for heroism on the show.

I was given the most precious gift—my life and a chance to live it. I had no idea at the time of the turbulence ahead.

Meanwhile, many social and military realities were taking place in 1952–54. I vaguely understood some of these events because my parents discussed them at the dinner table every night. Dad had been in the US Marine Corps during World War II and had strong opinions. Mom was his equal in the family debates. I remember family debates over the Communist threat, the beatnik movement, and civil rights issues. These conversations were far from being at the PhD level, but ideas and opinions sailed across the Formica kitchen table night after night. I sometimes would go to bed pondering these issues. I learned to hate the Communists, question the needless violence of the civil rights movement, and recognize the option of a beatnik lifestyle. Much later in life, I realized you need an anchor in life to meet its challenges, and I was building mine.

We moved away from the devil's pit. The memories were too troublesome—echoes from the soulless cistern, the chaotic rescue, and my lifeless blue body. I had no recollections of any of these events, but my parents did. Mom and Dad had many sleepless nights after the accident. Dad eventually regained normal sleep patterns, but Mom did not. The dark abyss that had taken her son would frighten her at night for decades. My family moved in the spring of 1953 to a new house across town.

But the devil's pit never left me. It resurfaces, on and off, to this day. In fact, I was constantly confronted with the devil getting me in my new house in Hopewell. Our new two-story asbestos-shingled house on Fourteenth Street was twenty-four feet by thirty feet, and I lived in a basement bedroom. One half of the basement on the back of the house was exposed to the outside, and the street side was underground. The first floor had two small bedrooms, a living room, the kitchen, and a full bathroom. The house was about 150 feet from the Hopewell railroad yard, so the hum of the trains, like the hum of the fans, often lulled me to sleep at night.

The houses on Fourteenth Street were a mixture of single-room railroad row houses left over from past eras, small, ratty white-clapboard houses, and a couple of upscale stone or red-brick homes. Like my past neighbors, families on my street worked in Main Street retail stores, in the Hopewell lumber and grain mills, in warehouses adjacent to the railroad, and in the railroad yard.

My downstairs bedroom had steep wooden steps to the upstairs, a door to the unfinished side of the basement, and a rickety door to the storage room under the front porch. Being a seven-year-old kid, I never liked that storage room door and seldom opened it because I thought the devil could come through the ground and into that room to reclaim me while I was asleep. It was an old fear in a new house. I always watched for shadows around that basement storage door and often imagined it opening by itself. I never told anyone about this fear. Intermittent nightmares throughout my life have ensured I'll never forget. When I wake up in a cold sweat and jump out of bed to defend myself against the darkness, I know that the devil's pit resides in the back of my mind.

My sixth birthday was a celebration of life—my life. Mom organized a big birthday party in August 1953 and invited about forty kids, relatives, and friends. She also invited a few firemen, police officers, and hospital staff to the party. Each of these individuals had witnessed some part of that cistern accident. The party was held in the home of my mom's parents. Nannie and Clarence Burk lived next to the Duncan River and Hopewell's water plant. River-fed oak and maple trees overhung the white-clapboard house with its big screened porch along one side. Black awnings protected the windows since there was no air conditioning. My party was the simplest of celebrations, but everyone knew it was much more.

They came in a variety of cars and trucks: Hudsons, Chevrolets, Packards, Fords, Oldsmobiles, and one police car. The policemen ran the police car lights and allowed the kids to crawl over this symbol of law and order. The police car was most popular among us kids, but I also liked a 1952 DeSoto that the parents of one of my friends drove. I felt grown up because Mom dressed me in a starched white shirt and a pair of dress blue jeans with skinny suspenders. It was my first time wearing suspenders; only men wore suspenders.

I remember fishing for prizes. Mom and Dad hung up a sheet, and kids took turns using a cane pole to throw over the sheet to fish for prizes. When we felt a tug on the pole, we pulled it up and caught a prize. After the fishing tournament, we competed in relay races for more prizes. I recall the glistening birthday cake and the six burning candles. The cake sat on a round, three-legged knotty-pine table about a foot in diameter. A crowd of well-wishers surrounded me, and with a mighty puff, I blew out the candles. The glow of life was around me.

My first year of school began in September 1953. The year 1953 saw Dwight D. Eisenhower sworn in as the United States' thirty-fourth president, the death of Russian Premier Joseph Stalin, and the execution of Ethel and Julius Rosenberg for revealing atomic secrets to the Soviets. Walt Disney's film *Peter Pan* had its premiere, as did the musical comedy film *Gentlemen Prefer Blondes*, starring Marilyn Monroe and Jane Russell. The Boeing 707 flew its first flight, and President Eisenhower offered aid to France in a peripheral war in Vietnam. IBM introduced the "Giant Brain," which used vacuum tubes to increase calculating speed a thousandfold. Information was fed to the machine from reels of magnetic tape. Senator John F. Kennedy married Miss Jacqueline L. Bouvier, and pictures of atomic bomb tests and the mushroom clouds were constantly replayed on television. These were my times.

Over the next year, I learned more about what happened to me when I fell into the well. Mom sat me down several times and read newspaper articles to me about that near-tragic day. One evening, we sat down alone on the family-room sofa, and she proudly showed me a scrapbook she had been working on. Dad was working late, as he often did. The cover of the scrapbook was an ugly brown leather. But inside, my mom had created the most wonderful childhood universe a six-year-old could imagine. Mom placed the scrapbook on her lap and began to take me on my six-year journey.

The scrapbook began with Mom's beautiful script noting my full name, birth date, weight, and the hospital where I was born. Each letter of every word was carefully crafted. Below this introduction, Mom had pasted a white cardboard oval and drawn clouds and stars. A baby's face peeked out of one cloud. In big letters it said, "A-Bit O'heaven," followed by:

God took a ray of sunshine,
A little star or two,
He took a pink and fleecy cloud,
Picked out from heaven's blue,
He put them all together,
To make a baby's charms,
And dropped them down from heaven
Right into Mother's arms.

My great-aunt wrote poems, and Mom included this one to begin my scrapbook. Each newspaper article, birthday card, and picture was glued or taped on the page with surgical precision. Handwritten notes and other poems were elegantly presented in celebration of my treasured life. The scrapbook was a monument to mothers everywhere.

"Mom, what does this article say?" I pointed to a newspaper article titled "Rescuers Save Boy after Fall into Abandoned Well."

"Davey, this is about Tommy rescuing you and receiving awards in New York. It was an article in the *New York Times*. Do you remember the TV show Tommy was on?"

"Tommy is a hero," I replied.

"Yes, he definitely is." She wrapped her arm around my shoulders.

"Mom, are you mad at Mrs. Hallman for not watching us?"

"Ah! Yes, at first your dad and I were mad, but you played around Mary's house hundreds of times with no accidents. On that day, Betty took her eyes off you for a while, and your adventure caught up with you."

"Mary said her Mom cried for days," I replied. After a short hug and a period of silence, I took a deep breath and asked, "Mom, was I dead?"

Mom paused, trying to figure out how to explain. "Sort of."

"What do you mean—sort of?"

Mom was silent as the amber rays of a setting sun shone through the venetian blinds of our family-room windows. "Davey, you were blue when you came out of that cistern. You had no pulse," Mom said, her voice high.

"What's a pulse?"

"It's how fast your heart beats," she responded. Mom placed my hand on my heart. With her hand cuddling mine, she whispered, "Do you feel your heart beating?"

"Yes," I said. I became aware for the first time of my heart dutifully beating.

"If you had no pulse, that means your heart quit beating for a while."

"So, Mom, I was dead for a while?"

"Yes."

I glanced at the diminishing sunlight to consider this news. My life had dimmed for a while, just like the sunlight I was watching. I wondered if my future would be as uneven and unforgiving as the walls of the devil's pit or filled with as much hope and love as my mother's embrace.

Mom looked at me and smiled with a calming presence. Her arm grew tighter around my body.

I realized I had survived my death. I could still see sunlight. I could still smell Mom's apple pie. I could enjoy trees. And I could feel the grandeur of my home and the warmth of my mother's love.

CHAPTER 2

Life on the Line

"Grandpa, let's go fishing," I said on a Sunday afternoon in 1957. Mom, Dad, and I had been to the First Christian Church and then to visit my mom's parents, Nannie and Clarence Burk. Our family was dressed up. I wore a starched white shirt, skinny tie, and big-boy suspenders. Mom wore a white Sunday dress with a white pearl necklace, and Dad was in a gray suit that didn't fit, and his slick hair was combed from left to right. Dad loved the Brylcreem, the TV commercials, and the jingle, "A little dab'll do ya!"

I was in the fifth grade and had turned ten years old in August. It was a partly cloudy October day, and the trees had begun to change color. I remember this day even now. It was a wonderful autumn day with a blue sky, cool wind, and family love.

"Ask your mom and dad if it's okay to go fishing," Grandpa said. He gave me the widest smile a human face can muster.

"Yes, it's fine, but change your clothes. Don't ruin that Sunday sport coat and pants," Mom replied.

I always kept blue jeans, old shoes, and extra shirts at Nannie's house for such events. I quickly changed clothes. It never occurred to me that Grandpa's only day to rest was Sunday. He had to go back to running a Louisville & Nashville Railroad locomotive at six o'clock on Monday morning.

Clarence was the chief engineer. In the fifties, trains were the lifeblood of the American economy. He was responsible for running the coal-fired steam engine on routes that crisscrossed Ohio, Kentucky, and Tennessee. He made over ten dollars a week during the Great Depression, so they were considered wealthy in Hopewell. Nannie could buy several big bags of groceries for two dollars, and of course, neighborhood gardens provided other foods.

When Clarence came home from his shift, he would walk around to the back of the house and take off his shoes, heavy coveralls, and sometimes his shirt. This short, stocky man was always covered in soot from head to toe. His arms, especially his forearms and hands, were oversized and as strong as an ox. Shoveling coal into a boiler was not a job for the weak. You did this type of work even if you were the locomotive chief.

Nannie and Clarence lived next to Duncan River, near the water and electric plants. Duncan River was hidden from tourists and heavy boat traffic and had a calming effect on everyone. Their house had a stone fireplace, a kitchen, a living room, two bedrooms, one bathroom, and a long screened-in porch on one side. It was a white-clapboard house, although one portion of the house had been a one-room log cabin in the 1800s. I treasured the house, the fishing dock, and the boat. Duncan River was probably too small to be called a river and too big to be called a creek, ranging in width from thirty to one hundred feet. It meandered through horse farms and farm fields. It was lined with determined oak and maple trees.

"Grandpa, do you want me to dig up some worms?" I asked.

"Sure, but go behind the garden," Grandpa said. Plenty of worms were always available in the rich black dirt next to Duncan River. By three o'clock, we were in the boat with everything we needed. In the afternoon, the fish were biting. The river came alive, and the setting sun created a kaleidoscope of light bouncing off the river's artifacts. And, if you were quiet, you could hear the animals and birds living their lives one movement at a time.

We decided to fish our way downstream toward the dam. We had a small motor on the boat, but we used our oars to quietly glide downriver, testing fishing holes along the way. The river current was lazy because of the dam. Occasionally, an audience of cattle or horses standing on the riverbanks watched us fish. The cattle and horses would huff and puff on the stage defined by the riverbank, lighted by the sun and framed by the trees. I often wondered what they thought of us drifting down the river. At times, we were less than six feet from them. Life surrounded me when I was fishing—in the sky and trees above, on the riverbanks, and in the river below. My devil's pit experience had taught me to honor life.

"Davey, throw your line in over by that dark spot in the river," Grandpa whispered so as not to scare the fish. I followed his suggestion and immediately got a bite. I reeled in a bass, probably about one pound. It put up a terrific fight, but I won the battle.

"Wow! That was fun," I said as I placed the fish in a wire basket. We fished that spot for about an hour and kept thirty of the bigger fish.

We fished that lazy river at all hours of the day. Grandpa taught me how to set up fishing lines and bait, how to hold the reel and cast, and what to do when the hook got entangled in trees or brush. Learning how to fish in shadows and deep holes, navigate the river, and clean the multitude of fish we caught was a magnificent way to learn about planning, executing the plan, and life.

"Grandpa, how did you know those fish were down there?" I asked.

"Well, Davey, I've fished this river for fifty years. During one of the major droughts, before you were born, the river almost went dry, so they built the dam. I walked five miles of this riverbed when I was young, and I still remember those natural potholes and ledges where fish hang out. We hit the right hole at the right time. It was fun, wasn't it?"

"Grandpa, let's go home," I said. "I'm tired after catching all those fish."

Clarence smiled. He put up his fly rod, and I did the same. "You steer us home," Clarence said. He moved to the front of the boat, and I went to the back. I started the motor when the sun was low in the sky. I navigated my way upriver as I had done many times before.

"Nannie, look at the fish we caught!" I yelled as we walked up the hill from the boat dock holding a heavy basket of fish. She looked out of her screened porch and said, "Wow! You outdid yourselves." Nannie would cook them in a way only a grandmother could cook, but there was no cleaning fish for her.

I began the ritual of cleaning fish—cutting off their heads, scraping off the scales, and gutting them. I used a black-handled knife with a steel blade about two inches wide and eight inches long. The razor edge of the knife could subdue the catch of the day or your finger. This was no time to be a klutz—you had to concentrate on your task. As I cleaned those fish, I wondered why man should be dominant over fish. Who set this order? I, like most people, found solace in order, and I was constantly searching for it. Fishing was orderly with just enough uncertainty.

And for a few moments, I tried to answer my own questions. I was sure our minister at church would say that God set this order, but I wasn't totally convinced. In my Bible study class the week before, we discussed Genesis 1:1. "In the beginning, God created the heaven and the earth." I thought this was true, but I concluded that a day for God, who has no clock, might be a billion years. God also said, if I remembered it right, that man was to have "dominion over the fish of the sea, over the birds of the air, and over every living thing that moves on the earth." *There you have it,* I thought as I began to clean fish on a heavy hardwood board by the garden. Those topics were too confusing to consider any longer, so I methodically cleaned fish for over an hour. I left the leftovers on the bank of the river, as Grandpa had taught me, so snakes, cats, foxes, and the like would have a convenient meal. A day later, everything was usually gone, but if it was not, we mixed it in with the garden dirt for fertilizer.

For a kid, it's a unique experience having a live thing on the other end of a fishing line. First, you have to prepare the rod and reel, the bait, and the boat. I learned how to maneuver a boat around obstacles, anchor it, and be safe. Then there's an ever-changing tactical strategy and ever-changing game plan to fishing successfully. Some of the variables are predictable, like the sun rising and setting, but some are not, like a sudden storm and lightning. Next, you learn how to set the hook when you get a bite and how to pull the fish in. Fishing teaches you about plans versus execution. You learn to try again if you fail cast after cast. It also teaches you to be independent. And I think you learn to respect nature. The fishing line connects you to nature.

It was dark, and I was a foul-smelling ten-year-old. I took off my putrid clothes on the steps of the screened porch, left them there, and ran to the bathtub. A single two-hundred-watt lightbulb on an electrical cord lit the screened porch and my way. Nannie would wash my clothes for the next fishing adventure.

Later that week, Nannie cooked a wonderful fish dinner for the four of us. Clarence was working. I often went to the grocery store with Mom or Nannie and discovered where this food came from and the expert decisions behind its selection. We shopped at Hopewell's Foodtown grocery store. A twelve-ounce box of Kellogg's Corn Flakes was twenty cents. New York T-bone steaks were about one dollar a pound. Swanson TV dinners were the rage, heavily advertised on TV at seventy-five cents each. A first-class stamp cost three cents, and a soda pop or can of Campbell's soup was about ten cents. Gasoline was twenty-seven cents per gallon. The Dow Jones Industrial Average was around three hundred, the average home cost about $20,000, and the hourly minimum wage was one dollar per hour. The national debt was $270 billion.

My parents and grandparents taught me many things, including not wasting anything. After we ate Swanson TV dinners, for example, Mom washed the three-compartment aluminum trays and used them for picnics and family gatherings. Leftovers populated our refrigerator.

Mom, Dad, Nannie, and I ate fifteen fish that evening, along with homemade cornbread and green beans picked from the garden. Dad built a fire in my grandmother's fireplace because it was a cool autumn evening. We knew how to eat fresh fish and seldom encountered a fishbone. We talked about family and world happenings, and I realize now that these family dinners and fishing trips ensured that the wisdom and knowledge of past generations was passed on to me.

One conversation focused on the Soviet Union's *Sputnik I*, a satellite orbiting Earth on October 4, 1957. "Does anyone know how that spaceship the Soviets launched stays up there?" I asked during dinner at my grandparents' house.

Mom and Nannie quickly admitted that they didn't know. Clarence said, "That's a good question, Davey."

"The paper says it goes so fast that gravity can't pull it down," Dad said. "I read it weighs 184 pounds and orbits the earth every 95 minutes at a maximum altitude of 560 miles. That's all I know. You should ask your teachers about how it stays in orbit on Monday."

"I will," I said. I gathered another scoop of green beans. This event shocked us as citizens of the so-called technology leader— the United States of America. The entire focus of the US education system changed that day. The media began a constant drumbeat: "We need more science, engineering, and math majors." It changed my life.

Sometimes my dad went fishing with us, and then three generations were in the boat. We had many laughs on those boating excursions, and they bound us together. If common blood doesn't tie you together, then life experiences can do it. We had both.

My dad was born in 1924 and graduated from Hopewell High School in 1941. His name was Hamlet Bourbon, and everyone called him Ham. He was handsome, six feet one, and about 190 pounds. He had worked for his father when he was a teenager, wiring houses and fixing electrical problems. His father also taught him how to test and replace radio tubes. In those days, most houses were on one electrical circuit, often with a couple of plugs and a light socket hanging down from the center of each room. After high school graduation, he worked in the Sun Shipbuilding and Dry Dock in Chester, Pennsylvania. The dry dock people thought he was eighteen years old, but he was actually seventeen. They built tankers and cargo ships that were desperately needed in the war effort. Dad could have received an exemption from serving in the military and stayed at the shipyard.

The Kentucky draft board records of December 1941 stated the following: "Mr. Hamlet Bourbon worked at the Sun Shipbuilding and Dry Dock in Chester, Pennsylvania. He installed and worked on layouts and blueprints for the electrical equipment on ships, engine rooms, and motors, worked for the ship's electrical contractor, and also understood refrigeration and air-conditioning. Even at his young age, he could run a crew and knew what to do."

During one Duncan River fishing trip with Dad when the fish weren't biting, he said, "I was working in the shipyard, and three of my high school buddies called me and said, 'Bourbon, come sign up with us for the Marine Raiders.' Adolf Hitler had attacked the Soviet Union in 1941, and the Japs attacked Pearl Harbor that same year. I could have had an exemption from US military service, given I was building ships for the war effort. But I wanted to join my friends and fight the Nazis and Japs before they landed on American beaches."

"So you quit your shipyard job and came home?" I asked with a puzzled look as our boat tugged on the rope that was tied to a riverbank tree branch.

"Yes, and the four of us drove down to Louisville, Kentucky, and signed up on January 26, 1942, for the US Marine Corps. We all went to boot camp together in San Diego, California. We thought we would be fighting side by side as Marine Raiders," Dad continued.

My heavy green fishing line straightened, and I landed a large, colorful perch. "Dad, this is a keeper!" I unhooked the fish and threw him in our fish basket. I baited my hook again, threw the line in, and asked, "What happened after boot camp?"

"Well, toward the end of boot camp, the four of us were being processed so they could cut our final orders. As one of my Hopewell buddies, Buddy Parker, was being processed, a USMC staff sergeant asked, 'Son, where were you born?' Buddy said, 'Hopewell, Kentucky, Sergeant.' The rest of us stood in line behind him. 'What do you want to do? Your aptitude and physical fitness test scores are good.' 'I want to be in the Marine Raiders, Sergeant.' 'Okay, you're in. God bless you!' The sergeant initialed his paperwork. Buddy moved forward in the line, but he was only a few feet from me.

"'Next,' the sergeant bellowed out. I stepped forward.

"'What's your name?'

"'Ham Bourbon, Sergeant.'

"'Where did you get a name like that?' the sergeant asked.

"'Sir, Ham is short for Hamlet—like in the Shakespeare play.'

"'Your test scores are even better than your friend's, Private Bourbon. Where are you from?'

"'Sergeant, I'm from Hopewell, Kentucky, too. So are my two buddies in line behind me. We all want to be Marine Raiders.'

"'How big is Hopewell, Kentucky, son?' asked the sergeant.

"Sir, I think it's about seven to eight thousand people,' I replied. After a short pause, the sergeant leaned forward in his bulky steel chair and across the steel table and said, 'Only one of you can do Marine Raiders.'

"'Why, Sergeant?'

"'The USMC has a rule that only one soldier per ten thousand people in a town can be enlisted in the Marine Raiders. Which one of you four wants to do it?'

"'I'll do it,' Buddy said immediately with a proud voice as he turned around and stood up as straight as a telephone pole.

"'Okay, you're in, son.' We'll stamp your orders, but not your friends'.'"

Dad went on to explain what else happened to him. As I remember the stories, my dad and the other two buddies were split up into different parts of the USMC. Due to Dad's high test scores, the USMC sent him to meteorology school in Newport, Rhode Island. Later, the military decided that women could become meteorologists, which would free men to go overseas and fight.

One popular World War II poster showed a woman in blue work clothes with a red bandanna wrapped around her head, drilling a steel brace. "Rosie the Riveter" was a cultural icon representing millions of American women who worked in the factories producing tanks, munitions, and airplanes. Another poster said in big letters, "Do the job *he* left behind." And women did.

Dad received orders to go to San Diego to teach USMC courses on electrical and refrigeration topics. Later, he was sent to Goldsboro, North Carolina, and he again taught courses on airplane systems. He had applied to go overseas several times and was always denied. Dad decided to make a call to his high school sweetheart. About 7:00 p.m., he walked up to the black telephone in a military base phone booth, paused, walked inside, and carefully shut the door. The phone booth was the only place he could have privacy on the base. Before he called her, he rehearsed what he would say, mumbling the words to himself. He picked up the phone, dialed the operator, and called Dorothy collect.

"Miss Burk, will you accept a collect call from Ham Bourbon?" the telephone operator asked.

"Yes."

"Mr. Bourbon, she is on the line," said the operator.

"Dot, they wouldn't let me go overseas. I'm stuck in the USA."

"I know that's what you want, but I'm glad they're keeping you home—it's safer," Dot replied.

"Dot, I was thinking—maybe this is a good time to get married. Will you marry me?"

"Well, that's a surprise! You mean now?" Dot was irritated by how the marriage proposal was being offered over the long-distance collect call, but she was happy. Dot worked in the Veterans Administration hospital in Baxter, Kentucky. She had seen the aftermath of war and knew there were no guarantees in life.

"Yes, now! I love you. You know that. Let's get married," Ham said as he nervously twisted the black cord of the phone with his fingers.

"Okay, yes! Yes!"

Dot borrowed twenty dollars from her family for a bus ticket from Hopewell to Goldsboro, and she married my dad in a minister's living room on June 3, 1945. Their wedding night was in a military barrack with individual rooms. Ham's fellow marines had tried to get him drunk at the wedding reception, but that didn't work. When Dot and Ham left the reception, they went back to the barrack. Dot went to the bathroom and sat down on the toilet.

"Oh my God! Those idiots put cold cream over the toilet seat," Dot exclaimed as she reached for a towel.

Ham jumped up to rescue her and began to laugh. About that time, the shades on the two windows came crashing down. Outside, the shadows of Ham's buddies were looking in and laughing. Few have had such a honeymoon night.

Dot was planning to live on the military base, or next to it, but two weeks after the wedding, Ham got orders to go to San Diego and then to Zamboanga, Mindanao Island, in the Philippines. Japan had seized the Philippines from US control.

Ham would be in charge of electrical systems and other maintenance on USMC airplanes. He would run a crew of men to keep "the birds flying." His USMC wing included pilots, supplies, maintenance, and communication personnel. They were supporting General Douglas MacArthur's reoccupation of the Philippines, mainly with F-4 Corsair fighter and reconnaissance planes. World War II intelligence required planes to fly over suspected targets and troop movements and take still pictures and video. There was no other way to gain firsthand knowledge of the wartime situation in the forties. Sometimes the planes and pilots came back shot up, but no pilots were killed in Dad's part of the war. The island-hopping Pacific War had experienced major battles at Guadalcanal, Admiralty Island, Guam, Corregidor, and Iwo Jima.

Dot moved back to Baxter and continued to work for the VA hospital there. She worked on the processing of VA loans to military personnel and occasionally helped out in the hospital, watching patients and doing odd jobs. Every day, Mom would see the carnage of war as soldiers with broken minds and bodies tried to figure out their places among the living.

On August 6, 1945, the United States dropped an atomic bomb, Little Boy, from *Enola Gay* on Hiroshima, Japan. On August 9, an even more powerful atomic bomb called Fat Man hit Nagasaki, Japan. The Japanese emperor decided on August 10 to end the war without his cabinet's consent, and Japan surrendered on September 2, 1945.

In November 1945, Ham's USMC wing was ordered to Peiping, China (now called Beijing). The trip was hazardous because numerous mines were still in the sea—many floating loose, and some scraped the side of the ship. They shot at the mines they could see, sinking them or triggering explosions. His job had always been the same: keep the planes flying.

Dad was honorably discharged from the USMC on June 7, 1946, and returned home to Hopewell. Of Dad's four Hopewell buddies who signed up for the US Marines, two came back to Hopewell, one died in combat in Germany, and Buddy Parker, who was selected for the Marine Rangers, was killed in action. Sometimes your place in line is all that matters.

It didn't take long for Dad to get back into the swing of things. On August 3, 1947, at 1:47 p.m. at the St. Vincent Hospital in Baxter, Kentucky, I was born with crystal blue eyes and brown hair. I weighed eight pounds and two ounces. An uncle who saw me while I was still in the hospital said, "Ham, that kid is going to be a good football player. Look at those big strong legs!"

I was part of the postwar baby boom generation. We were born between 1946 and 1964 to men and women who came home from World War II to restart their lives. Given our heritage, we expected people to work hard and be motivated to professional accomplishments. We thought we had to outperform the Russians. We would become the me generation. And these same characteristics would drive my future endeavors.

World events were happening all around us. In 1947, the French were fighting in Vietnam, Al Capone died, strong disagreements between Russia and the US over what to do with Germany were unresolved, and Andrei Gromyko, the Soviet representative on the United Nations Security Council, objected to the US plan for international control of atomic weapons. US Secretary of State George Marshall proposed the Marshall Plan for rebuilding Europe after the war, Jet Pilot won the Kentucky Derby, Britain granted India and Pakistan independence, the Soviet Army took over US Vacuum Oil and UK Steel refinery as their German assets, and Chuck Yeager broke the sound barrier by going over six hundred miles per hour in a Bell X-1 rocket plane.

I watched world events play out in the media and listened to discussions between my parents and grandparents. Nannie told me stories about how, in the twenties and thirties, remnants of old soap bars were thrown in a box, and once every three or four months, my mom and my grandmother would melt them and make new bars of soap. Another story Nannie told me was how she fed hoboes during the Great Depression. We were sitting on the screened-in porch one Saturday afternoon with a view of the Duncan River and the background hum of electrical generators from the water plant next door.

"Davey, I would cook fried apple pies for Clarence to take on his two-to-three-day trips on the L&N train," Nannie said as she fixed a pin in her bird's nest hairdo. "I always cooked a dozen extra for the hoboes who were down and out. They would politely knock on my kitchen door and ask for food. I would give them a pie, and they were so hungry they ate them on the kitchen porch immediately."

"Nannie?" I would ask. "Weren't you afraid the hoboes would rob you?"

"No, they were good people. They were proud people. Usually the men knocked on the door, but sometimes, I could glimpse a woman or kid in the shadows of our yard. Men would take one bite of the pie and hand it into the shadows to a woman or kid for their bites. They usually came around dinnertime as the sun was going down. They knew which houses to go to in Hopewell. When you are hungry, Davey, word travels fast. More people kept showing up at my back door, so I cooked more pies. A few times, I cooked as many as three dozen fried apple pies and gave them to the hoboes. When I ran out or didn't have any food for them, I told them, and they would go away."

"How many hoboes did you feed, Nannie?" I asked.

"Oh, hundreds." She hugged me and gave me a radiant smile. "Davey, we are fortunate. Clarence has a good job that pays well, so we share it."

Clarence would take me over to the water plant about once a year. I always wanted to see the oil-fired furnace that generated steam for the huge electrical turbines. Hopewell had generated electric power for itself since the twenties, and the electric plant wasn't decommissioned until the fifties.

I sat there with Grandpa on a concrete ledge and marveled at this old system of technology. "Grandpa, how does this thing work?" I asked on one Sunday afternoon visit.

"David, we buy oil and use it to heat the furnace. Many thick pipes run along the walls of the furnace, and inside each pipe is water that becomes steam. The steam builds up lots of pressure and is forced into the electrical generators that turn the rotors. This rotation creates electricity." I listened to his every word. The hum of the generator provided background music for our conversation. It was intoxicating.

"How come we can't see electricity?" I asked.

"It's a force, a hidden force. You'll have to study to answer that question for yourself. I don't really know," Grandpa replied. He grabbed my hand and began to leave the power plant. I grudgingly left this testament to human ingenuity. The power of that room will always be within me.

I marveled at the size of Grandpa's forearms. They were like Popeye's, and they seemed to be ten times the size of my forearms. I often studied the muscles and veins in his forearms and wondered how a human could be that strong. He was my grandpa, and I was proud of him. He lived his life around the biggest, most powerful machines humans had produced—big, black steam locomotives, intense steam-generating furnaces, and powerful electric generators. Yet, he respected nature more, I think.

I loved Grandpa. I wish I had told him so, but maybe I did in indirect ways. At that time, I had no idea I would see him thirty years later, and he would save my life. But this is a story for another time.

Our close family ties and the small town of Hopewell reinforced a sense of togetherness, hopefulness, and the confidence to never give up. We were on our way to fulfilling the American Dream.

CHAPTER 3

Blue Meadows

The Hopewell railroad yard and train station were historic relics of the American Dream, and they were adjacent to my home on Fourteenth Street. The rail yard was built in Hopewell in 1882. It was the center of economic commerce in central Kentucky until the early 1900s.

My playmates and I explored every aspect of the railroad yard and often played for hours on the big black switch locomotive that always stayed in the yard. Such a locomotive used four or more axles and low gears to move railroad cars and other locomotives around the dozens of parallel tracks in the yard. The remnants of an old turntable facility remained where railcars and locomotives once turned around. An exhausted boxcar repair warehouse anchored one end of the yard.

The L&N depot was a handsome, tall building with powerful overhanging gables and roofs to protect cargo and passengers. Many central Kentuckians used this depot to go off to war or school before the automobile and airplane became America's dominant transportation options. One of our favorite pastimes was to have BB gun fights on Sundays using an old red L&N caboose and the switching locomotive as our platforms for battle. Sundays were the only time yard operations were shut down when the occasional train zoomed by. We would position ourselves on top of the locomotive and caboose and under the big iron wheels for cover during our battles. The ping of BBs hitting steel thrilled us and reinforced the authentic nature of our battles.

For six days a week, the yard and its machines—trucks, trains, wagons, and boxcars—were in constant motion. People got hurt tripping on rails, getting hit by trucks and forklifts loading and unloading supplies, or being struck by lumbering railcars pushed by the switch locomotive. Every few years, someone was killed. At night, mile-long trains hummed by the Hopewell rail yard and my house. You quickly learned to look down with one eye and watch where you were walking—and up with the other eye to keep track of a train's progress.

My closest neighborhood playmates were Jimmy McMaster and Emmett Neely. Jimmy was a tall, skinny eleven-year-old whose dad worked at the Hopewell Grain and Storage Company. Jimmy's slick black hair was combed straight down his forehead. For some reason, he always looked pale. Emmett was ten years old, and his mom worked at the Hopewell J. C. Penney store. He was a little heavier than me and wore a flattop haircut. He often put this obnoxious grease on his hair and combed it vertical. Emmett might have had a slight mental problem since his conversations hopscotched around.

Jimmy, Emmett, and I were the leaders of this crew, and we were looking for new adventures with our BB guns. Playing inside with toy soldiers and forts and outside with BB guns was the norm in 1958. Our playgrounds were three-dimensional physical entities. We could not imagine a virtual world then.

The global backdrop for our aggressive play was the Cold War. On television, we'd watched the US Navy launch the *Forrestal* aircraft carrier, the largest in the world, on December 12, 1954. I built a plastic model of that ship. The images of atomic submarines, aircraft carriers, and atomic bomb blasts, and Khrushchev and the Communist Party, defined the Cold War. My parents and playmates took the arms race seriously. Good and evil were clearly delineated, we thought.

Our BB gun battles were also a reflection of our troubling national times. Federal troops were sent to Little Rock, Arkansas, when Governor Faubus defied federal law and ordered the state militia troops to stop black students from entering a white high school; *Sputnik* was launched on October 4, 1957, and achieved orbit, beginning the space race; Khrushchev became the head of the Communist Party and declared they would conquer capitalism; and my schoolmates and I were practicing H-bomb drills by hiding under our desks.

"Jimmy, Emmett. Let's go over to the Thoroughbred Meadows Farm and have a BB gun battle," I said decisively. It was a snowy Sunday afternoon in February. For Christmas, the kids on my street all got BB guns for presents. We were a motley crew, ranging in age from ten to twelve. Now fifth and sixth graders, we had endured several years of elementary school together.

"Okay, let's move out," Emmett ordered when we'd assembled in my front yard. We wore heavy blue jeans and coarse wool sweaters. Since we had to shoot our BB guns, we wore no gloves, and our hands would eventually turn blue from the cold.

On that February day, we assembled a platoon of six and began the trip to the Thoroughbred Meadows Farm by going through the railroad yard and crossing city streets to a limestone wall. Central Kentucky rock fences were famous for craftsmanship and durability. Irish and Mexican immigrants built the fences in the late 1800s and early 1900s. The limestone rocks were interwoven using no mortar. The amazing feat was that many of these hand-built rock fences were still intact a century later. We were climbing over history and didn't know it. White wood fences circled the horse farms, often inside the boundaries of the rock walls. We meandered through this maze with our BB guns. We had no fear. We were masters of our neighborhood.

Gentle rolling hills, meandering streams, lazy country roads, and the sheer beauty of nationally known horse farms surrounded Hopewell. Some central Kentucky horse farms were secluded, and tourists never saw them. But the Thoroughbred Meadows Farm was our playground.

We formed two teams and set rules for our battles. The most important rule was never shoot the BBs above the waist. We had discussed the consequences of hitting someone in the eye with a BB. If you hit someone above the waist, you had to drop out of the battle and go sit under an oak tree. The team of the last man standing won the battle. We followed the rules. The one rule we didn't follow was that our parents thought we played around our working-class neighborhood. They never realized we played in the rail yard or hiked miles to the edge of one of the most famous horse farms in the world.

With snow on the ground and a Sunday afternoon temperature of twenty-eight degrees, six of us were in the middle of a battle on two sides of a frozen tributary of Duncan River. Jackson Creek was about twenty-five feet across. Jackson Creek had a series of small concrete dams about every five hundred feet. On cold days, these miniature waterfalls were frozen and silent. We were left to our own ingenuity to avoid falling in. We hid in the snow and small bushes on each side of Jackson Creek as one team chased the other. Occasionally we would slide across the creek on the ice on our feet or hips while firing our BB guns. It was exhilarating!

In one epic battle, Emmett and his teammates had pinned me down behind a small stone wall that was part of one of the dams on Jackson Creek. Jimmy and another friend were on my team, and we were trying to outflank and surround the other team.

"Jimmy, cover me, I'm going to move to the other side of the creek," I yelled. I darted out of my hiding place and began to run on the frozen creek on the high side of the dam.

"Get Bourbon," Emmett yelled to his teammates as they shot BBs at my legs. I jumped at the sound of their air rifles trying to hit me, and when I came down, I heard a cracking sound. My feet hit the ice as it gave way, and I found myself in four feet of ice-cold water, hanging onto the dam. The high side of the dam was where the water was deepest, and my gamble had not worked. Immediately everyone yelled, "Time out!" as they ran to my rescue.

"Bourbon, you sure did yourself in," Jimmy said as two of them, standing on the ice on the low side of the small dam, reached out to help me. "Yeah! Get me out of here, dammit," I yelled as the cold water began to overcome my body. They pulled me out of the high side of the dam and over to their low side, where the shallow water was frozen solid. I was now officially out of the battle, and it was three against two.

"Fellows, I'm going home," I said as I picked up my BB gun. "See you tomorrow." I began to walk away from the battle scene.

"We're going to finish out this battle," Emmett said. "We'll be home soon."

With everything below my chest soaking wet, including my school shoes, I walked the mile and a half back to my house in defeat. In an instant, I had made a decision and taken a chance, and it did not work. This event, like so many before, taught me responsibility for my actions. The penalty for my decision was high: cold feet, ruined shoes, soggy and heavy wet clothes, and a long march back in the middle of winter to contemplate my miserable situation. And, of course, a head cold was only days away. I walked to the basement door, which I had left unlocked, and slipped into my house.

"Is that you down there?" Mom shouted down the basement steps.

"Yes, Mom. I'll be up in a minute," I replied. I took off my clothes and put them in the washer, dried off, and set my shoes out to dry.

The next morning, I put on those damp shoes and wore them all day at school. At school, we joked around about who shot whom and how it was done, and of course, "Bourbon fell into the creek" was the news of the day.

It never occurred to us during our BB gun battles that each of those manicured fields had thoroughbred horses worth millions of dollars running around with us, probably even a Kentucky Derby winner. Moreover, we could have been seriously hurt. In the heat of battle, we often found a group of thoroughbreds watching us from the hill above. The stark beauty of the snow-covered rolling hills with noble black thoroughbred horses silhouetted against the snow was a magnificent sight that few have the opportunity to witness.

Sometimes one-ton racehorses would run straight at us only to stop, look us over, and take off again. We often stopped our battles to watch horses race each other across the fields. Steam would be blowing out of their nostrils like boilers. I would look into their big clear eyes, and we connected. They knew we were in their home and that we respected their every move. Their elegant muscles would flex, and we could see their awesome power. They kicked up the turf and snow in a fury of exhaust. Thoroughbred horses were bred to run, and run they did. They knew their trade. They took risks too. We were of the same breed.

A moment's reflection during our rest breaks from battle brought back memories of walking on Jackson Creek on cold winter days with the crystal clear ice cracking. When we did fall in the creek, and nature won, the rescue effort would begin. The creek was only one to four feet deep, and we simply stood up to save ourselves in the bitterly cold water as I had done many times.

When we sat by the creek to rest, we would close our eyes and imagine proud Indian tribes walking in our footsteps centuries earlier. The main Indian tribes in Kentucky were the Shawnee, Cherokee, Yuchi, and Chickasaw. During the Indian removals of the 1800s, most of these tribes would be moved west to reservations. But for centuries, they camped along Duncan River and Jackson Creek, raised their families, hunted buffalo and deer, and fought the white man to defend their land and way of life. Shawnees lived in small round dwellings called wikkums or wigwams—not tepees. The men hunted, and the women farmed and took care of the children. They moved by walking, using dogs as pack animals, and paddling dugout canoes. There were no horses in North America until Europeans brought them over, so Shawnees adopted horse transportation later. Tecumseh, a tribal chief, was probably the most famous Shawnee. We felt as if their shadows watched us play.

Every once in a while, one of our crew would find a flint arrowhead, and I would wonder about its history. *Did that arrowhead conquer a white man intruding on Indian land? Did that arrowhead defeat five deer? Did the arrowhead save a family from a bear attack?* If artifacts could talk, humans would be much wiser.

The word "Kentucky" comes from an Iroquoian Indian word "Kentake," which means "meadowland," and I was right in the middle of this Kentake. The limestone underlying the rivers and creeks was sturdy, the water clean, the horses tough, the grass glistening, the oak trees benevolent, and the dirt black and rich in nutrients. The land and its props were authentic, like its people.

Whether I realized it or not at the time, I was in the middle of a history in which rugged individualism and freedom flourished as settlers moved west. Daniel Boone first saw this land in 1769, and he may have walked the very fields upon which I played. This was Kentucky, and it was the long-forgotten heart and soul of American values.

We played on these farm fields for more than a year, but during one of our battles, a bright-orange farm truck came bouncing across the field. Having no place to hide, we quickly stood up and waited for the truck to arrive.

As the truck slid to a halt in the open field, two men got out. "Boys, what'n the hell you doin'? Get in the back of the truck. You're goin' to the farm office," hollered a farmhand.

Our platoon loaded up in the truck and entered the office— mud, snow, grass, and all.

"Boys, I've seen you all out in the fields before, but we have nine horses in that field today. One is a Kentucky Derby winner, and two others have won stake races," the farm manager said. "What're your names?" He wrote them down.

"If you spook a horse, and it breaks a leg, I'll be fired, and your parents will be sued. The next time I see you in the field, I'll call your parents and the police and charge you with trespassing. Got it?"

"Yes, sir."

"Now take the road home and don't cross the field," the farm manager said.

As we walked the long way home, about three miles along the roads, we realized that our battles on those manicured farm fields were over. We were in need of a new adventure but couldn't find it.

Television provided a diversion from our defunct BB gun battles, so I found myself watching more TV with Mom and Dad. Dad loved to watch *The Honeymooners.* The show began in 1952 and starred Jackie Gleason as Ralph, Sheila MacRae as Alice, Joyce Randolph as Trixie, and Art Carney as Ed Norton. The show's main character, Ralph Kramden, was a blue-collar bus driver who consistently failed in most things and often tried get-rich-quick ventures. Ralph often acted as if he was going to punch someone in the nose, only to back off his insults and threats. Beneath Ralph's antics was a man with a friendly and warm heart who loved his wife and pals. Ralph Kramden was the inspiration for the animated character Fred Flintstone. One of Gleason's famous lines, which my Dad loved, was "How sweet it is!" *The Honeymooners* made us laugh and escape the reality of the local and national news, which was generally depressing.

One evening, I was watching our black and white television with Mom and Dad when a commercial for powdered milk came on. The commercial claimed you could get ten gallons of milk from this jar. I listened intently and said, "Dad, you can't cram that much milk down into that little jar."

They laughed, and Dad replied, "Son, you add water to the powdered milk."

"But Dad, they didn't tell you that in the commercial."

Another favorite family show was *Davy Crockett*, which began in 1954. I was an avid viewer from day one. I idolized the six foot six Fess Parker, who played Alamo icon Davy Crockett in the television series. Up to five thousand coonskin caps were sold per day in those days. I had a Davy Crockett rifle, coonskin cap, and lunchbox. The marketing power of television was demonstrated by this TV show, as over $300 million in Davy Crockett apparel sold within a year after the show debuted. I bought the record "The Ballad of Davy Crockett" and played it hundreds of times. I, like many of my generation, was swept up in Walt Disney's Davy Crockett phenomenon.

One day after school I came home to find a new Zenith Flash-Matic television in our small living room. Prior to this, the family procedure to operate the TV was to get up, walk across the room, and manually turn the TV knobs to switch channels, mute the TV, and turn it off and on.

"Dad, how does the flash tuner work?"

"I'm not totally sure, son, but I think this handheld tuner sends out a radio signal to change channels." Dad knew about radios since he'd worked for his dad testing vacuum tubes for radios in the thirties. My questions continued. "Wow, it even mutes the TV so we don't have to listen to commercials," I said. "Dad, does it send out a different radio signal to mute the TV?"

"Son, I'm not sure. You'll have to study how it works."

"Dad, does the radio wave hurt us?"

My dad was getting irritated by my barrage of questions. "No, son, they wouldn't sell the TV if it would hurt someone."

Without the challenge of BB gun battles on the farm, our days consisted of boring activities like school, watching television, and playing neighborhood baseball games. One day after school in March 1958, Jimmy, Emmett, and I were playing baseball in a field close to my home.

"Jimmy, have you noticed that new water tower they're building on the hill in the Thoroughbred Meadows farm?" Emmett asked.

"Yes. We ought to go over there with our BB guns and check it out," Jimmy replied. Our BB gun skills had eroded after we got kicked off the Thoroughbred Meadows Farm. School and home were confined spaces, but the blue meadows of the farm were open and free. "Okay, let's check it out, but I bet it's locked up tight. Besides, the construction site is on the corner of the farm," I replied as we ended our three-man baseball game.

The next Sunday, we assembled our battle group of six friends, including Jimmy, Emmett, and me. With our BB guns in hand, we worked our way to the construction site. We discovered that a contractor was building a new million-gallon water tower for Hopewell, and an eight-foot steel fence with barbed wire on top surrounded the site. We peered through the fence and were confident it would not keep us out.

We crawled under the fence that protected the construction site. Nothing could keep this battle-hardened platoon out. We were masters of the neighborhood. We examined everything at the site: a crane, mountains of steel trusses and big pipes, welding machines, and many huge locked toolboxes and sheds. Steel cables randomly lay on the ground with no real purpose except to trip us. We watched over this site in the ensuing months as men in steel helmets and heavy boots built the water tower.

"Jimmy, look at me," Emmett exclaimed as he sat in the driver's seat of the big crane. Emmett kicked the big steel links of the crane tracks and then joined Jimmy in the control cabin of the crane. I climbed onto a pile of steel trusses and pipes, sat down, and surveyed our future battleground. The marvels of America's industrial might were in front of us. Fortunately, we could not start the crane's diesel engine or unlock the big toolboxes or sheds. But on weekends, we held BB gun battles at the construction site—our exciting new venue.

By the end of April, the water tower had gained eight steel legs, reaching to the sky with a big center steel column. Each of the eight steel tubes was about four feet in diameter, and the center post was about double that. The steel was a mottled rusty color. I thought the half-finished water tower looked like an ugly, dead spider on its back. Steel guide wires and concrete anchors were everywhere. The stained legs of the tower went up in the air over one hundred feet. The wind moved these cathedrals to the sky around a lot, and we would hear the squeaking of steel, anchors, and wires. It was a dangerous venue.

Some days after school, we would take our usual hike to the farm and construction site, sit on a white wood fence five hundred feet from the construction site, and watch the men climb the ladders inside the swaying steel legs to the top. The crane lifted huge pieces of curved sheet steel to the top, and the men welded them into place. After a few weeks, the bottom half of the storage tank was completed.

At that point in the construction, we thought the water tower looked like a champagne glass with eight legs. The men added a platform on one leg and a walkway with a handrail around the bottom of the tank. Some of the guide wires and anchors came down. The water tower now had the strength to withstand the wind and rain. The total structure would be about 160 feet tall.

And since it sat on the highest hill about two hundred feet above Main Street, to us it was the biggest structure ever built.

One evening in May, the BB gun crew decided to hike over to the water tower. It didn't get dark until about nine, so we thought we had plenty of time to have an evening battle with the water tower as our stage. The construction crew was gone, and the steel chain linked fence was locked.

"Jimmy and Emmett, pull the gate this way. Jack, pull the other side of the gate the opposite way," I said.

Several of us got inside the gate. Then we repeated our gate-pulling exercise until everyone was inside the construction site. We walked around the battleground, surveying the latest changes.

"David, come over here," Jimmy whispered. "The door to this leg is unlocked." We slowly opened the heavy steel door, which squeaked loudly, and looked into the tube.

"Guys, there's a ladder in here," Jimmy said in an excited voice. As each of us peeked in, we knew our fate. We were going to climb up. We had no fear or experience.

"Who's going up first?" Jimmy exclaimed.

"I'll go," I said in a calm voice as I tried to reassure my platoon that this adventure was safe.

I swung my BB gun strap back over my head and shoulder so the gun was on my back. I got inside the hollow steel tube and looked up. "Wow, it's a long way up there," I said in a burst of excitement.

At the very top of the vertical tunnel, there was a small opening of light. It seemed far away. The first step on the steel ladder reverberated up and down. I began my climb, taking one step at a time. The echoes from my steps blended together into a constant ringing. After I went up about forty feet, I looked down to my comrades and said, "Come on up."

"I'm on my way," Jimmy said in a shaky voice.

Along the way, I would stop and look up and down to see small openings of light at both ends. I was in the middle, and it seemed crowded in there. The echoes were getting louder as more of my friends ventured up the tube with me. I never thought about the challenges of what I would find at the top or the trip down. I could only think about the beautiful view I was about to see. What would it be like on top of the water tower?

Finally, I reached the end of the tube and the outside platform. My hands were aching. I held on tightly with every step I took. I walked out on the precarious platform about 120 feet in the air and surveyed the view. Like a tree, the whole structure was swaying back and forth in the wind. "Guys, it's perfect up here, but the steel is slick!"

I was out of breath. I could see Hopewell—the courthouse, the church steeples, Jackson Creek, the railroad yard, and the gorgeous horse farm below. Instead of snow-covered hills with stark black trees and roads, it was summertime. The grass was green, of course, but sometimes it bloomed with a small blue flower. Everyone called it bluegrass.

Eventually, Jimmy, Emmett, and I made it to the platform. The other three decided not to climb up. Instead, they stood below, looking up at us. The entire town was laid out before us. The water tower was on the highest hill, so our elevation was more like three to four hundred feet above the town. The view was spectacular. As the wind blew, green waves rolled across the meadows. Sometimes two waves would cross and end in randomness. Occasionally, our eyes would catch a glimpse of blue from the tint of the bluegrass flowers. The closest fields were manicured for thoroughbreds, but in the distance, we could see burley tobacco and golden wheat waving in the wind.

The three of us sat there for thirty minutes with our legs hanging over the edge of the platform, inspecting the countryside and the clouds. We were living on the edge. The sun was beginning to set, and faint purple and orange bathed the clouds. It occurred to me that clouds don't know we were there and don't care. They go about their business, unaware of their purpose.

The water tower platform was my cloud. It was my perch, and I could see everything I knew. It was like a thousand-piece puzzle below me. I felt the cool air across the platform as nighttime was trying to overcome the heat of the day. I loved everything about that place as I sat on my cloud.

The adventure was not over. I decided to climb up the ladder welded to the platform and peek over into the steel bowl. This feat was more dangerous than climbing up inside the steel tube. The ladder was perched outside, and the wind was high. I climbed up the ladder and looked into the saucer-shaped steel bowl. It was magnificent. I wondered how much water this steel bowl would hold. I climbed over the edge of the steel plates and into the bowl. The bowl was sturdier than the platform and outside ladder. I walked around inside the half-finished bowl, and it swayed several feet back and forth. I shot my BB gun into the side of the bowl and listened to the BB bounce around. Jimmy climbed the outside ladder and peeked over the edge of the bowl, but he did not crawl into it.

"We could have a great battle inside this bowl," Jimmy yelled.

"Yah! It would be fun, but we could never get six of us in here. It's too dangerous. I'm coming out," I said. My heart was beating fast.

Jimmy and Emmett watched me retrace my steps over the edge of the bowl and down the side of the slippery steel plates to arrive on the platform.

"Be careful, David!" Jimmy said. I positioned myself stomach first over the edge of the half-inch steel plates—with my hands and feet on either side of the plate. As he finished saying my name, my right foot slipped on the shiny steel frame of the platform. I slid to the right and caught myself only with my left hand, my weaker hand, and arm.

"Ah!" I moaned, and I glanced down at the top of a shed 130 feet below. I caught myself and grabbed onto a vertical platform bar with my right hand. I swung both feet over the platform, with Jimmy and Emmett holding my legs, and dropped to the platform.

"Ugh! Sorry, fellows. Whew!" I said as I sat down on the platform and rested. I had totally underestimated how difficult it would be to get back to the platform.

Jimmy and Emmett were silent. We didn't talk as I motioned to them that I was out of breath by waving my hand at them. After a five-minute rest, Jimmy and Emmett went down the ladder inside the tower leg first. I sat on the platform and continued to rest. I had survived a stupid feat, and we all knew it, but I wasn't going to admit that to my friends. The sun was orange, and we would soon lose our light. I took my last look at the wonderful place where I lived, stepped inside the steel tube, and put my foot on the first step down. Somehow the trip down seemed much faster. Once the three of us were safely on the ground, we celebrated our accomplishment and bounded off toward home.

"That was a great time," Emmett said as the six of us walked home across a manicured bluegrass field highlighted by a setting sun.

"What was it like climbing into that bowl?" Emmett asked.

"Great, like being in another world, but I won't do it again."

As we walked home, my hands were aching and raw, and I realized my underwear was wet from the stress of my adventure. I now had some experience and knew what fear was like. I never figured out why my underwear was wet, but it was probably a combination of urine and sweat. Of course, I didn't admit it to my platoon members, but I was scared to death much of the time I was on top of my cloud.

The next day, I learned that the police heard of our stunt. An article in the newspaper stated that kids had been spotted on the water tower the day before. The article went on to describe the hazards of such escapades. The next time we surveyed the site, we found a large lock on the entrance door of the steel tube. Our one-time adventure would not be repeated. Since I had never flown in an airplane, being on the water tower was like witnessing the beauty of where we lived from the sky. Blue meadows provided the setting for these youthful adventures.

CHAPTER 4

Bluebloods

My first Hopewell cotillion resulted in social paralysis. For me, it was a terrifying experience to ask a girl to dance. The more I wanted to dance with a certain girl, the less likely I was to ask her. The cause was uncertain. It was easy to go to school, play sports, or lead the charge in a BB gun battle, but it was far more difficult to ask a young lady to dance. I kept looking at a certain girl, and from that point on, my life changed. It was Mom's idea for me to join cotillion—to learn new social skills and how to dance—in January 1959. Only because my dance card was filled out beforehand did I dance at all. Of course, I hardly spoke to my dance partners. During a dance, my objectives were to not step on her feet and to remember the steps to the bop, stroll, and foxtrot.

For the monthly dances, the guys dressed up in sports coats and suits, and the girls wore dresses. The guys were too bashful to ask girls to dance, so the dance cards had a list of dance partners on the back. More and more dance-card slots were left blank toward the end of each school year, which meant the guys had to fill them in by asking someone to dance. The dance card was a social invention, and it worked.

I remember one cotillion at Teen Circle. Teen Circle was a large building next to the county courthouse in downtown Hopewell. It had a big dance floor with wooden booths fortified with many coats of paint and Formica tabletops to cover up past sins and mistakes. Once a month, some of us were assigned to take buckets and putty knives and scrap off the chewing gum that was stuck to the underside of the tabletops. The back of the room had a place for spinning forty-five RPM records, or where a band could play, and a small refreshment stand. The other end of the large room had picture windows that looked out over the majestic Hopewell courthouse. The view at night with the lighted courthouse was inspiring.

Teen Circle served as our social haven, and we could dance and interact in a social scene. We would stand by the Teen Circle windows and watch our friends come and go. We checked out the cars driving by. My favorite car at that time was the Plymouth Fury—with its sharp fins molded onto the rear fenders, the four big headlights, and the front grille. From the front, the car looked like an oversize frog's face. It was cool. I wanted that car when I could drive in four more years.

Dancing seemed easy on the television show *American Bandstand*. Dick Clark was the host of the show, which began in 1957, and I found it interesting to see how other kids dressed and danced. America copied whatever *American Bandstand* kids did. We were no different. We danced to songs like "Twelfth of Never" by Johnny Mathis, "Peggy Sue" by Buddy Holly, "Wake Up Little Susie" by the Everly Brothers, "Come Softly to Me" by the Fleetwoods, and "Tammy" by Debbie Reynolds.

Mom had other things going on that winter, including having my baby sister. In February 1959, Katie was born. I remember going to the hospital and seeing her for the first time. "Wow, Mom, you sure did a good job," I said as I watched Mom and Dad holding my new sibling. Having been an only child for eleven-plus years, I wasn't sure that it would work. But once Katie got home, I realized she was cute, fun to play with, and completed our family. The eleven-year difference in age meant there was no sibling rivalry. I played sports, studied algebra, and investigated girls, as Katie learned to walk, talk, and spell.

At our monthly dances, I kept noticing a young lady. Beth DeMoss had curly brown hair and wore simple but classy dresses. One dress had small polka dots and a black belt that showed her figure. It buttoned up the front, and what I thought was so cool was that it had a high lace collar with a black bow. In those days, young women didn't wear things high around their necks. Beth wore white socks and beautiful black-leather dance shoes with thin straps. Beth always looked great, but I was too shy to ask her to dance, and she had only showed up on my dance card once. During that dance, I was nervous and stepped on her feet, and of course, I never looked into her eyes.

Mom told me that Beth's family owned a horse farm that had been in the family for a century. It was a small farm where they bred horses and raised tobacco and soybeans. They owned horses that won a few stakes races, but no big winners like the Belmont, Preakness, or Kentucky Derby. That was all I knew about Beth, but I wanted to know more.

I spent most of one April evening trying to get up enough courage to ask Beth to dance—with no results. I had been tortured by the sequential playing of songs like the "Witch Doctor," "Yakety Yak," and "Book of Love." I kept glancing at her, and I think she realized something was going on. Beth looked me right in the eyes and smiled. I choked on my soda pop. And then Elvis Presley saved me. The DJ announced he would slow things down by playing "Love Me Tender." This was my chance! The dance ended in thirty minutes.

I walked over to Beth, not looking into her eyes, and bashfully said, "Beth, would you like to dance?"

"Sure," she said in a friendly way. So off we went to the dance floor. I held my left hand and her right hand out to the side, and we danced about one foot apart. I thought I was doing the foxtrot, but I'm not sure.

"I saw you play in the small fry football game last week," Beth said in a kind voice.

"Oh! Really? I didn't think you even knew who I was."

"Everyone knows you, David. It's a small town." Her comment came as a surprise to me. As the song came to an end, we stood on the dance floor longer than normal. I wanted to say something else, but it wouldn't come out of my mouth. Fortunately, the next song was "Young Love" by Tab Hunter, so we danced again. This time we were only six inches apart.

As the evening ended, I said, "Uh, Beth, would you like to go to a movie? We could meet at Mildred's Drug Store and then go."

"When?"

"Oh! How about Saturday at six?"

"Yes, that would be fun," Beth said as her mother came to pick her up.

Mildred's Drug Store was on a Main Street corner, and the single-screen theater was two blocks down. Mildred's was a classic fifties drugstore with an art deco flair. The outside décor and sign were chrome with a light-green tile background. A neon sign in the window spelled out, in script, "Mildred's Drug Store." To the left was a soda fountain counter with chrome stools fixed to the floor. Running the length of the fountain across from it were three booths with vinyl seats and Formica tabletops. To the right was the pharmacy, and pills and liquids filled dark wood cabinets and shelves. I still marvel at the craftsmanship of those cabinets today, and I thought they conveyed the integrity of the medicines that were dispensed to trusting townspeople.

The drugstore was a beehive of activity with shopkeepers, businesspeople, and kids constantly coming in and out of its doors. It was the center of downtown. Since Mildred's Drug Store was on my way home from school—and in those days we walked to school—I often stopped in for a soda. I'd listen to the jukebox and see if any of my friends were there. The chrome jukebox was always playing the latest songs: "Jailhouse Rock" by Elvis Presley, "Rock Around the Clock" by Bill Haley and the Comets, and "Flying Purple People Eater" by Sheb Wooley.

The movie house had the traditional small-town ticket window, and the theater marquee, outlined by red-and-white-neon lights, hung over the sidewalk. The marquee used big metal letters to announce the times and names of the movies that were showing. The movie house was two blocks from the drugstore. At night, the theater was a beacon of light in an otherwise colorless Main Street. For teenagers, especially the ones who didn't drive, the theater was a way to escape the oversight of teachers, coaches, and parents. It was a venue for freedom and a gateway to the outside world.

I arrived early at Mildred's Drug Store and sat down at the soda fountain for my first real date. I wore a solid white dress shirt, thinking that all my plaid shirts looked too ordinary for Beth.

"Do you want a menu, son?" the fountain manager asked.

"Yes, but I may eat in a booth," I replied.

He nodded as I scanned the menu. I found that a bacon, lettuce, and tomato sandwich was forty cents, and a banana split cost twenty-five cents.

A few minutes past six o'clock, I caught a glimpse of Beth's mom dropping her off in a big pink car with a white top.

"Hi, David," Beth said. She entered the drugstore with a big smile on her face. She was wearing an immaculate tan dress with white lace borders.

"Wow, you look great," I blurted out.

Beth sat beside me on a chrome stool with a green vinyl seat.

"Do you want to sit in a booth or here at the fountain?" I asked nervously.

"Let's sit in the booth," Beth replied with a giggle. We stood up and moved to an empty booth. The booth seats were covered in the same green vinyl, and the Formica tabletop was white with flakes of gold embedded in it. As we moved, I couldn't help noticing her perfectly proportioned legs and the thin belt around her small waist. At that moment, a feeling came over me and surged through my body. I wasn't quite sure what the feeling was, but later I knew it was sexual desire.

The fountain manager came over to the booth, handed us menus, and asked, "What do you want to drink?"

"Cherry Coke would be fine," Beth replied.

"I'll have the same," I replied and struggled with what to say next.

We didn't say anything for a while. I looked into her pedigree green eyes. In fact, that might have been the first time I ever looked into any girl's eyes. Whew¾stressful.

"Ah, I saw you drive up in a nice car. Is it new?" I asked trying to say something—anything.

"Oh! It's not new. It's a 1955 Lincoln Capri," Beth said.

"It sure looked new."

"Yes, Mom and Dad bought it for four thousand dollars, I think," Beth replied with a proud smile.

The fountain manager brought us our Cherry Cokes and asked, "What do you want to order?"

"How about a hamburger with everything—lettuce, pickles, cheese, and ketchup—but no fries," Beth responded.

"I'll have a BLT with fries," I said. "So Beth, you live on a horse farm off Randle Road, right?"

"Yes, you'll have to come out sometime. We can hike around the farm."

"Okay, sounds like fun. My friends and I play on Thoroughbred Meadows Farm all the time," I proclaimed with pride.

"Yes, we go over to their house for Derby parties every year. It's fun," Beth replied.

I wondered how one gets invited to a Derby party. I then made a futile attempt to explain how my life tied to horse farms by saying, "My dad and I were called over there on a cold February night when the power went out because of an ice storm."

"Oh! What for?" Beth asked.

"Well, when the power went out, they needed a backup generator installed because a mare was having a baby. We quickly loaded up the truck and set it all up in a stall so the veterinarian could help deliver the foal. I helped set up the lights and heaters and got to watch the birth."

As I was telling her this story, I was thinking about the chandelier in the entrance to the stable that night. That's right, on the Thoroughbred Meadows Farm, where Derby winners and hopefuls roam, barns were not quite as you might imagine. They were very well-maintained buildings with heating and ventilation systems that the world's poor would love to live in. I had always thought that the chandelier was a bit too much for a horse barn. But I expect the horses enjoyed its many sparkling lights at night. Yes, the horses' nightlight was a chandelier!

"Yes, Dad has taken me to watch several live births. It's amazing," Beth replied. "Was the foal a pedigree? What was its bloodline?" Beth innocently asked.

"I don't know, Beth. I'm not in the horse industry," I said as our food was delivered to the table. We ate our food and talked some more, and we topped it off by sharing a strawberry milkshake with two straws. We sucked on our straws at the same time, making a loud noise, and for the second time that night, I looked into her beautiful eyes. It was fun as we learned how to date and interact.

While we waited for the check, I said, "Do you still want to go to the movie?"

"Yes, Mom says *South Pacific* is a wonderful movie," Beth replied.

"Okay, then we'll go after I pay."

South Pacific was a musical that I wasn't thrilled about seeing, but the Hopewell movie house was a one-screen theater, and there were no other choices. Since we could not drive, we would walk Main Street that evening. Beth and I walked the two blocks to the theater, and I paid seventy-five cents each to get in. This was a higher price than I normally paid in Hopewell, but it was *South Pacific*. A big *South Pacific* poster was on the theater wall in a glass case.

"It looks like this was a Broadway play," I said as we examined the colorful yellow-and-red poster.

"Yes," Beth said. "We saw the play in New York."

We entered the theater, bought Cokes and popcorn, and sat in the next-to-last row in the back of the theater since it was almost full. I was impressed with the powerful music and island scenery. We shared our popcorn and napkins, and toward the end of the movie, we were free of food and drink. I reached out to hold her hand. At first, I held her hand stiffly, but eventually I rubbed my thumb over her soft palm. Beth turned and smiled at me, and our hands tightened. At the end of the movie, before the lights came on, I abruptly leaned over and kissed her on the cheek. To my surprise, she didn't move away.

I followed her out of the movie house, watching her body sway back and forth. Once outside the theater, we walked back to Mildred's Drug Store, and we were holding hands. The April sky was clear, and the air was brisk. As we were walking, I thought it seemed natural to hold her hand. We went back inside the drugstore to use their phone to call her mom to come and pick her up.

"David, I enjoyed the night. Thank you."

"Yes, I did too," I replied as we stood inside the drug store's glaring lights.

"Let's go outside and wait," I said.

Main Street was filled with people walking and driving their cars—it was Saturday night. People were talking, laughing, and having fun as music from the car radios poured into the air. Beth's mom drove up in her Lincoln Capri, her eyes surveying our every move, and Beth leaned over and kissed me on the cheek. "Good night! Talk to you later!" Beth said and closed the door of the car.

I walked home that April evening pondering our fate. I was happy. I had a successful first date. *Wow! Maybe I'm in love.*

For the rest of our sixth-grade school year, Beth and I went out, but it was not as frequent as I would have liked. We both were busy, and I was too young to drive, so dating was dependent on parents, school, sports, and church schedules.

Beth invited me out to her house several times. I met the family, including house servants and farm hands. Her two-story house had about a dozen rooms and rose-colored flowers and immaculate trimmed bushes around it. Her bedroom included a four-poster bed from the 1800s, and her window overlooked a pond. The kitchen was bigger than the first floor of my house. We hiked her farm fields, watched thoroughbreds and saddlebred horses gallop over rolling hills with white-planked fences defining each field, and found time to relax, hold hands, and kiss in the serenity of an isolated horse farm.

The end of my sixth-grade year brought several changes in my life. I would soon begin working in my dad's business. I continued swimming for the Hopewell Country Club swim team, and I got ready for the upcoming football season. Junior high sports began next year. I thought I could become the next Johnny Unitas of the Baltimore Colts and play college football for the University of Louisville, as he did from 1951 to 1954. I would turn twelve years old in August and enter the seventh grade in September. Our junior high football team began practice in early August.

In June 1959, I began summer work in my dad's business. After having seen the worst of the outside world, my dad went into business with his father, John Bourbon. We called him "the Boss." The Boss's wife, Ruth, had died of tuberculosis. The Boss, my grandfather, had begun a radio and electrical contractor business in the twenties in Hopewell. Their office and warehouse was on a major downtown street. We often had breakfast at one of the downtown restaurants. He usually was in bed by nine weeknights, was up at five, and was eating breakfast downtown by six.

My grandfather opened the shop every day at seven. He drove a green 1952 Ford F-100 pickup truck. The front of the truck had two big wide headlights, a huge front grille, and an engine hood that defined durability. The cabin would hold three people. It had flat seats, a high roof, and gauges for voltage, temperature, miles per hour, and oil and fuel levels. The back tires were encased in fenders that surrounded the entire wheel well. The bed of the truck was not large, but the Boss seldom carried loads of materials to and from the jobsite. I always thought the running boards were the best part of the truck. All shop trucks were Fords.

The Boss was a slender man, six feet and one inch tall. He had a bald head and wore gold wire-rimmed glasses. He was a diabetic, smoked cigars, and wore an old-fashioned railroad watch on a gold chain. The unique and funny thing about this watch was that it had two sets of hands. At the end of the workday when his employees were ready to stop, the Boss would pull out that watch, show it to them, and say, "Why are you stopping? See here—it's only four o'clock, not five o'clock." Once they got the inside story, everyone would laugh and go along with his antics. Every new employee—and I mean every one of them—had to go through this ritual. The other employees always played along with my grandfather. He would stare at the new employee on the first day of work and tell him he had to work one more hour. It was as humorous to watch my grandfather play this game for the fiftieth time as it was to watch the faces of the new employees.

The townspeople thought my grandfather was a spirited character. He was inseparable from his Ford F-100 truck, watch, cigars, and of course, the shop. He frequently gave friends appliances and work at his cost, and of course, these practices greatly upset my dad. While his generosity was a fine way to make friends, it was not too good for making a living. Without my dad, the Boss would have been financially broke. To the Boss's credit, he always went on service calls to help people who had lost their electricity to storms or lightning, or when furnaces were out on cold winter nights, and he never failed to help elderly folks. He grew up in a different era where hard work as a young boy was the norm. He was tougher on family than friends.

As the co-owner of an electrical contractor business, Dad studied the blueprints, estimated job prices, hired and fired the men, planned the work, ordered the materials, priced bills, and managed the crews on a day-to-day basis. He did it six days a week, often working at night. He was constantly running between jobs and trying to keep multiple crews busy. Managing your own family business is not an easy task. Dad, like his father, sometimes didn't charge enough, and once he made money, he was terrible at long-term investments.

In July 1959, Beth approached me at the Hopewell Country Club swimming pool on a late Sunday afternoon. I had quit swimming practice laps and was drying off with a fluffy brown towel. I was tired after my swim. She had finished eating in the club dining room with her family. Beth, in a beautiful white-lace Sunday dress, rigidly said, "David, can we go somewhere and talk?"

"Sure. How about over by the tennis courts on the bench?" I sensed that Beth was upset.

"So what's up?" I smiled at her and sat down.

"I have been trying to tell you for a week that I'm leaving Hopewell. I'm going to a women's boarding school in Virginia."

I was shocked. I twisted both ends of the towel around my neck. "Oh. Why?"

"Mom and Dad want me to get a good education, and they are worried it might not happen in the Hopewell school system," Beth replied.

"Ah! Beth, this is not fair." I reached for her hand.

"The seventh grade begins there in three weeks."

"So we won't see each other until Christmas?" I replied in a puzzled voice.

"Mom says we'll be traveling over the holidays, so I may not have time to see you."

"I don't understand why you're leaving," I said. I stood up with the little energy I had left and stared at the vacant tennis court in silence.

Beth stood up, and we hugged. We walked back to the pool area holding hands, but we did not talk. Privately, I didn't understand why my first girlfriend had to be taken away so abruptly. I tried to act nonchalantly, but inside I was very upset.

After a few weeks of reflection after Beth was gone, I realized this was my first experience with dating and the elite blue-blooded horse families. I sort of knew they let their kids go to public schools with us commoners during elementary school, but then they were sent to some of the finest boarding schools in the United States. Blue-blooded horse families would not let a commoner of local heritage infiltrate their families. My introduction to the ways of the upper class was a shock. I think Beth knew this but was not about to hurt me or try to explain it.

Protecting bloodlines was important for both horses and horse people. My bloodlines included coal miners and laborers from England; Beth's included wealthy aristocrats from France. And to my surprise, although we both lived in Hopewell, these worlds were destined not to mix.

The term "blue blood" has an interesting history with both biological and societal explanations. One idea of blue bloods derives from medieval Europe and its kings, queens, and castles. Pure European nobility is based only on hereditary criteria, not wealth. The medical explanation begins in early European history, when nobles seldom were exposed to the sun, whereas peasants and ordinary folks were outside, working. Therefore, their skin tanned. Nobles were pale. Their veins stood out with a blue tint, and their skin seemed to be blue in color. A genetic explanation centers on some families with recessive genes that develop a condition called methemoglobinemia. Here, hemoglobin does not carry an adequate amount of oxygen in the blood, and at certain levels, causes the skin to be blue and lips to be purple. And some drugs, metals, and chemicals can cause human skin to turn blue. Beth and I, however, were not facing a medical or chemical challenge, but one based on social status and wealth.

Although my focus had been on school, work, and Beth, outside the haven of Hopewell, the seeds of change were everywhere. Fidel Castro was fighting President Batista's troops in the hills of Cuba, and King Faisal of Iraq was overthrown in a bloody coup d'etat. Communist insurgents in South Vietnam assassinated many South Vietnamese officials and began to move supplies into South Vietnam via the Ho Chi Minh Trail. The Cold War between the Soviet Union and the United States was firmly in place, with the US nuclear submarine *Nautilus* sailing under the North Pole ice cap, and a cosmic rocket carrying a hammer-and-sickle emblem on a Soviet-launched *Lunik* satellite flew past the moon. Alaska became the forty-ninth state, the "Southern Manifesto" of US Senator Harry F. Byrd, Sr. was signed by more than one hundred government officials to prevent integration initiatives by passing certain laws, and the seeds of the US women's liberation movement were germinating with the promise of the birth-control pill.

My sleepy existence in Hopewell would not be insulated from these upheavals or the ways of blue bloods.

CHAPTER 5

Taff Lane

It was the first day of the seventh grade, and I sat behind a new girl with long, black double ponytails and brown eyes. "Hi, I'm David. What's your name?"

"I'm Sally Leonard," she said in a shy voice.

"How long have you lived in Hopewell?"

"Two years. My parents moved here from Ohio. My dad is a raw-materials buyer at Jacobson Mills," Sally said as she swirled around in her seat and moved her long legs toward me.

"Don't they make shirts and shorts?" I replied as I subconsciously sized her up.

"Yes, they do. Have you been in the factory?"

"Yes. My dad's business keeps that factory going. He does all the electrical, heating, and air conditioning work," I said proudly.

Over the next few months, Sally and I talked and worked on algebra and geography homework together. Sally was smart, most likely smarter than me. Her radiant personality—and the fact she was a fresh face—attracted me. We became friends, and Sally learned to tolerate me. My favorite pastime was to stick glue or tape things to her ponytails since my seat was behind hers in class. These things attached to Sally's hair included weeds, tree sticks and leaves, paperclips, bubble-gum wrappers, and notes telling classmates behind her to pull her ponytails. It got to the point where her classmates always checked her ponytails after class to warn her of an impending attack.

Our classes were held in a massive three-story structure that housed seventh- and eighth-grade classes. Four huge Roman pillars crowned by a cornice framed the front steps of the school, which was built in 1908. The capitol-like steps leading up to the entrance and the dome atop the building gave it an air of grandeur. In the early days, this building was home to grades one through twelve. My father, mother, and other relatives had gone to school there. This dignified building was a tribute to how families and communities supported education back then. The building had served its purpose well for fifty-plus years, but it was scheduled to be torn down to make way for a circular auditorium and a band room. I thought we might be part of the last class to run its noble hallways.

School desks in the building were heavy wood with black iron frames, a shelf under the desktop, and an inkwell hole that once had a purpose. Each classroom had row after row of these desks firmly fixed to the hardwood floor with heavy black screws. Often I would study the grain of the hardwood in these desks, trying to decipher the wood's character and wonder whether this tree had known its fate. The writing boards were black and required the use of dusty, white chalk. Each classroom had a cloakroom with coat hooks. The ceilings were ten or twelve feet high, and bright lights hung down from thick iron pipes. The building embodied the permanence of American education.

One day, our teacher, Miss Mildred Fletcher, was lecturing on the provinces of Canada, and we were supposed to be writing down the answers in our workbook. Sally was wearing a pretty flowered dress with a tie around her neck that held up the front and back of her dress. I had a crush on her but wasn't sure what to do with my feelings. She had tied the straps in a beautiful bow at the back of her graceful neck. I had been tempted to untie this bow since the beginning of class, and the agony of not doing it finally overcame me. Toward the end of class, my hand slowly approached her long neck. I managed to grab one end of the bow and pull it. The front and back of her dress fell straight down, and our classmates gasped.

"Wow! Look at Sally!" one of my classmates yelled. Since I was in back of her I could not see her chest, but I could see the back of her white bra. Her entire body flushed. I had finally gone too far.

Sally grabbed the front of her dress with one hand and pulled it up over her chest. She turned, and with her right hand, Sally slapped me as hard as she could. The slap echoed up and down the hallway. *Wham*—what a hit! My face stung for an hour. Sally jumped up and ran off to the women's restroom, clutching her dress in the front, but her bare back and bra were for all to see.

Miss Fletcher immediately grabbed my arm and took me to the principal's office. Our classmates, of course, were snickering and talking. "Bourbon, you're going to be expelled," one of my classmates proclaimed.

"David, did you do this?" the junior high principal said in a stern voice.

"Yes, sir, I did."

"Then I have no choice but to suspend you for the next three days," he said. I collected my books and coat and walked home. I felt terrible about my antics. I had embarrassed that wonderful girl in the first few days of school. I really liked Sally. I kept asking myself, *Why did you do this, you dummy?*

My next challenge was to go home and explain this to Mom and Dad. I knew how Dad would react, but I was not sure what Mom would say. The problem was that Mom was on the school board. In fact, she was the first woman elected to it. Not only would this hurt Sally and her family, but it would also embarrass my family. Everyone in Hopewell would know of the incident—everyone.

On the way home, I stopped at Mildred's Drug Store, bought a twenty-five-cent chocolate ice cream cone, and sat on the stool, pondering my stupidity and fate. The store's jukebox was playing "It's So Easy" by the Crickets. My walk home was slow. I was lugging a heavy bag of books, and my headache was building. When I got home, Mom was standing in the doorway. The principal had called her and told her what happened.

"David, what on earth were you thinking?" Mom said.

"Mom, I'm sorry. I horsed around too much."

"Well, we'll wait for your father to get home, but I suspect you will be grounded for some time."

When Dad got home, they talked, and sure enough, I was grounded for two weeks. That meant I had to come home immediately after school and miss football practice *and* two games. I stayed home for two weekends. I had to go over to the Leonard home and apologize. I also apologized to my geography class and to Miss Fletcher.

On my return to school, Miss Fletcher said, "Class, David has something to say to you."

I stood up at my seat and said, "I'm sorry I embarrassed Sally, and I have told her so. I also disrupted our class, and I apologize to everyone. I am an idiot! I'm sorry."

Over the ensuing weeks, I tried my best to make up for what I had done. I quit putting stuff in Sally's hair. I brought her small flowers from the schoolyard. I tried to strike up casual conversations. I told her I was sorry about once a day.

"Sally, can I walk you home today?" I asked about a month after this episode.

"Sure," Sally said with a smile that turned my logical thinking into mush. I could tell that Sally's heart was kind. She was a classy young lady.

"Sally, would you go out with me?" I mumbled in an embarrassingly weak voice. "I didn't mean to hurt you, but I did. I'm sorry."

"David, it's okay," Sally replied. I finally realized she accepted my remorse as genuine. "Yes, let's go out. When?"

Sally and I began dating in October 1959. We visited Mildred's Drug Store and the movie theater. We were not old enough to drive, so we walked to sock hops and sporting events. We would smooch and hold hands, but that was it. I walked her home from school when I could.

One day as we walked home, I said, "I hear we're going to integrate with Dunbar High School."

"Yes, I've heard that, too. It's scary. Your mom's on the school board—she should know," Sally said.

"Yep, but Mom doesn't talk to us about some things the board discusses."

"I don't know how it will go," Sally mused. "It took federal troops to protect two Negroes so they could walk into that all-white high school in Little Rock, Arkansas."

"Yes. The governor of Arkansas hates Negroes," I said. "I hope we don't have troops here." In 1958, the US Supreme Court upheld a ruling that integration was legal, and Governor Faubus's actions were deemed unconstitutional. But Governor Faubus ignored the ruling and closed Central High School. The two students did graduate, and the racial hatred and violence in Little Rock was exposed on television for all to see. This race-based fear was unspoken in Hopewell. Television ensured it was on everyone's mind.

We reached the street corner where Sally turned left and I turned right to go home. "Are you playing football?" Sally asked as we looked at each other like two young, puzzled deer in a romantic encounter.

"Yes, but getting expelled from school, and Mom and Dad grounding me, means I lost my starting quarterback job."

"Oh, really," Sally replied with a flip of her hair and a sassy smile.

"Yes, but I'm going to win it back," I declared as we began our separate paths.

Twenty-five kids were on the Hopewell Junior High Thoroughbreds football team, and the starting offensive line averaged 158 pounds. Our seventh-grade team ended the season with five wins and one loss.

My biggest source of pride was being awarded my first junior varsity football letter. I bought the letter jacket for thirty-nine dollars with the money I earned at my summer job. I took the jacket and my orange JV letter to the Thimble Fabric and Sewing Shop on Main Street and had the letter sewed on the jacket.

I wore that black jacket with orange leather sleeves as if it signified I had won the Nobel Prize. All team members wore their jackets with immense pride. We did not have big houses or expensive cars, and we didn't own horse farms. There were few symbols of status for ordinary people in small-town America, and for me, my letter jacket was a true status symbol.

Sally wore my letter jacket even on warm days. My sister was two years old, and she frequently wore my letter jacket around the house. Of course, the bottom of it dragged along the floor as Katie wandered the house. Even Mom would wear my jacket at times. Dad couldn't join the fun since the jacket was too small. That letter jacket was definitely an icon for the family. We all jockeyed to wear this symbol of achievement, which I still have to this day.

The winter brought numbing cold. It was a time for basketball. I was about six feet tall in the seventh grade and played forward. The University of Kentucky had won its fourth NCAA basketball championship in 1958, and I followed the team closely. Players like Johnny Cox and Vernon Hatton were constantly on the news because Kentucky was a hotbed of college basketball. Coach Adolph Rupp's "Fiddlin' Five" team compiled a record of 23–6 on its way to the national championship and its nineteenth Southeastern Conference championship. Like many young kids, I wanted to be a sports star, so I worked hard in practice and the games. Our seventh-grade team won seven games and lost four during a cold winter.

The school year ended, and while a lot of kids my age couldn't find a summer job, I had the opposite problem. I continued to work in my dad's electrical contracting business. The work was hard, but the pay was good at $1.85 per hour. I had my own money to buy clothes and date, but no time to do much in the summer. I was up at six and working nine-hour days, five days a week.

I found being a blue-collar worker to be in conflict with being on the country club swim team and trying to be a stallion with the girls. On the weekends, I would swim for the Hopewell Country Club in tournaments around central Kentucky. The members of some of these country clubs were very wealthy. But during the week, my teammates sat around the pool and walked Main Street. I was in dirty work clothes riding around Hopewell in an electrical contractor's truck—not exactly a glamorous way to attract country club girls.

My friends soon realized that during the week there was little point in calling me to go out for a night. I was exhausted. Sally had a part-time job, so we only saw each other on the weekends that summer.

Fortunately, when the summer work ended, I could practice football in August and have more time to see Sally. Sally went out for the JV cheerleading squad and made the team, so we were together during our six JV games. The girls only played basketball and ran track at my high school in 1960. Other activities for young women included the band, Future Homemakers of America, the speech club, the Latin club, and choir.

One time, I asked Sally, "Would you play girls' sports if our school had more of them like golf and swimming?"

"That topic came up in class the other day when Betty gave a book report on the Olympics. She said no girls were in the first Olympics in 776 BC. I heard they were going to start girls' golf at Hopewell High School sometime," she replied.

"But do you miss not having more sports opportunities?" I persisted.

"No, we have plenty to do, and it costs too much to have boys' and girls' coaches and teams," Sally replied.

Since we could not yet drive, we had three main places of refuge on Main Street in Hopewell—Mildred's Drug Store, the one-screen movie theater, and the Teen Circle. Sally and I made great use of these hangouts, as did all of my classmates. These iconic places were within walking distance of one another and provided venues for us to socialize and be free.

Teen Circle had a jukebox that played songs of the day, including "Witch Doctor" by David Seville, "Itsy Bitsy Teenie Weenie Yellow Polka Dot Bikini" by Brian Hyland, "It's Now or Never" by Elvis Presley, "Bird Dog" and "Wake Up, Little Susie" by the Everly Brothers, and "Puppy Love" by Paul Anka. My favorite song was "The Book of Love" by the Monotones. I can still sing every word to this day. Teen Circle opened for sock hops and dances and sometimes hosted cotillions. Sally and I did all of it; we were becoming soul mates.

At Teen Circle, my friends and classmates could build friendships and have face-to-face discussions about an array of topics, such as who was dating whom, race relations, sports, nuclear war, and rock 'n' roll. We often decorated the ceiling with lights and balloons for sock hops. We helped the parent chaperons clean up after each event, which always ended by eleven o'clock. The chaperons were wonderful, but we could tell that the driving rhythms of our music and our uninhibited dancing bothered them. Rock 'n' roll was gaining momentum. Kids with cars could park outside and go into Teen Circle. The Hopewell police didn't allow us to loiter outside around the cars. Teen Circle was an important part of our lives throughout our teenage years. Once we turned twenty, we couldn't get inside.

A new face in politics emerged when Senator John F. Kennedy announced on January 31, 1960, that he would run for president. To us, he seemed too young to be a politician. Adults, including this possible president of the United States, were old people with gray hair, wrinkled faces, and fat hanging under their chins, which we called "gizzards."

A lunch counter sit-in by blacks in Greensboro, North Carolina, on February 1, 1960, caused a ruckus when white waitresses refused to serve them. We watched the black and white races struggle to find balance, ironically on black-and-white televisions.

Sally and I, along with a multitude of friends, escaped some of this turmoil by walking up and down Main Street talking and having fun. We walked a lot in those days. The town was alive with young and old interacting in a family atmosphere. We felt safe in Hopewell, compared to the chaos we saw daily on television. The shopkeepers knew everyone by name, and they knew our parents, so our behavior was generally good.

The movie theater was another refuge for Sally and me. I learned how to hold and caress Sally's hands. The dark theater enhanced our focus on touch. Our handholding helped us fall in some sort of love and led me to tantalizing sexual fantasies.

Occasionally, my hands found their way to her waist or breasts but always with her blouse fully on. I had no idea what came next. As eighth graders, we were growing up together. We learned how to share, dance, fight, and make up. The only time we did not hug and kiss was when we watched movies like Alfred Hitchcock's *Psycho,* which was totally frightening to us.

Besides these three places on Main Street, there was school. At school, I sometimes tried to misbehave when I knew Sally was at recess or lunch. I was in my eighth-grade homeroom when Sally was at lunch. Often Sally would go outside and wait under the second story cloakroom window, hoping I might peek out or drop a note to her. My eighth-grade homeroom teacher had been teaching for two years. She tried her best to control the boys, but we were a lot to handle. Besides, we were much bigger than most of our teachers. She would often send me and other misbehaving kids to the cloakroom for not paying attention or disrupting class. I think this practice was better for her since she didn't want the principal to know she couldn't control the class.

My other pastime when I resided in the cloakroom was folding notebook paper on the floor to make water bombs that I intermittently threw out the cloakroom window. I became a legend around the school as the cloakroom hero. Every cloakroom had a white-porcelain washbasin where I could fill the bombs. I remember being very quiet as I folded the paper and slowly turned on the water faucet. I often took my shoes off so I did not make noise. Many other skills were required to be the perfect cloakroom hero, such as knowing where to walk on the wood floor to avoid squeaking boards. Through careful thought and practice, I perfected the processes necessary to execute these achievements. Our teacher didn't seem to look in the cloakroom much. I think she was happy to have me out of sight so she could complete her memorized lesson plan.

One day, as I had planned, I was sent to cloakroom purgatory for talking in class. I meticulously prepared the perfect water bomb and crept up to the open window. I peeked over the windowsill and observed about a dozen kids standing around and talking during their recess. Sally, wearing my letter jacket, glanced up and saw me evaluating the potential victims of my perfect water bomb.

My radar identified my target as Marvin Jacobs, standing about ten feet from Sally. I launched my missile. The trajectory was perfect, I thought, as my work of art arched toward its prey making a *whoosh* sound. At the last minute, Marvin moved, to be replaced by Coach Strickland, the Hopewell basketball coach.

My water bomb hit Coach Strickland squarely on the shoulder. He turned around and looked up at the window. "Who did that?" He ran up two floors to the cloakroom. Before I knew it, he was standing at the other end of the cloakroom, yelling, "Bourbon, get downstairs. We're going to see the principal." Immediately, a chorus of cheers erupted from my classroom and the recess crowd below. The legendary cloakroom hero had struck again.

I was expelled for two days and repeated my long walk home and my two weeks of home internment. Of course, my classmates loved it and thought I was the hero of the year. And I have to admit that I liked the admiration. Later, everyone was patting me on the back in the hallway. This was the second time I had been expelled from school. By the next time I entered that cloakroom, the window had been nailed shut, and the cloakroom door was left open for the rest of the school year. My career as the cloakroom hero had abruptly ended.

My teammates and I excelled in JV football. Our eighth-grade team's record was again five wins and one loss. I permanently lost my quarterback job, but I played as a fullback and offensive and defensive end. For a Class A (small school) football program, we were good, and we were getting better. Many of my classmates were much better athletes than I was. Going ten and two in our two years in junior high foretold our futures in high school football. Sally cheered as I played, and we shared many good times during these games.

I found a new adventure in March 1961 when Connie and Danny invited us to drive around with them in Danny's car. Sally had become friends with Connie Burden, who was in the eleventh grade. Connie's boyfriend, Danny Kruger, was also in the eleventh grade. Sally and I were close to ending our eighth-grade year. We enjoyed going out with them because we got to cruise the Circuit—that is, drive from the downtown courthouse up High Street, to Jerry's Drive-In Restaurant on the outskirts of town, and back down Main Street to the courthouse. The Circuit was about an eight-mile loop. It was fun. This Hopewell ritual was supposed to be for the older kids with driver's licenses. We got to experience it before our time.

The Circuit was a tour trip back in time. Many historical and magnificent buildings anchored this treasured route, including the courthouse and town square, Teen Circle, Mildred's, and Jerry's. The courthouse, for example, had an interesting history. The first log courthouse was built in 1787, overlooking Hopewell Springs. The courthouse square included streets on all four sides. In 1799, the original log and lumber courthouse structure was torn down, and rebuilt with stone. It had a cupola, and in 1816, a tall spire was added. One of the earliest engraved drawings was an 1862 depiction of John Morgan capturing Hopewell during the Civil War, which read, "The rebel Morgan with his guerillas bivouacking in Court House Square after levying contributions on the inhabitants." Much of this structure was destroyed in an 1872 fire.

Hopewell's third courthouse was built in 1873 from large granite blocks from a nearby quarry with a 113-foot-high clock and bell tower. Wisely, the designers included fireproof vaults and rooms in the new building. A photograph from 1899 shows the square packed with people, horses, and carriages celebrating the USA's victory in the Spanish-American War. The third courthouse burned down in 1901.

People forget that in this time period, knob-and-tube wiring, coal- and wood-fired stoves, and no sprinkler systems meant that buildings burned down. The fourth and current Hopewell courthouse was finished in 1905 and was fashioned after the US Capitol and the South Carolina capitol buildings. Hopewell's 1905 courthouse was placed on the National Register of Historic Places in 1974.

Each of the four Hopewell courthouses was a tribute to democracy at the local level. The building represented values, such as hard work, law and order, and freedom. Local leaders assessed taxes and allocated county and city funds, laws were written and improved, property records were meticulously kept, court trials were conducted, jury verdicts were decided, and many celebrations and town events happened at the courthouse square.

When I drove by the courthouse, I saw much more than a building and town square. I saw thousands of speeches, auctions, elections, and celebrations. I saw the birth and growth of a nation built upon sturdy pioneer values. I know where I came from—Kentucky, the heartland of the United States in bygone times—and I shall forever be grateful.

One Saturday night in May, Sally and I were in the backseat of Danny's car as we cruised the Circuit. We were always excited to ride with Danny and Connie because we could hug and kiss, yell out the window to friends, and enjoy every aspect of driving around the Circuit.

"David, Sally, what time to you have to be home?" Danny said.

"We need to be home by eleven o'clock," I replied.

"Good, then we'll take you to Taff Lane," Danny said with a laugh.

Taff Lane was a lonely, narrow country road known by the high school students as Lovers' Lane. Sally and I had never been to Taff Lane, and we thought it would be fun. Taff Lane was a winding road that crossed a shallow rock-bed creek. On the other side of the creek was a barn protected by a fence and gate. Cars had to drive through the creek because there was no bridge. In heavy rains, the road was impassable. Trees and bushes lined the roadside, broken only by occasional entrances to farmhouses and barns. The road was narrow in many spots, and only one car could pass at a time. Cars coming and going often had to back up to the nearest gate. The cars' bright headlights were irritating to young lovers' eyes.

On the way out to Taft Lane, Danny and I talked about a track meet we had both participated in. I did enjoy throwing the discus and came in second or third in most JV meets. Danny ran the one-mile and half-mile races in high school meets and occasionally came in first.

Danny crossed the creek and parked in front of the barn. Connie and Danny wasted no time making out in the front seat. In the past, Sally and I had done much kissing and rubbing, but we were normally in public places. But now we had no such constraints. This was a liberating experience for both of us. *Now what am I supposed to do? Should I try to go all the way? Did I know how to go all the way?* Unfortunately, my answer was no. Suddenly, I was nervous—really nervous.

Sally and I took a break from kissing. We could hear the creek rushing by. It sounded good—cold and crisp. The radio was playing songs like "Come Softly to Me." I think she was nervous too as we held one another.

After a while, Danny and Connie got out of the car, opened its trunk, and pulled out a heavy blanket. "David, Sally, we're going to the barn for a while. I left the keys in the ignition. You two behave," Danny said with a laugh. He pitched me a small package. I held the package up close in the dark to discover it was a condom.

"What is that, David?" Sally asked innocently.

"It's ... a rubber," I mumbled.

"Oh," Sally replied with a surprised giggle. I had put on a rubber in my room to see what it was like, but now I had to do it in the dark, with Sally watching. It was much more stressful than a school exam or a football game. I put the condom down on the seat.

Sally and I began to kiss. Now my hands went all over her body. Being a rookie at the proper procedures for such endeavors, I spent an eternity trying to unbutton her blouse. I awkwardly helped her pull her blouse off and then unhooked her bra. This movement created a rush of adrenaline through my body. I took off her skirt and panties, but these procedural matters seemed to take forty-eight hours.

We did not talk. Her back was red hot. I kissed and fondled her. Then I realized I still had all of my clothes on. I had forgotten half of the procedure—getting myself undressed. This wasn't going to work. *Now what am I supposed to do? Do you stop what you are doing and get yourself undressed—or does that blow the whole deal? And that damned rubber is still looking at me from the seat.*

I retreated from her most tender spot and proceeded to take my pants, underwear, shoes, and shirt off. Now I only had on my T-shirt and socks. I was worried that Sally might change her mind while I was taking an eternity to get undressed. But Sally was silent. And then I opened the condom package and fumbled around to put it on. After I got it on, I wondered if I put it on inside out, and wondered if that mattered. But there was no time to worry about my puzzlements.

Sally slowly opened her long legs and placed one leg high on the backseat. As soon as I glanced at those beautiful legs spread out, I moved myself between them. Almost two years of sexual restraint were about to explode. By now, I was swirling in the air with no place to go. After two unsuccessful attempts to hit the target, I was getting upset. How in the hell did you do this? Fortunately, Sally was patient as I continued my haphazard attempt at lovemaking. And then I had an epiphany. Why not use my hand to guide myself in? Meanwhile, Sally was graciously smiling at me and giving me all the time I needed. I was thinking that all this was taking way too long. Sally might stop me at any moment. I could write a symphony in the time it took to get my clothes off, put on a condom, and meander around trying to hit the target.

On my third try, I used my hand to find the target. Ah! Our bodies twisted and turned. Somehow our inhibitions vanished. Time, which was so important earlier, didn't seem to matter now. We moved on each other in unrehearsed ways, but it was so soft and pleasant. The car seemed like a furnace. We were soaking wet as I lay on top of her. The world was irrelevant. Sally and I shared a new world.

I wondered whether it was over. Now what was I supposed to do—quickly retreat and get dressed, or was there a winding-down procedure, too? I was a future scientist so "procedure and process" was the way I thought, even at fourteen years old. I was trying to do everything right. I wanted Sally to be happy. We held hands, and all was perfect.

After resting for a while, I stepped out of the car and held Sally's hand as she followed. We were naked, but I still had my socks on. We walked to the end of the car as I held Sally. I stepped into about a foot of creek water and washed up. The water was clear and clean, like our first lovemaking encounter. A half-moon provided a nightlight. I could see her shadow waving in the water. I grabbed her, and we kissed as the world rushed by our feet. I realized my socks were soaking wet. "Sally, I've still got my socks on," I said with a laugh.

Sally laughed, too. "David, let's get dressed. I'm cold." I held her on the short walk back to the car.

Sally and I had lost our innocence, our virginity. Like many before us, it might have happened too early or too late, but it happened. We got dressed and sat back down in Danny's car. I closed the windows and ran the car heater. We didn't talk—there was no need to. We smiled at each other, kissed occasionally, and held hands. We must have been faster than Connie and Danny because they didn't come back for another twenty minutes. When they did, they simply said, "Did you two have fun?" We nodded but said nothing.

On the way home, none of us said much. Danny and I made a few comments about the track meet. Danny took Sally home first and then me—we were both home by eleven o'clock that night. To Danny's credit, he said nothing about the events of the night. *So that's what it's all about,* I thought. The next day, I called Sally, and we talked, but not specifically about the previous night.

For the rest of the school year, Sally and I continued to hang out together. About every other week, we would go out driving with Danny and Connie and continue our intermittent sexual adventures. Our encounters in the theater, and elsewhere, were more intense now. We were in some type of starry-eyed love. I wasn't quite sure if it was the real thing or something our parents called puppy love. Even holding hands was different now. We shared everything. It was a special time. It was a first time.

My work at the shop that summer was long and hard, and I was winning a few races for the Hopewell Country Club swim team. In mid-July, Sally called me one weekday and said in a poignant voice, "Can we meet at Mildred's Drug Store tonight?" When I walked into the drugstore, Sally was sitting on a stool at the soda fountain. She had been crying.

I said, "Sally, are you okay?"

"David, Dad got a promotion at Jacobson Mills. He'll be a purchasing manager in Louisiana."

"What?" I sat down on the stool besides her. "What?"

"Yes, we're leaving. He just got the job offer," she moaned.

I stood up from my stool and hugged Sally. The fountain manager gave us space by moving to the other end of the counter. I was totally confused by what was happening.

Sally was crying, and I was trying not to. True love was being truncated on short notice, and neither of us had any control.

"Sally, I'm in love with you," I said in a defiant voice.

"Yes, I know."

During those last weeks, Sally and I saw each other as much as possible. We promised to visit one another, but I had hardly been out of Hopewell County, much less all the way to Louisiana. Sally planned to write me with her new address once she got settled in her new home.

One early August morning before football practice, I watched as the Leonards loaded their station wagon and followed the moving van out of town. I hugged and kissed Sally for the last time and walked home crying.

CHAPTER 6

Silver Fangs

"Don't be a sissy! Run to the finish line! Run! Run!" Coach Humphrey yelled. It was the first day of football practice in August 1961, and we were running laps around the field. I was in the ninth grade. Our junior varsity football team had won ten games and lost two during our seventh- and eighth-grade years. Hopewell expected a highly successful varsity football team. We were the class that created the buzz in Main Street conversations.

Getting into shape for football season was not the easiest thing to do in the August heat. The heaviest players often walked the last few hundred yards, and the rest of us lumbered our way across the finish line. After a rest and water break, it was time for calisthenics. Next, we walked through offensive plays and defensive schemes. Practice ended with fifty-yard wind sprints. Most of my teammates worked during the summer, but we somehow had enough energy for both work and football practice. When we had one practice a day, I also worked half a day at my dad's business. When we had practice twice a day, I didn't work.

The next week we began hitting and scrimmages, and the aches, pains, and bruises started. But after a while, a head-on collision at full speed didn't seem to bother you. Your body adjusted and got into football shape. These collisions were necessary rituals in football practice. No one gave the possibility of a concussion a second thought. The competition was intense. Freshmen challenged upperclassmen for starting positions. You learned that anyone could take your job at any time.

The whole town came to our gridiron practices, especially when they were in the evening. My dad would attend practice and scrimmages in the evening, and he talked to parents and townspeople about the events of the day and our football team. It was embedded in Hopewell's culture and football heritage. The Hopewell High School football tradition went back to as early as 1909, when the sport of football was being developed, including the flying wedge and leather helmets. In those days, it took three downs to get a first down, field goals were worth four points, and touchdowns were five points.

American football was growing in popularity in the fifties and sixties. In Kentucky, for example, we watched Johnny Unitas play for the University of Louisville in the fifties. I dreamed of being like Unitas. He set college passing records and helped develop the power of the forward pass in American football. The Pittsburgh Steelers drafted him for the NFL in the ninth round, but he did not make the team. He worked in construction in Pittsburgh for a while to support a wife and child, and he played on a semipro team called the Bloomfield Rams for six dollars a game. In 1956, Unitas joined the Baltimore Colts and went on to win the NFL championship in 1958, and several NFL most valuable player awards.

Our high school football field was located between an old quarry and Duncan River. The edge of the quarry cliff was a hundred feet tall. The precipice revealed the strength of the gray limestone, and there were no places where one could climb its walls. It provided a unique amphitheater where football battles would be won and lost and football heroes made. Duncan River wandered through Hopewell and provided the gift of pure limestone-filtered water. Townspeople said that this water built strong bones in the thoroughbred horses that encircled Hopewell.

Beyond Hopewell and our revered football field, the outside world was boiling in 1961. In January, John F. Kennedy was sworn in as the thirty-fifth president of the United States, and a chimpanzee named Ham completed a successful one-day flight in a test of the Mercury space capsule. The Strategic Air

Command launched the first solid-fuel rocket, the Minuteman, an intercontinental ballistic missile. The US-led Bay of Pigs invasion of Cuba failed. Yuri Gagarin, a Russian cosmonaut, became the first person to orbit the earth. As the US and Russia disagreed over the future of Germany, thousands of Germans were fleeing Communism to West Berlin. A month later, the Communists built the Berlin Wall. The American army presence in South Vietnam increased to sixteen thousand, and the war went from being perceived as a guerrilla war to a real, full-scale war. And Chubby Checker's 1960 song "The Twist" was one of several songs that signaled the beginning of several simultaneous US social revolutions: the women's liberation movement, the drug culture, and peace demonstrations.

High school football was Hopewell's retreat from this turbulent background. The year before, I had lost the JV quarterback job to Kevin Castillo. My dream of being the next Johnny Unitas had evaporated. Moreover, I wondered if something was wrong with me since both Beth and Sally had moved away. I was trying to keep my chin up, but inside, I was depressed. I had conquered the devil's pit, fishing, the water tower, academics, and even cotillion and dating, but I seemed to be losing my more recent challenges. And the outside upheavals bothered me more and more as I grew older.

I was trying to earn a starting job as a fullback or a defensive end. My freshman classmates and buddies—Eddie Russell, C. J. Moxley, and Rick Shaffer—were challenging older players for their starting positions. This was not going over well with the older players, but Coach Humphrey didn't care. He saw only one thing—a shiny silver Kentucky State Class A Championship trophy sitting on his desk.

Eddie Russell had been my friend since the seventh grade. He was close to starting as offensive guard. He grew up on a farm and was a strong, big kid weighing about two hundred pounds. He would work on the farm and tobacco fields most of the day and take off work to practice. Eddie would show up for practice with a sunburned face, blond hair cut in a short flattop, and stains on his hands and forearms from harvesting burley tobacco. He was a no-nonsense guy who began his sentences in a sort of slow and metered John Wayne-style by saying things like "Well-a, this ain't gonna work, my friends." Or "Did ya see that son of a bitch hit that halfback?" Or "Look-a the tits on that girl." He was stubborn, and his views and values were cast in stone. It was futile to convince him of new ways of thinking. But on the football field, Eddie never gave up, and his endurance was limitless. He would fight you until he couldn't move. He was as tough as the limestone that oversaw our football field.

Rick Shaffer was the son of the factory manager for Jacobson Mills. Rick, at 190 pounds, had won the starting job as offensive center. I had known Rick since the fourth grade, when his family had moved to Hopewell. In the summers, Rick worked in the tobacco warehouses and mowed grass for Jacobson Mills. His hair was black and rich as Kentucky dirt, and his legs were as thick as fenceposts. Rick was somewhat callous, molded by a robotic father and a case of acne so bad that classmates constantly teased him. Unbeknown to either of us, I would soon have a similar fate. He was smart enough to walk up to the line of scrimmage, see different defensive schemes, and call out who should block whom before we snapped the ball. These were not easy football tasks. Rick was a little edgy; if you ever said the wrong thing or challenged him or played a joke on him, he would get riled, and he played that way on the football field. Rick also played defensive linebacker, as did several players who played both offense and defense. All those characteristics combined to create a very good football player. He would later make the all-state team.

Chuck John (C. J.) Moxley's dad owned an insurance agency, and he was close to winning the starting offensive tackle position. Coach Humphrey also tried C. J. at defensive tackle. His joking and exaggerations concealed what I knew was a soft heart inside. We had grown up and played together since the first grade. C. J. worked in about every job in town, including as a retail-store clerk. At about 210 pounds in high school, he later played a few years of college football. He was always doing the unexpected and was sort of a nomad and free spirit around town. C. J. had a matter-of-fact attitude that "shit happens, so deal with it." He was not the most patient guy and was once fired from J. C. Penney for stuffing a customer's clothes in a bag and saying, "You wrap the son of a bitch!" When C. J. wasn't playing football, he was fixing cars. He could rebuild any car, including the engine and transmission. He'd show up for football practice with thick automotive grease on his clothes and hands. Later in life, he took motorcycle trips to Alaska and the four corners of the USA. He was the gypsy, risk taker, and entrepreneur of our class. C. J. was often in conflict with himself—not the world—as he made abrupt decisions that didn't always work out.

I was the son of an electrical contractor one day and a country clubber the next. As a result, I learned to adapt quickly to new situations and people. I might have been the smartest among us, but I was definitely the smallest at 170 pounds. And my endurance was not good; therefore, I would wear down as the football game went on. I tried to compensate for my average athletic capabilities by being smarter than my opponents. I was an overachiever, like my dad and grandfathers, who thought life's challenges could always be overcome by persistence and hard work.

The four of us forged a core group within our football team where the sum of the parts was greater than the whole. A football team needs core groups like this to play for the school and the team, but most important, for one another. You cannot let down your buddy on the battlefield. The football field became the furnace where our personalities and behaviors would be tempered and tested. We learned about teamwork and trusting one another to do a job. We had then, and even now, common bonds that only growing up together can forge. No one else can enter this special club because time, location, and events protect our unique experiences.

Off the field, we sometimes confronted the uncertain environment around us. For example, one day after practice, the four of us were walking home when we began discussing the future integration of our school with an all-black high school.

"What do you think about integrating with Dunbar High School next year?" Rick asked.

"Well, I hope we don't have any trouble with these colored people," Eddie replied with a sigh.

"Eddie, we shouldn't say 'colored people.' They don't like it," I shouted as a noisy truck drove by.

"That's what my dad calls them. He says Hopewell once had 'colored toilet' signs. So, what the hell do I call them?"

"Negroes, I think," C. J. said.

"Okay, I'll call them Negroes," Eddie replied in an irritated voice.

In the sixties, what you called another race or ethnic group was not always clear. Social norms and terminology were in transition. Dr. Martin Luther King, in his sermons and speeches, often used the terms *Negro* and *black*. Our World War II-era parents called the Japanese "Japs" and the Communists "Commies," generally accompanied by a cuss word before or after these terms. Consequently, there was considerable confusion in the media, and among us, about what to call whom when.

"I'm not looking forward to next year," Rick said.

"Did you see the stuff on TV about those Freedom Riders in Alabama?" I said.

"Yep! They tried to sit in the white section of buses and restaurants down there," C. J. replied.

"The whites beat the Negroes with pipes and bats," Rick said. "If this happens here, there won't be a football season."

"Negroes eat in our restaurants and sit wherever they want. They ride buses in Baxter anywhere they want. We don't have that problem here," I cautiously reminded them.

Standing on the street in front of Mildred's, Eddie said in his slow drawl, "We ain't going to solve this she-it today. Let's go home." And with that, we turned and headed to our homes.

In May 1961, the Freedom Riders took their fateful trip from Washington to New Orleans to test the Supreme Court decision in the Boynton versus Virginia case, which outlawed racial segregation in restaurants and buses that crossed state lines. Their trip took them through towns like Rock Hill, North Carolina; Atlanta, Georgia; Montgomery, Alabama; Jackson, Mississippi; and New Orleans, Louisiana. In Montgomery, Alabama, the city erupted in violence. US Attorney General Robert Kennedy ordered federal marshals to Montgomery while the Reverend Martin Luther King, Jr. spoke and tried to quell the unrest. These turbulent events would define the environment for next year's school integration, and I was worried it would come unraveled.

On August 22, 1961, I was playing fullback as a ninth grader in a full-contact scrimmage. It was the second-string offense going against the first-string defense. Our football coach, Bob Humphrey, was a master motivator. Coach Humphrey walked up to the huddle and said, "Run 235 X and see if you can block somebody."

This play was a handoff to the halfback to go through the gap between our left tackle and end. As the fullback, I was supposed to lead the halfback through the hole and block whoever was in the way. I had good balance and peripheral vision and always seemed to be able to square up on the defensive player and block him. My success was due more to technique and the ability to make quick decisions than my athletic skills.

We broke the huddle in a cloud of dust. The quarterback barked out the signals, and the ball was hiked. The offensive line did a good job blocking the first tier of defensive players as we kicked up dust clouds. The halfback followed me, and we quickly found ourselves eight yards past the line of scrimmage. If I could block the defensive back, we had a touchdown. As I approached the defensive back, he backpedaled and fell flat on his back. I lunged forward to block him, fell forward, and found my head at his feet. The halfback sailed by for a touchdown, and everyone was yelling and celebrating, including Coach Humphrey.

As I fell, my mouth hit the top cleats on the shoe of the defensive back on the ground. His shoe and cleats went right under my facemask and hit my mouth.

"David, your mouth is bleeding pretty bad," Rick said as he came running over to the scene.

"Get a towel! David's cut his mouth," Rick shouted.

My face was numb. My vision was blurry. The coaches and trainers rushed over and used a towel to carefully wipe my mouth. Blood was pouring out of my mouth as I spit out my flimsy mouth guard.

"Call David's parents—now," Coach Humphrey commanded.

As I walked to the locker room with a trainer holding the towel to my mouth, I asked, "How bad is it?" Pain was radiating from my mouth.

After a short pause, the trainer said, "I can't tell where the cut is, but you broke your two front teeth."

The trainer and one assistant coach helped me get my football gear off. They looked at me but said nothing. I had to see the damage for myself. I looked in the mirror and saw that my two front teeth were broken off in a perfectly shaped upside down V. Thoughts raced through my head. What would the girls think of me? Would people tease me? Can this be fixed? My tears were not only from physical pain now.

By the time I had taken a shower and dressed, my mom was there. As I was walking out of the locker room, the team was coming in. I had no way to avoid them.

"David, how bad is it?" asked one teammate.

I simply wanted to get out of there. But by then, the word was out about my broken front teeth. As I left the locker room, a teammate said, "Old V-Tooth has a problem now."

In the hospital's emergency room, it was determined that I had cut the inside of my lip badly. The doctor put stitches in my swollen lip, and I was discharged. He recommended that I go to a dentist immediately.

The pain was immense, and the pain medicine the doctor gave me didn't help much. I had a pounding headache. I didn't sleep that night. I kept looking in the mirror at my two broken front teeth and hoped that the dentist could put caps over them. The anguish exceeded my physical pain.

The next day, Mom carted me off to our family dentist. Dr. Stanley Jacobs was an old-time dentist who was close to retirement.

"David, we're going to have to put two caps on those teeth. Let's schedule an appointment for tomorrow and get this done," he said. "Here's a prescription for a stronger pain medication. Take only two pills every six hours."

We left the dentist's office with a good solution—or so I thought. The next day, I returned to the dentist's office and sat down in the chair. The dental assistant came out with a tray of dental tools and two silver caps. I stared at the two shiny silver caps on the tray like they were shackles in a prison. I went into shock. "Mom, I don't want those silver caps. I thought they would be white porcelain caps," I said in an anxious voice.

Dr. Jacobs came in. "Are you ready?"

"No, I'm not. I thought these caps would be white porcelain," I said.

"David, white porcelain caps would be permanent. You're young, and your teeth are not fully developed, so you can't have porcelain caps yet. You'll have to wear the silver caps for a few years until your teeth are fully grown," Dr. Jacobs explained.

Mom accepted Dr. Jacobs's explanation, but I was upset. This old-time dentist, who had put gold and silver caps on thousands of his patients before me, had condemned me to a social prison clad in silver. I reluctantly accepted my fate. The silver caps were installed, and I left the office in disbelief. Mom didn't quite get the magnitude of the situation, but she soon would.

I went to practice and kept my helmet on and mouthpiece in place. I didn't smile or laugh. My teammates didn't say much, because they knew if they teased me, there would be an immediate fight.

During the weekend, I tried to settle down. I told myself the kids would understand and leave me alone when school began on Monday. But I dreaded that day because none of the girls or teachers had seen me since the football mishap. Once they had seen my teeth and the novelty wore off, I would have some peace. I figured there would be some light kidding. I prepared myself for it and assumed things would work out fine.

In the first minutes of my first day of school, as I was walking down the halfway to my first class, I heard someone say, "There goes Silver Fang!" I turned and saw half a dozen kids giggling, but I couldn't identify who said it. This incident foretold my fate. I had been a rising high school star, but now the playing field had been leveled. And I wasn't about to date with those silver fangs.

During the entire school year, the "Silver Fang" salutations were frequent, especially when my back was turned. The notes and poems I found pushed through the vents in my hallway locker about my silver teeth were relentless, unmerciful, and anonymous. Examples include "I sang with my fangs," and "You started out on top and now your silver teeth weigh you down. Ha ha!" Other notes I kept included "Who wrote the 'Book of Love' for Silver Fang?" and "No girl will kiss you now, Silver Tooth. Your teeth must be slick and cold!"

Braver students would say things as I passed them in the halls. They'd snicker, "Why don't you smile for me?"

I dreaded the bell that signified changing classes because I had to expose myself to more teasing. I had already been expelled from school twice, and they knew that if I started a fight, I would be expelled again. They would also say things during class—where the classroom environment protected them. I kept thinking the relentless kidding would stop, but it didn't.

During football practice and games, my teammates were too busy to focus on the trivial pursuit of teasing me. They seldom teased me because they knew I was a fellow warrior and such an injury could happen to them at any time. Besides, my freshman class had been listening to the hype about us marching to a state championship, and we were serious about our football. The football field became a haven for me because looks didn't matter—how you played did. For me, the roughness of the game was an outlet for my frustration and anger.

Other than going to school and playing sports, I stayed home. It was easier to stay home than cope with the teasing. I watched a lot of television shows and reruns like *American Bandstand*, *The Mickey Mouse Club*, *I Love Lucy*, *Rawhide*, and the movie

The Shaggy Dog starring Annette Funicello. I rekindled a love affair with my childhood sweetheart, Annette Funicello, of *Mickey Mouse Club* fame. And I watched our new president, John F. Kennedy, struggle with the Soviet Premier Nikita Khrushchev and Cuba's Fidel Castro while the arms and space races were raging. For a fourteen-year-old, I was more up to date on the social and political events than my classmates.

Our first football game was at home against the Marshall Musketeers on September 8, 1961. By halftime, we were ahead 21–6. Early in the second half, we scored another touchdown and led 28 – 6. At the beginning of the fourth quarter, I heard an assistant coach call my name. "Bourbon, where are you?" As a freshman, my pulse rate went up fast. The coaches were going to put me in my first varsity game. I jogged up to the sideline, trying to get my helmet on and chin strap buckled.

"Bourbon, get in there and block," Coach Humphrey said. I ran onto the field. I was excited. I was playing fullback in front of about a thousand people, many of whom I knew. To me, it was like playing in front of all of humanity. Wow! Junior varsity games were lucky to have a hundred people in the stands. Coach Humphrey substituted more and more young players to give them experience. Eddie, C. J., and Rick were in the game too, and we all shared the experience together. With only five minutes left in the game, we were leading 35–6.

With about three minutes left in the game, we ran a pitch out to our star halfback. My job was to block any linebacker who came our way. The play was called in the huddle, and off we went to face a beat-up Marshall team.

As the ball was hiked, I moved to my left and our quarterback pitched the ball to our halfback. Their middle linebacker shot through the gap between the end and tackle, and I decided to hit him low. My shoulder pads caught his legs perfectly, and we were both on the ground. I had thrown the perfect block. I hoped my dad saw that block. He did, of course, and he complimented me after the game. Our halfback soared past everyone else, and we watched him run sixteen yards for a touchdown.

Once back in the huddle, the coaches called a play where the fullback (I was the fullback!) ran the ball to try for the extra point. This would be my first varsity carry, and all I could think was, *Do not fumble and let the Musketeers return it for a touchdown.* The ball was hiked, and I took the handoff and burst through the line to score with two defenders tackling me. I was excited and relieved. I had played in my first varsity game and made no mistakes, an extra-point run, and a touchdown-breaking block.

Our team sent a message that day to good Class A football teams across the state. We had 439 yards to Marshall's seventy-two yards. We had stopped a good, average Class A team in its tracks. The Hopewell newspaper noted, "Hopewell fans were encouraged by the sparkling performances of several freshman and sophomores who saw varsity action for the first time." We ended that football season with nine wins and one loss, but the team we lost to went to the state playoffs, not us. We had to reload and try again the next year.

One day in December, I was in my freshman shop class, sitting on a stool at a workbench. I had endured my silver teeth and their ramifications for months. At the workbench a seat behind me was Perry Session, a ninth-grade classmate. As the teacher wrote on the board, Perry said to me, "Buck-toothed Silver Fang, would you move your head? I can't see the board."

In an instant, I turned and hit Perry in the mouth as hard as I could. He fell to the floor with his mouth bleeding profusely. He held his mouth with both hands and rolled from side to side on the floor in pain. I didn't knock a tooth out, but I did cut him badly.

I walked around the workbench, stood over him, and said, "Perry, say that again."

He lay at my feet with blood everywhere. He didn't say a word. At that moment, I would have fought anyone until I was dead. That day in shop class, I changed my tactics. I decided to fight when people said derogatory things to me.

I was expelled from school for a third time. I went home to my upset parents and was grounded. Mom was still on the school board, and my antics were embarrassing. The rest of the school year, I was determined to fight if anyone said anything to me about my silver teeth. The fight did stop most of the direct hazing—but not the notes slipped into my locker.

I made it to the Christmas holidays and didn't go out. I tried everything from making fun of myself to an all-out fight in the middle of class. No matter how I reacted, the kidding didn't go away. Once school was out in June, I worked in Dad's business and was the happiest kid alive. The guys at the shop did not tease me.

In late June 1962, my mom said, "David, we are going to Baxter to see another dentist. I called around, and this dentist is good." My parents had discussed the situation with teachers and friends and decided the silver teeth had to go. Baxter was a much bigger city, about twenty miles away.

"Okay, Mom, that's good," I said. A lift of my eyebrow signaled a slight sense of hope. "I've tried to be patient. I thought eventually they would quit, but they're vicious. If the dentist can help me, great."

"I know, David, I know," Mom said with a loving smile.

On the drive to Baxter, I was hopeful I wouldn't have to wait until I was eighteen or twenty-one before I could get porcelain caps. The dentist met with Mom first. I'm sure Mom had talked to him on the telephone and was explaining the relentless teasing and how it had affected my life. I had been in a state of turmoil and depression for almost a year because of those stupid silver teeth.

After examining my teeth and reviewing the X-rays, the new dentist said, "David, we are going to put porcelain caps on those two teeth. Make an appointment next week, and we'll grind them down and take molds. In a few weeks, you will have white teeth that match the color and size of your other teeth." Several weeks later, I walked out of that dentist office with two white front teeth. I was free of my deformity.

I began to hang out at Mildred's. I went over to the country club and swam. In those sacred hangouts, I yearned and searched for Sally, but she was a thousand miles away in Louisiana. I truly needed Sally to help me get through the torment. We had traded many letters, but talking long distance on the telephone was too expensive for both families. I also found myself talking to girls again after almost a year of isolation. Amazingly, the kids realized I was normal again, and as quick as the drop of a guillotine blade, they went back to old routines and practices. They didn't understand what they had done or how they had acted.

But I had changed. I would be fifteen in August, and I had learned an important lesson that year. Two silver teeth had changed how people treated me. What if my skin was black? What if I was fat or skinny? What if I stuttered or lived in a wheelchair? I was still me—with the same values, thoughts, and behaviors—before and after those silver fangs.

The silver fang episode was an important predecessor and learning experience for the next chapter in my life. My all-white high school was to be integrated with the all-black high school next year. The tsunami of sixties-style school integration had reached the sleepy little town of Hopewell, and I was about to be right in the middle of it.

CHAPTER 7

Black and White

There we were—two lines of football players facing one another on the first day of practice—one with white faces and the other with black faces. I remembered those black faces. They had been chiseled by decades of struggle and discrimination. We looked at one another with uneasy eyes, not knowing what lay ahead. Would we be on television, like so many before us, with stories of hatred and turmoil? Or would we work together on and off the field and be stronger for it?

It was August 6, 1962. I was fifteen years old and entering the tenth grade. The Hopewell Thoroughbreds, an all-white school, integrated with its crosstown rival, the Dunbar Tigers, an all-black school. The sixty of us were the first to meet in our newly crafted school.

As we stood in those two lines, facing one another, we were uneasy about how school integration would work given the racial troubles we viewed daily on TV. We stood tall. No one sat down or squatted. The dust was high in the air because, much like a herd of wildebeests, we abruptly came to a halt in unison after running laps around the football field.

Coach was a short, dumpy man with a receding hairline. He walked bravely between us. His strength was as a motivator. "Young men, today is a special day. We know our two schools are combining. Now there will be one school, one team." He watched beads of sweat slowly run down our faces as he gained momentum for his next words.

"We are stronger as one than we are separate. Our first goal is to win the conference. Our second goal is to win the state championship. It's that simple. Now learn your plays, pay attention to what the assistant coaches tell you, don't take cheap shots in practice, and drink plenty of water. Let's get to it."

As I walked to the offensive unit, I thought the coach was right—we would be stronger as one. The bad news was that some gridiron heroes had seen their last play—they would be sitting on the bench as second stringers. The coaches, of course, were delighted. They could already see the conference and state championship trophies sitting on their desks.

Last year, we'd won nine games and lost one. We experienced success and liked the feeling. I also found clarity in the game of football. There were rules of the game, and I knew when I achieved success or failure. It was simple: You won, or you lost. You gained a first down, or you did not. You made the tackle, or you did not.

The Dunbar Tigers were a Class A school with a worse record than ours. The previous year we had beaten Dunbar High School 58–7. I wouldn't take such a loss kindly, and I'm sure our black players didn't either. It was not the ideal last memory as we began practice.

I stood in the heat and dust of the Hopewell High School Football Field, looking at a row of strained black faces. I doubt my predecessors since 1909 envisioned a mixed-race football team on this field, but here we were, competing for playing time.

Although my white teammates never talked about it, I also think we wanted to show these black guys that being white didn't automatically mean we were given everything on a silver platter. We were tougher than they thought. Only one of us came from a wealthy family. We were the sons of plumbers, farmers, insurance salesmen, factory workers, automobile mechanics, and retail clerks. Although we didn't understand the harsh realities of racial prejudice, we knew how to work. Our WWII parents had not been tempered by air-conditioning and vacation homes, and neither had we. And so the battle was on to see who would play, who would stay, and who would quit.

After practice, I walked home with C. J., Rick, and Eddie. We didn't have much to say—we were tired mentally and physically from a hard first practice. We stood on the corner for a minute looking at one another, and then Rick said, "I think coach is right—we can win it all." We nodded and split up to go home.

I walked in the door and said hi to Mom. Dad was still working. At dinner Mom asked, "How did practice go?"

"Fine, Mom, no fights. Coach told us we could win the conference and state championships together," I replied as a Frigidaire window air conditioner began humming behind Dad's chair.

"Good," Mom said. Three-year-old Katie knocked her spoon on the floor.

Halfway through dinner, we heard Dad's truck drive up. He came in with a bunch of blueprints for a bid he was preparing. Dad cleaned up and sat down at the table with us.

"So, how did your first practice go?" Dad asked.

"Good. The coach says we can win it all with the two schools combined," I repeated.

Dad replied, "Yes, Dunbar has some good athletes."

We ate for a while, and then Dad said, "The paper this morning said Marilyn Monroe died of a pill overdose."

"Yes, I heard that. She tried to kill herself before," Mom remarked. "Why would someone with everything give it all up?"

"I don't know. It's sad," Dad said. Of course, I knew, having worked at the shop, that Dad and the guys loved to look at the posters of Marilyn they had hung up in the men's bathroom.

After dinner, Dad sat in his reclining chair. Mom and I cleaned the dishes. I asked Mom why there was so much hatred between the races.

"David, most Negroes have been denied a chance to get a good education," Mom began as she finished rinsing off the last plate. My job was to clean up the dinner table, put stuff in the refrigerator, and dry the dishes.

"Is that why they're not in my math classes?" I replied.

"Well, yes," Mom responded after a few moments of thought.

"So, will it get better for us—and them?" I asked.

"Yes, but it will take a long time. We need to educate a whole new generation. That's why I strongly supported combining Hopewell and Dunbar schools. You have to start somewhere. I probably won't get reelected because of my vote to combine the schools, but it's the right thing to do." Mom took off her apron and sat beside Dad in her rocking chair.

Katie and I sat on the sofa. Nannie had knitted an Afghan in a hexagonal black, brown, and green pattern, which lay over much of the back of the sofa. Katie and I played together as Mom and Dad read and listened to our Stomberg Carlson table radio. We were exhausted from the day.

The next morning, after much thought, I said, "Mom, you're right. I don't think skin color has anything to do with people's intelligence."

Mom nodded with a self-assured smile and said, "Get out of here. You'll be late for school."

I was proud of my mom. She did her housewife job very well. She was the only woman on the school board. And Mom bravely voted to integrate Hopewell's school systems. Mom was gentle as a kitten but brave as a racehorse thundering down the hillside.

The town was mainly segregated. Creeks and railroad lines separated the black and white neighborhoods, and therefore, the boundaries were distinct. Few blacks were educated after decades of school segregation. They worked in grain mills and farm fields. White people held the good jobs. Few blacks could afford decent housing. White people went to white churches, and black people went to black churches. The local country club had no black members. Mixed-race dating, at least in public, was taboo. Yes, blacks and whites ate together in the town's restaurants, rode buses together with no concern about where people sat, used the same restrooms, and sat beside one another in the movie house and at football games with no problems, but there definitely were physical and social lines of demarcation in 1962.

Hopewell's school integration and its sports teams were an integral part of America's march toward equality. And we were about to play football together a century after President Abraham Lincoln's 1863 Emancipation Proclamation.

The next Monday, the news was about East Germany constructing the Berlin Wall. Its soldiers began to string barbed wire along the border and then built a concrete block and cement wall. It split Berlin into an East German, Communist-controlled sector and a West German Allies-controlled sector led by America, Britain, and France. Before the wall, more than 3.5 million East Germans defected from East to West Germany. The Berlin Wall stopped this massive emigration with twelve-foot walls that grew to cover more than ninety-seven miles of Germany; about twenty-seven miles of that wall divided the city of Berlin. The wall became a monument to the Cold War between the USSR and the United States and its allies.

The evening after our fourth football practice, several of us were walking home together. C. J. said, "This German wall is a bunch of crap. They're shooting people who try to cross the border."

"Yeah! President Kennedy told Khrushchev the US would go to war to protect Western Europe," I replied.

"We'll be over there fighting these Communists when we graduate," Rick said.

We kept walking and pondering Rick's comment. Then we changed the topic to who was dating Peggy Sander. "Peggy's got quite an ass on her. Is she dating anyone?" Eddie said.

"Are you interested in her, farmer boy?" I joked as I pushed Eddie off the sidewalk. "You screw sheep, don't you? So you ought to be ready for Peggy," C. J. said as we laughed. Eddie laughed, too.

"Ask her out, you big dummy," Rick said.

"Well, I think I will," Eddie replied in his drawl.

For the first ten days, we practiced twice a day—in shorts with helmets and shoulder pads. Slowly, we began to size up everyone. We learned everyone's name. Out on the field, there was little time to talk, but in the locker room, we eventually began to kid around. It was an interesting learning experience for everyone. The blacks checked out their preconceived notions about whites and vice versa. The most prejudiced white football players discovered, to their amazement, that if a black human body bumped up against them in the shower, they didn't catch leprosy. We had never seen a naked black body, and I assumed they hadn't seen a naked white body either. And in this way, enlightenment starts to happen—one tiny impression at a time.

The week before our first game, the starting lineups were set. The attrition was over; there were thirty-two players on the final roster. Eight black players earned starting positions, and all of us played on offense, defense, or special teams. We accepted promotions or demotions without complaint. In those days, you went along with the coach's decisions without bickering or whining. You did whatever you could do to help the team win.

I was the starting right defensive end. I was a sophomore, six foot one and 170 pounds, and still growing. I seemed to be able to break blocks. I knew when to blitz and how to play the pitch out, and I could turn the play inward so my teammates could make the tackle. I was probably the surest tackler on the team. I hit them low, wrapping my arms around the ball carrier's lower legs. They always hit the ground. Smart football skills allowed me to stay on the field, often getting the most tackles during the game. At times, I also played offensive end, mainly to block. I knew how to square up on the defensive man, keep my feet, and drive him back.

We won our first two games of the season with ease against two Class A schools—Bishop Shamrocks and the Bracket County Bulls. The first game was at home against the Shamrocks. We ran through a big paper hula-hoop with the band playing. Our starting tailback, Donnie Dorin, was the star player; he scored four running touchdowns. Donnie was a very good black athlete with short hair and a handsome smile. He probably did well with the women, but black players and white ones seldom shared personal stories in 1962. We were equal, especially on the football field, but separate in our personal lives and neighborhoods. Donnie was quick, yet he was strong enough to throw the shot put in track and field. He eventually played college football.

On one offensive play in the first quarter of the season, Donnie broke through the line and ran for about fifteen yards. A Shamrock cornerback hit him late while he was already on the ground. The referee didn't call it. Rick and I ran over and promptly picked him up.

"What was that little shit's number?" Rick said as the three of us walked back to the huddle.

"Twenty-four," I said.

In the huddle before our quarterback called the next play, I said, "If you get a chance to hurt number twenty-four, do it. He took a cheap shot at Donnie."

Donnie smiled as we broke the huddle.

Later, C. J. and Eddie Russell managed to slam that wiry guy between them. As the dazed cornerback began to get up, Eddie said, "Don't mess with our fullback." We harassed that cornerback the entire game, and what was important was our team knew it. Episodes like this permeate race and wealth boundaries and build personal relationships and a team spirit. We were building ours. If you mess with one of us, you mess with all of us.

The huddle is where you plan. The huddle is where learning takes place. In the chaos of a game, eleven players stop after each play and reconfirm their allegiance to the team, execution, and winning. The huddle is where the agreement to play as a team is honored. Few events in life allow you to make a plan and then immediately go execute it. At the end of each play, you know whether you were successful or failed. What more can you ask for? I savored these moments in the huddle then, and I realize today how important they were. Competent managers and politicians would love to play in such a system, while incompetent ones would prefer to hide under the guise of longer-term plans and feedback. The football huddle is a forum for real-time feedback.

Dad always brought home the high school football programs. Mom and Dad liked to look at the ads, and they were frequently the focus of dinner conversations. They were a testament to the character of small-town America in the sixties. Other than big companies like JC Penney and Sears stores, most Hopewell businesses were family owned and operated. The ads in the football program provided a glimpse of Hopewell's business and social structures:

- *Bert's Restaurant—Specializing in Steaks, Lobster, Shrimp, Pompons, Chicken & Seafood*
- *Bus Station Cab Service—Radio Controlled*
- *Carl's TV & Antenna Installation and Repairs*
- *Emmitt's Coin Laundry*
- *Farm Bureau Insurance Services*
- *Hopewell City Club*
- *Hopewell Lions Club*
- *Hopewell Stock Yards*
- *Jacobson Mills—A Good Place to Work*
- *Jacob's Food Town—The Sign of Quality and Home of Low Prices*
- *Jackson's Grain & Storage*
- *Lucky's Machine Shop*
- *Mildred's Drug Store & Soda Fountain*
- *Nora's Cut & Curl*
- *Patterson's One Stop Food Center & Quick Clean Laundry*
- *Stepsons Women's Clothes Exchange*
- *Thimble Fabric & Sewing Shop*
- *Tom's Appliance & Repair Company*
- *Webster's Radio & TV Repair*

The lifestyle of Hopewell was defined by these family-operated businesses. A walk down Main Street was a joyous experience. We knew one another, young and old, and we were forever connected. Nora, the owner of Nora's Cut & Curl, was raising three kids alone after her husband had died of lung cancer. Carl, the owner of Carl's TV & Antenna Installation and Repairs, was in the navy during World War II when Dad was a marine. The Marine Corps is technically a branch of the US Navy, so Dad and Carl constantly kidded one another with jarhead jokes. A jarhead is a term navy personnel use to describe a marine with a haircut that looks like a mason jar. Carl's brother died in the war.

Even the structure of a small town defines togetherness. Hopewell's Main Street was only forty feet wide, including sidewalks. Horse-drawn carriages and cattle drives down Main Street defined its width long ago. The coin laundry was always busy because only about half the townspeople owned a washer and dryer. Sooner or later, everyone in Hopewell used Emmitt's Coin Laundry. And in the sixties, when equipment failed, it was repaired. You didn't go out and buy a new appliance or radio every time one broke down.

The newly minted Hopewell High School officially opened its doors on August 27, 1962. It was crowded with many new faces. We football players knew one another, but for other students, it was their first day in an integrated school. I did notice less talking and horsing around in the hallways the first week, and none of the black students sat in the front rows. I was also surprised and saddened to see that no black classmates were in my solid geometry and trigonometry classes.

During the first week of school, I was elected vice president of the sophomore class. After the Silver Fang hassle, I thought most people hated me, so I was surprised. Marvin Jacobs, a very smart guy who was on the golf team, was elected president of the class. Peggy Sander was elected treasurer, and Danny Ingels, the class communicator, was elected secretary.

The next Friday night, we lost our first game against a Class AAA powerhouse, Castle County Wolves. We should never have scheduled this game, but Coach Humphrey thought if we played bigger schools, we would receive more state media attention.

I remember the bus trip to the Castle field. We dressed in a new football locker room that was four times bigger than ours. Thirty-two of us ran out onto the field with a small contingent of our fans yelling and hyping up our adventure into the big leagues. The reality of what was about to happen hit me when I watched more than eighty Castle High players run onto the field with the precision of an invading army.

"Eddie, they look like an army," I said as we did our stretching exercises.

"Yep! We're outmanned, but Coach thinks we can beat them," Eddie Russell said with a chuckle. The final score was 33–14.

The smallest school in the state had sort of played with one of the biggest. Coach thought this was great, but most of our players thought we should only play Class A schools. Football is a leveling experience. Fortunately, none of us got hurt, but we were banged up. In fact, the next week we lost to a key Class A competitor, and our record was now 2–2. I don't think Coach Humphrey understood the toll playing a Class AAA school like Castle High took on our team.

Integrating schools and playing football were not the only changes going on at the time. Cuba, for example, was a growing problem that was on everyone's minds. Fidel Castro, a rebel Cuban leader, seized twenty-eight marines near the American naval base in Guantanamo in 1958; he overthrew the Cuban government of Fulgencio Batista in 1959; he nationalized the Texaco oil refinery at Santiago de Cuba in 1960; and he agreed to trade the USSR oil for Cuban sugar cane. The cumulative effect of each event was an added level of anxiety that permeated everything from the locker room to Main Street conversations. In April 1961, anti-Castro forces attempted to invade and overthrow Castro in the Bay of Pigs. Nikita Khrushchev, the USSR premier, and John Kennedy, the US president, began a heated and public debate on the failed invasion.

My family had nervously watched parts of Fidel Castro's 1961 May Day speech on our Zenith Flash-Matic television. Our family made a point to eat dinner and be seated in front of the television for the 6:00 CBS Evening News with anchorman Douglas Edwards. On May 1, 1961, Castro spoke in front of a massive crowd in Havana, Cuba, in his customary green drab military uniform, full beard, and plain box hat.

The revolution has no time for elections. There is no more democratic government in Latin America than the revolutionary government.

If Mr. Kennedy does not like socialism, we do not like imperialism. We do not like capitalism. We have as much right to complain about the existence of a capitalist imperialist regime ninety miles from our coast as he has to complain about a socialist regime ninety miles from his coast.

What kind of morality and what reason and what right do they have to make a Negro die to defend the monopolies, the factories, and the mines of the dominating classes?[1]

Fidel Castro declared Cuba officially aligned with the USSR and the Communist Bloc. He yelled, "Do you need elections?" And his followers shouted back in unison, "No!"

"Damn," my Dad said in disgust after watching the evening news. "We finished the Japs and Hitler, and now we'll have to fight the Cubans."

"Thank goodness they don't have an atomic bomb," Mom replied.

"Dad, why do the Cuban people support Castro?" I asked.

"Son, the damn Communists got into Cuba and started this. The poor people of Cuba have nothing to lose—they might as well follow Castro," Dad replied.

The battle between the two ideologies intensified when President Kennedy banned all trade with Cuba in February 1962. A Cuban military court convicted 1,179 Cuban exiles of "crimes against the nation" for the Bay of Pigs invasion, and they were sentenced to thirty-year prison terms. In April, Castro offered to trade the prisoners for five hundred tractors, but the US turned

---

[1]   Source: http://news.bbc.co.uk/onthisday/hi/dates/stories/may/1/ newsid_2479000/2479867.stm

http://www.historyofcuba.com/history/speech1.htm

down the offer. In a prison-for-ransom agreement, the US agreed to pay $62 million for the release of the prisoners.

"Go do your homework," Mom said to me with a gentle smile. She pulled out the family checkbook and began paying bills at the kitchen table. Mom was the family's bill payer. Dad took a nap to recover from his demanding workday. Dad seemed to be the most frustrated with the news; he was exhausted from World War II, running a family-owned business, and being a family man.

I went off to my basement bedroom to work on geometry problems that Ms. Anita Zeiger, my math teacher, had assigned. Ever since the Soviet Union launched *Sputnik* into orbit in 1957, everyone said, "The Russians are ahead of us. They have to be really smart to launch *Sputnik*, so work hard on your math and science skills."

On April 12, 1961, the Russians put Yuri Gagarin into orbit and brought him safely back to Earth. A continuous stream of Russian space successes justified the frenzy that America was behind the Russians technologically, and therefore, the space race was on. Consequently, a whole generation of baby boomers, including me, worked hard to study math and science to fulfill the space race mandate and catch up with the Russians.

The year was full of immense turmoil and conflicts—East and West Berlin, John F. Kennedy and Fidel Castro, and black and white school integration. I lay in bed contemplating bits and pieces of these dilemmas until I mercifully fell asleep.

CHAPTER 8

Pain

"Men, we can play with 'em. If we hadn't fumbled, we'd be ahead. They didn't think a Class A team could whip 'em, but we can. From now on, when we run 235X, I want the fullback to double-team their tackle. He'll play in college. Get 'em on the ground!" Coach said at halftime. He broke the piece of white chalk in his hand. "Our defense is playing well. We need to get more offense." It was a 7–7 ballgame.

It was October 12, 1962, and we were playing another Class AAA high school, the Mercer Titans. It was a brutal game, and the referees barely kept control. Penalties were few, and injuries were many. During football season, pain comes and goes in waves. Don't play football unless you can play with pain—mental and physical pain—and you prepare for it. You trade winning now for tomorrow's agonies.

In the previous two weeks, we had won our games against Class A opponents. Our record was 4–2. We were not thrilled about the Mercer game, given our previous loss to Castle County. Coach Humphrey, of course, wasn't the one out on the field getting beaten up by bigger, stronger football players. These bigger schools had begun extensive off-season weightlifting programs while we had one set of old weights crammed into our football field house—and no weightlifting program.

"Now, get up here!" We held our arms and hands up toward a central point and huddled in a circle. "Men, give it all you've got!"

We yelled "Beat Mercer! Beat Mercer!" and then broke the huddle. Mercer's football field had lights, so we were playing a night game on a damp, cool Friday evening.

We kicked off to Mercer to begin the second half, and they marched about twenty-five yards down the field before we stopped them. Our offense took over and moved down the field sixty-five yards to score. We ran for the extra point, but didn't score, and we led 13–7. Our star tailback, Donnie Dorin, sprained his ankle on the play. Losing Donnie was an omen of things to come.

On our ensuring kickoff, Mercer's offense advanced down the field to our twenty-yard line. On a third and six yards to go, they pitched out to their halfback toward my side of the field. The herd was coming at me in all its fury. I used my hands to fend off the blocker, made a diving tackle, and caught the tailback's ankles before he had a chance to turn upfield. He hit the ground at the line of scrimmage. My saving tackle felt good. Mercer tried to kick a field goal but missed. The score was still 13–7.

We took over the ball and drove to our thirty-yard line. It was the fourth quarter. Rick had his hands on his hips, and I couldn't quite catch my breath. Mercer had been using many more players than us, and their depth was an important factor late in the game. We had to hang on for six more minutes to win.

As our offense trotted on to the field, Coach yelled, "Bourbon, get in there and help block their damn tackle." Mercer's right defensive tackle was about 220 pounds. I ran onto the field, determined to block this future college player who was causing havoc in our backfield. I reminded myself I needed to keep my feet and stay low when I blocked him. Physically, I knew I was no match for this quick, strong athlete. With Donnie Dorin hurt, the coach substituted Bob Hardy at tailback. Bob was a young white kid without much football experience. He was a ninth grader who was learning the game, and he was a good athlete.

The first play we ran was a pass play over the middle that went incomplete. Our starting guard shuttled in the next play, which was a handoff to Bob through the "one" hole between our center and left guard. In our play numbering system, each gap on the left side of the offensive line was an odd number, and on the right side, an even number. As a left end, I was supposed to block the defensive end outward if possible and then try to block downfield. We broke the huddle and lined up to snap the ball.

"Hut, one, hut, two, hut, hut," and the ball was snapped to our quarterback, Kevin Castillo. He quickly handed the ball off to Bob to go through the one hole. Bob lunged through the hole. Mercer's linebacker broke through the hole and hit Bob with a jolting crunch. Whack!

After the play was whistled dead with no gain, we began to walk back to the huddle. But before I got to the huddle, I saw Bob was flat on his back. The referees blew the whistle. One referee herded the defensive team away from Bob. Several of us stood about three yards away as the coaches looked him over. C. J. clenched his fist. Eddie's shoulder began to sag. A faint quiet began to overtake the crowd.

"Ask the stadium announcer to ask if there's a doctor in the stands," Coach Humphrey yelled as he walked up to Bob lying on the ground. "Hurry!"

"*Attention, attention*! Is there a doctor in the stands? Please report to the field at once!" the announcer boomed out over the loudspeakers.

Two medical doctors came running. Meanwhile, Bob had not moved one millimeter, but his eyes were open, and he was breathing. I took one step closer and looked into Bob's eyes. They were empty. The blades of grass surrounding Bob were moving, but Bob was not. Everyone became silent. I backed away. The doctors crouched over Bob and began to examine him.

"Bob, can you feel this," one doctor asked as he ran a plastic comb down Bob's arm and leg. Bob did not answer as he lay there in a cross-like position. Time had stopped for Bob. The next few minutes for me seemed to slow down. What was happening didn't seem real.

"Bob, move your arms or fingers," said one of the doctors. They continued to probe Bob's motionless body, but Bob did not respond.

"Call an ambulance," one doctor said in a miserable voice.

One of our assistant coaches ran to the field house to use the telephone.

For about five minutes, I stood in silence with Rick, Clifton, C. J., and Kevin in the middle of the field. Clifton Porter was a tall black kid who played right offensive end. I remember the emptiness of the situation. The crowd didn't yet realize the abyss that Bob had fallen into. As young football players, we were full of hope and promise, and we did not understand the perils of the game. The grass seemed to quit moving. It stood in homage to Bob.

The crowd began to recognize the gravity of the situation. A pale shadow of despair overwhelmed the scene. One thousand people in the stadium were now quiet—some were praying. The only sound was the passing of automobiles on a nearby street. How could this happen? Why?

The ambulance drove out on the football field, bouncing all the way and digging deep ruts in the field. They quickly carried a stretcher to Bob's side. They bandaged Bob's head and neck and carefully lifted him onto the stretcher. Into the ambulance, he went with his mom and dad. Bob's mom was crying. The ambulance left the field much more carefully than it had entered, and Bob was off to the hospital.

My teammates and I didn't talk. No one dared say the word "paralyzed," but we knew it was not good. I was fifteen years old, and the gravity of the situation made me think: *Maybe I'm not invincible. Maybe horrific things can happen to me.*

After the ambulance was out of sight, the coaches directed us to the sidelines. They met in the middle of the field and decided to continue playing. I didn't want to play, and neither did my teammates. It was only a football game.

It was third down, and we promptly ran one more play and punted. Mercer's offense worked their way down the field and scored a touchdown with less than a minute on the game clock. We lost 14–13. The bus ride back to Hopewell was terrible. One of our courageous young players' lives would forever change. Bob did nothing wrong. He was such a fun-loving kid. We held out hope that Bob would recover.

At school on Monday, we learned that Bob was paralyzed from the neck down. He did not have use of his arms or legs and had problems breathing. After a few weeks, we were allowed to visit him in the hospital. We learned that the damage to the spinal cord was around the C4–C5 vertebrae, and there was slim chance of recovery. As Bob lay there in a neck brace in a reclining bed, C. J., Rick, Donnie, Eddie, and I gave him cards and balloons and kidded around with him. We wore our letter jackets to try to cheer him up, but after we saw him, we knew our task was futile.

Donnie, with a forced smile, said, "Hey, Bob, hope you get better."

Bob's eyes moved, but the sparkle was gone. We assumed he could hear us. Bob's mom left the hospital room. I am sure she left because she didn't want any of us to see her cry. Bob's skin looked puffy and pale.

Bob's dad slumped down in a bedside chair with his potbelly protruding and tried to tolerate our visit. He said, "Thanks, Donnie. Yes, he will get better. Thank you, guys, for coming."

We held our cards and balloons in front of Bob, hoping he could see them and stumbled through comments like "Bob, we'll do whatever we can to help you." "See the cheerleader I drew on the card—she's after you!" "Bob, we're going to have a fund-raiser for you." "C. J. is going to sing—that ought to bring out the people." "We'll check on you later, okay?" Then we left the room with an empty feeling. We said nothing on our way down the hallway to the exit. We had experience and fear, and there was no justice in what we saw.

We won our next Class A game 21–12, and our record was 5–3. Two of our losses were to much bigger AAA high schools. We had no game scheduled that Friday, October 26, and we had a chance to rest and reflect on Bob's situation and the rest of our football season.

Halloween was coming up, and our high school was planning a Halloween sock hop in the school gymnasium. I was in charge of ticket sales, and others worked on getting the band, chaperons, security, nonalcoholic beverages, best costume awards, and a table of snack food. All profits from the sock hop went to the Bob Hardy Rehabilitation Fund. I decided to charge a high price of two dollars for the sock hop for stag (single) or three dollars for drag (a girl escorted by a guy). The dance was set for eight until eleven, and the Sheltons were hired as the band. I made up flyers for advanced ticket sales and posted them around school.

I asked a blonde named Edna White to the sock hop. Edna was in my math classes, so we knew one another well. Edna was smart, and rumor had it that she sometimes dated an older college guy. In advance of the dance, we asked the Sheltons to play hit songs like "Monster Mash" by Bobby Pickett, "Travelin' Man" by Ricky Nelson, "The Twist" by Chubby Checker, "Duke of Earl" by Gene Chandler, "Soldier Boy" by the Shirelles, and "Sherry" by the Four Seasons.

I was going to the Halloween sock hop as Davy Crockett since I still had the plastic rifle and coonskin cap from my childhood. Dad provided an old leather vest, a heavy plaid wool shirt, and big boots to complete my outfit. Edna worked on an Annie Oakley costume based on the ABC television series. She found a solid tan dress from her grandmother and sewed tassels on the underside of the sleeves and around the bottom of the dress. I gave her my old toy cap gun and a cowboy hat. We looked forward to the dance because it offered us a break from the reality of television, school, and the Bob Hardy tragedy.

High school Halloween dances were crazy events, so we set up only one entrance and exit out of the gymnasium. I arrived at seven o'clock to help set up and sell tickets at the door. Edna came later, and we worked the entrance ticket table as the chaperons oversaw things. Although the chaperons were supposed to check for alcohol as we entered the gym, my classmates were geniuses at getting small containers of vodka and whisky into the gym. The cheerleaders made a ten-foot banner saying "Contribute to the Bob Hardy Rehabilitation Fund" and hung it from the basketball goal. Others hung orange and black streamers and plastic pumpkins on the stage, basketball hoops, tables, and chairs. All the food the teachers and parents brought was orange and black—our Hopewell High School colors. Rich Shaffer and his friend Sandra Pelfrey were the first to arrive, dressed as Tarzan and Jane.

C. J. dressed as Fred Flintstone—complete with a five-foot Stone Age club.

"Where's the band, Bourbon?" Rick asked.

"They better show soon. We have to empty the gym by eleven o'clock," I replied.

About that time, Donnie Dorin came in with his date, Estill Fisher. They were dressed as witches in black caps and long wigs, black pointed hats made from cardboard, and painted black broomsticks.

"Dorin, can you fly on the football field?" C. J. asked them as he walked up to the ticket table.

"Yes, if you would block, I could," Donnie replied with a chuckle.

Without the band, we stood around and sat on the bleachers, talking with classmates and chaperons. Fortunately for the band and the organizers of the dance, including me, the Sheltons showed up around nine o'clock, greeted by jeers from the crowd of about two hundred. By 9:30, they had played "The Twist," by Chubby Checker, and that seemed to calm the crowd down. Almost everyone danced on the gym floor except a few loner guys. Costumes ranged from a simple black T-shirt with a skeleton drawn on it to more elaborate costumes, such as Bullwinkle, monsters, Top Cat, goblins, Deputy Dawg, and of course, the forerunners of hippie-type costumes.

One ominous costume was a girl dressed as a dead Marilyn Monroe, with black eyes and painted lightning bolts on her face and legs.

"Did you come alone, Marilyn?" Eddie asked through an ugly monster mask.

"Yes, darling. I'm dead," she replied.

"Would you like to dance?" Eddie said with a laugh.

"Sure, handsome," she said as they walked to the floor to dance the Twist. The dance ended with the song "Purple People Eater."

The dance revenue came to almost $500 with a net contribution of $348 to the Bob Hardy Fund. We presented the check to Bob's dad in the school library a week later, and a small crowd of students attended. Everyone displayed a positive attitude about Bob's recovery, but inside, I think we all felt totally helpless. Occasionally, Bob's mom and dad would give teachers, students, and the school board updates on Bob's health and the latest research on quadriplegics.

During the next few years, many fundraisers were held to help Bob's family cope with expenses. Bob did not get better, although he did use a motorized bed and wheelchair and was the guest of honor at a few Hopewell home football games. When he came to games, we tried to focus on the game, but the reality of his complicated wheelchair and his struggling mom and dad were never more than a glance away. At any moment, everyone is living on the edge of trouble.

The urgency of Bob's situation faded with time. Bob would flash into my memory when I was asleep or when someone was hurt during a football game. I can't imagine the pain Bob and his family endured. Bob died two decades later, before his fortieth birthday. There was nothing benevolent in how or why he died. I had beaten death once in the devil's pit. Bob should have been given a chance to live his life.

On Monday, October 29, 1962, my family was glued to the TV to watch President Kennedy address the nation. Kennedy revealed that the USSR was building missile and bomber sites in Cuba and shipping missiles and planes to Cuba. We saw pictures of the Soviet cargo ship *Krasnograd* with jet fighters on board. In fact, the first nuclear-tipped missile was installed by the Soviet Union in Cuba in early October 1962. While the Soviets said these sites were for defensive purposes, the US asserted that they were offensive and could strike "most of the major cities in the Western Hemisphere." Kennedy had previously announced a naval blockade to stop the shipment of more offensive military equipment. He threatened to retaliate against the USSR if missiles were launched from Cuba against any country in the Americas.

Fidel Castro immediately mobilized Cuban military forces and called Kennedy's action "an act of war."

Secretary of State Dean Rusk said, "I would not be candid and I would not be fair with you if I did not say that we are in as grave a crisis as mankind has been in."

The Strategic Air Command increased its war status to DEFCON 3 for the first time ever, and B-52s were loaded with nukes and awaited orders. We didn't know at the time that the US Joint Chiefs of Staff recommended to President Kennedy that we attack Cuba within thirty-six hours to destroy the Soviet missiles and their nuclear warheads. Khrushchev proposed a summit meeting, and it was reported that several Russian ships bound for Cuba had changed course.

Immediately, Dad decided we needed to have a makeshift atomic bomb shelter at home. Consequently, we cleaned out the five-by-six-foot basement closet under the front porch, which was underground, with an opening into my basement bedroom. Since our house sat on a small hill, the front half of our concrete-block basement was underground, and the back half opened to the backyard. The front porch (and roof of the closet) was eight inches of poured concrete. We stocked the family bomb shelter with plastic jugs of water, tools, canned food, and heavy blankets.

Within a week, Dad gathered the family and said, "Be alert and if you hear of any attack, run to our house and go to this closet. Don't stop for anything."

"Everyone's got a job. Dot, you get Katie (my sister was three years old now) and all the canned goods and beverages you can carry. David, you fill the bathtub and sinks with water, get our winter clothes, and all the food you can carry. I'll get batteries, flashlights, tools, first-aid kits, and electrical cords. I'll get the gun and rifle, but don't you handle them. If you don't show up, then I have to go look for you—so show up no matter what!"

"Now, go around the house and inventory what we have and where it is. Does everyone understand?" he said in a deliberate voice.

"Dad, what if I'm closer to a friend's house or school? Should I stay there?" I asked.

"David, you come home no matter what. I want us all together if this ever happens—period," Dad commanded.

On November 1, Khrushchev agreed to a United Nations mandate to stop sending missiles and planes to Cuba—if the US would end the blockade. Kennedy's response was to show further evidence of a speed-up in building the missile sites, although he did direct US representatives to negotiate with United Nation leaders. The Pentagon revealed that a U-2 spy plane was missing over Cuba and reported that many planes had been fired upon. It also called more than fifteen thousand US reservists to active duty. Khrushchev made an offer to dismantle the missile sites in Cuba if the US would do the same with US weapons in Turkey. On November 8, the US and the USSR agreed to these conditions, and nuclear war was avoided.

Elated, we refocused on football. Our first season as an integrated school ended in disappointment with six wins and four losses, and we did not qualify for the state playoffs. Coach Humphrey didn't seem discouraged, but I think he finally realized we should play Class A competitors and not venture into bigger AA and AAA games. Besides, we had fifteen of twenty-two starters coming back the next year.

The holidays were a welcome break from school and football. I rested and enjoyed Christmas in small-town America. Main Street was decorated with lights, storefronts were aglow with holiday decorations, and churches and civic groups were holding holiday events and caroling around town. The holiday spirit had a calming effect on us. We had much to celebrate, including avoiding nuclear destruction. And I had time to reflect on what had happened to Bob Hardy. I thought there was much more chaos and pain in the world than I had imagined as a youngster.

School began on January 7, and we seemed refreshed to begin 1963. During the winter months, I played basketball. Our team included four seniors, three juniors, and five sophomores. Jerry Dent and Johnny Hammond were guards, Frank Davenger and I played forward, and Kevin Castillo was a center. Dunbar High School contributed five new basketball players. Joe Wickens, Darryl Tipton, and Warren Stow were competing at the forward positions, Clifton Porter was a center, and Calvin O'Connor was a guard. We already knew one another since we played football together.

One day after practice, toward the end of our basketball season, I was walking home with three fellow basketball players—Joe Wickens, Warren Stow, and Clifton Porter. We had become friends, not close friends like with Rick, Eddie and C. J., but friends.

"Bourbon, why do you white people call us Negroes?" Joe asked.

"Well, that's because, uh, that's what my parents said as I was growing up," I replied.

"Some whites call us 'blacks' and others use 'Negroes,'" Clifton chimed in.

"What do you want to be called?" I asked.

"I prefer 'black,'" Joe said. His friends nodded in agreement.

"Okay, I'll use 'black' and will tell my friends," I said, "but for whites, that's a new term. What do you call us, Clifton?"

"Whites."

"It makes sense, doesn't it?" I replied.

When we reached the corner of the school grounds, we split up. I went home to my white neighborhood, and Joe, Warren, and Clifton went home to their black neighborhood.

Our basketball team went 18–12 our first year as an integrated school. After we lost the last game of the season in a district tournament game, I knew my basketball career was over. I would not go out for the basketball team the next year. Joe Wickens ended my basketball career, though I never told him. He was quicker, more agile, and could jump higher than me, and I knew it.

Another change going on—the women's liberation movement—was gaining momentum. Birth control pills were introduced in 1960 and became popular. More than 1.2 million American women started taking them under the brand name Ortho Novum. However, the manufacturer received more than one hundred reports of blood clots, and eleven deaths were attributed to taking the Pill. The predecessors to tie-dyed shorts, miniskirts, long hair, no bras or girdles, and drugs were beginning to make their way into American culture. The beehive hairdo of the fifties was obsolete. Out with it went the puritanical attitudes of the fifties. My mom was unhappy with these changes, and one of her responses was to vote for a dress code in 1963 at Hopewell High School.

A woman's role at home and in the workplace was changing, too. Abortion and reproductive rights received national attention. The Society for Human Abortion, for example, established in San Francisco in 1963, challenged various contraception and abortion laws and provided information. A movement began to provide childcare so women would be able to work outside of the home. In big cities, women's health clinics and rape-crisis centers developed. Mom supported many of these initiatives but realized she would not be the beneficiary. Like the school-integration plan, Mom thought it would take generations to make these dramatic shifts in society. Consequently, Katie would be in the first generation to fully benefit from the women's liberation movement of the sixties.

The shadow of the Vietnam War was methodically rolling across the American landscape. The United States announced in 1960 that thirty-five hundred American troops would be sent to Vietnam. South Vietnam President Ngo Dinh Diem was elected with about 80 percent of the vote, while North Vietnam's Communists continued to kill South Vietnamese in an effort to topple pro-Western President Diem. In November 1961, the US military announced that over the next two years, sixteen thousand troops would be deployed to South Vietnam. In February 1962, President Kennedy said that US troops were committed to staying in Vietnam until the Viet Cong were defeated. By June 1963, 136

American troops had died in Vietnam. Given the troubles with Berlin, Cuba, and Russia, the Vietnam War was not on the average American citizen's radar in 1963.

President Kennedy and other US government officials were considering starting a draft lottery to conscript men for military service. They were debating what ages they should target, what criteria to use for exemptions and student deferments, and whether married men with or without children should be drafted. I was aware of these debates from television and reading newspapers. One summer day on our way to work, I asked Dad if he thought I could go to college or would they draft me into the military service once I graduated from high school?

"Son, if they can draft Elvis Presley, they can draft you," Dad replied.

"So what should I do?"

"Ask your mom. She knows most government officials in town," Dad suggested.

I would turn sixteen on August 3, 1963, and be in the eleventh grade that autumn. The big deal for me was to be able to drive a car, any car. And I was beginning to worry about a military draft and whether it would stop my plans to go to college. The Hopewell High School class of 1965 was fast approaching its day of reckoning. It was a daunting time for all.

CHAPTER 9

The Rambler

"Davey, your dad is bringing the new car home," Mom said in an excited voice.

It was Friday, July 12, 1963, and we were happy. My parents had always bought used cars. This was our first new car. Dad worked, and then he went to pick up the new Rambler at the dealership. At 6:30, Dad drove into our driveway in a shiny burgundy car. Mom, Katie, and I hovered around this new status symbol, examining every nook and cranny.

"Wow, Dad. What a great car!" We all took turns sitting in the passenger seat.

Dad got out of the driver's seat so Mom could sit there. American Motors built the 1963 Rambler Ambassador 990 four-door sedan. This one had been a dealer's car. It had two thousand miles on it, so it wasn't exactly a new car, but to us it was new. It had chrome and aluminum trim, four headlights, one-inch whitewall tires, push-button controls, full-wheel disc brakes, and a 196-horsepower cast-iron V8 engine. The model, *Ambassador*, was displayed in script type on each side of the rear fenders. To us, it was a status symbol—the American dream of a two-car family.

"Dad, thank you so much!" I said as I sat behind the steering wheel. "It's beautiful."

Mom and Dad hugged each other as they watched me practice steering the car. On my sixteenth birthday, I could get my driving license permit. Mom and I would share the Rambler, and Dad would cruise around with the family on weekends.

After Mom and Dad went into the house, I stayed by the Rambler to examine it further. I followed the flawless chrome trim down the side of the car with my hands and thought it was classy. I liked the script lettering on the sides. I was so proud of Dad for making the money to buy such a classy car.

I sat down in the driver's seat and pushed every button and control, surveying my new opportunity for freedom. I discovered a lever on the seat. When I pulled it, I watched with amazement as the front seat fell back flat—and I mean really flat. The entire experience played out in my mind in slow motion. I leaned across the front seat and found a similar passenger seat lever, pulled it, and with the precision of an orchestra, it too neatly dropped down flat.

Now in a state of utter euphoria, I lay across this portable bed. This was the definition of convenience. Wow! I imagined the girls who might lay their heads on this magnificent invention—the 1963 Rambler Ambassador with airliner reclining seats! It was a dream come true.

The next day, I bumped into one of my buddies on Main Street. "C. J., we got a new car," I announced.

"What is it? A convertible?"

"I wish. It's a Rambler with push-button controls. And guess what—it has reclining front seats," I continued.

"Man, you're lucky," C. J. replied. "You have a moving bed."

The word got out quickly among my classmates. "Bourbon has a car that turns into a bed!" I couldn't wait until I got my license. I had the perfect setup: no silver teeth, a career as a rising football star, some sexual experience with Sally, and a moving bed. What more could a sixteen-year-old boy want than to take a portable bed to Taff Lane?

On Thursday, August 3, my birthday, I arrived at the Hopewell County Courthouse at eight o'clock to take my driver's permit written exam. I skipped work that day at the shop. A state police officer handed out the exams. After finishing the exam, I waited in the majestic stone and marble hallway for the officer to post the scores on a bulletin board. I watched the clock on the wall as minutes went by in the heat of the non-air-conditioned courthouse. I would have waited all night to see my scores, but after an hour, the officer posted the scores. I had passed with a 98 percent score. Cruising the Circuit in a mobile bed was a powerful motivator to study for the exam.

I needed to be sure I would pass my driving exam, and I practiced every chance I got. Mom and Dad endured various driving maneuvers: parallel parking, backing up, parking on hills, and driving country roads and major highways. Many of the county's single-lane roads were dangerous. Main Street had high curbs, narrow streets, and a steep hill next to the courthouse. These obstacles presented a challenge to any driver.

On the day of my driver's exam, I went to Mildred's Drug Store and ordered a chili hot dog with onion for fifty-nine cents and soda fountain drink for fifteen cents. As I sat at the counter, I saw two of my classmates eating in a booth.

One of the guys said, "Hey, Bourbon, I hear you got a new car. That's out of sight."

"I'm taking my driver's test today at four o'clock, and I'm a little nervous," I replied.

"We want to see that car," he said with a laugh.

When I arrived to take my driving test, the burly officer and I got into the Rambler. He asked me to turn on and off the turn signals, wipers, and emergency brake. Then he said, "Back out. Let's go driving."

We drove around the city streets, and I followed his directions—everything was going fine. He asked me to parallel park on Main Street. This was difficult since traffic was behind me, the street was narrow, and the concrete curb was high—not to mention other obstacles like the parking meters. I turned on my blinkers, stopped traffic, and parked the Rambler perfectly. He was impressed and wrote down some notes on his clipboard. We drove on a major highway, and he asked me to pull over to the side of the road and then reenter the highway. I was very careful to do this safely and followed everything I learned in the driver's manual.

As we returned to the courthouse, we drove up the steep hill. He abruptly asked me to park the car on the hill and not use my parking brake. I had practiced parking on hills, but this hill was about forty-five degrees steep. I began my parking with a few jerks and tried to turn the wheels so they angled up against the curb and held the car. The car rolled back some, but it came to a stop.

"Well done, son," the police officer said with a big smile. "You did such a good job on the routine driving exam that I thought I'd put you to the ultimate test. Few drivers can park on this hill." And with that, he told me to drive back to the courthouse. He signed the papers. I had passed the exam with a very high score. I left the courthouse that day the happiest guy on the planet. I could cruise the Circuit. I could park at Jerry's Restaurant and Teen Circle as I had seen the big kids do for years.

My parents were proud of me for passing the driver's exam with such high scores on the first try. Mom and I both had more freedom now. Mom would use the Rambler when I was in school and at practice, and I would use it at night and on the weekends. Dad was working six days a week and used his truck. Dad only drove the Rambler when we went to church or took a Sunday drive.

The entire football team and some band members had inspected the Rambler in August before school began. They had to pull the reclining seat levers or have me demonstrate how both front seats went down. Their comments, in stark contrast to their Silver Fang remarks, were funny.

One classmate asked, "Will you rent this car to me one night? How much?"

I found a bunch of notes in my school locker. "Can I go with you? Can two couples lie down?" or "Quit your job. You can rent this sucker 24/7."

Every day, Eddie said, "Bourbon, you're gonna get a lot of ass in that car."

We were about to begin a new football season. We finished the previous season with six wins and four losses. Everyone in Hopewell thought it could be a conference or state championship year. We practiced in the August heat as we had in past years, but one thing was different. Except for two sophomores, everyone who started the previous year kept his starting position. We were stronger and more mature, and we knew how to play the game. We had no fear, and we had experience.

We attended Peggy Sander's pre-school opening party. Peggy's house was a beautiful two-story, white-clapboard Victorian house with a wraparound porch. Picnic tables were set up with plenty of food and sodas. Most of us were talking, and a few were playing badminton. Only half a dozen black football players attended the party, but they all were invited. The party was a huge relief from my summer job and the dusty heat of football practice. I felt civilized. I was standing with a group of guys and gals when Glenda Woodbury turned toward me. She was a senior with hair down to her shoulders and brown eyes, the captain of the cheerleaders.

"Hi, Glenda. How's your boyfriend, Doug Radford, doing?" I asked.

"Oh, we broke up last month. Hadn't you heard?" Glenda replied with a flip of her glistening black hair.

"No, I didn't know you broke up. Sorry to hear that. Doug's a good guy," I replied, trying not to jump out of my skin and drop my car keys.

We talked about the upcoming football season and what it was like to be a cheerleader. As we talked, I had a certain feeling about this young woman. It was a feeling I would eventually learn to recognize. I had felt it with Sally, but I had been too young to define it. I cleared my throat and said, "Let's go to Jerry's for a soda, and then I'll take you home."

"Okay. I need to call my parents to tell them what I'm doing. I'll need to be home by eleven o'clock. Is that okay?"

"Sure."

We left the party and, traveling one leg of the Circuit, cruised out to Jerry's Restaurant, and pulled in a drive-in parking space. "Three O'clock Thrill" by Kalin was playing on the radio.

"What do you want?" I ask Glenda.

"How about a Vanilla Coke?"

I pushed the drive-in speaker button and ordered one Vanilla Coke, one Cherry Coke, and a hamburger and fries for me. Pat Boone's song "Speedy Gonzales" began playing, and I quickly switched the radio channel. "I don't like Pat Boone. Do you?" I said.

"No. He's old."

A girl with black-and-white saddle Oxfords and a short orange dress with "Jerry's" embroidered on the front delivered our food. Some of the curb-service attendants had used roller skates to cruise around the covered drive-in parking area, but an automobile accident ended that way of delivering food. I paid, and we sat in the car and talked, ate, and listened to songs like "Pink Shoe Laces" and "Coming of Age" by Dodie Stevens, "Save the Last Dance for Me" by the Drifters, "Runaway" by Del Shannon, and "Return to Sender" by Elvis Presley. We knew the words to every song and sang them together as we gyrated around the front seat, attempting to eat food and talk.

"How's it going with the black players?" Glenda asked.

"Okay, I guess. We've had time to get to know them, and they're good guys," I said.

"Some of the white girls think Warren Stow is handsome," Glenda said.

"Well, I wouldn't know about that. All I know is you sure are cute."

And with that, Glenda leaned over and kissed me on the cheek. I took her home that night at exactly eleven, walked her to the door, and didn't try to kiss her. Her mom was peeking out the window at us, and the porch light was on. It was a great night— and maybe I had a new pal.

We began our football schedule with Class A-rival Benton County at home on August 30, 1963. This was our year, townspeople thought, and the stands were full of two thousand fans. We kicked off to the Benton County Sabers and promptly stopped them. On our first set of downs, Kevin Castillo threw a perfect pass down the sideline to Warren Stow, and he ran fifty yards for a touchdown. Unfortunately, we missed the extra point.

It was a defensive battle with some rugged hits. A thunderstorm dumped over an inch of rain on our battlefield. It was muddy. We led at halftime 6–0.

The Sabers kicked off to us. We gained about thirty yards, and they stopped us. The game continued to be a defensive battle. The heavy rain had stopped, but the field was like jelly. At the beginning of the fourth quarter, Benton County had the ball on our forty-five-yard line, after we fumbled at midfield. C. J. Moxley was the right defensive tackle, Rick Shaffer was the right side linebacker, and I was the right side defensive end. The three of us had to coordinate our efforts to be most effective.

"C. J., they are going to run it down our throats," I said as we waited for the Sabers to break the huddle.

"That fullback is a good lead blocker," C. J. replied.

They hiked the ball and ran straight at us. C. J. and I took out the blockers, and Rick made the tackle. On second down and seven, they ran a second play straight at us. I threw off my blocker, and within a millisecond, I found my head squarely in the runner's stomach. I made the stop, but my neck was numb. I lay on the ground much like Bob Hardy had one year ago. I wondered for an instant if I was paralyzed.

"Get up, you idiot," C. J. said. He reached out his hand to pull me up. "Good play."

"Are you okay?" Rick asked.

"I'm taking myself out for a few plays," I replied. "My neck is numb."

I jogged off the field, slowly took off my helmet, and sat on the bench, carefully moving my neck. I was finished for the night. The trainer wanted me to get an X-ray on Saturday morning at the Hopewell Hospital.

We stopped Benton County on that set of downs. They scored later, but they missed the extra point. The game ended in a 6–6 tie. We were disappointed. Our quest for a conference or state championship had been dealt a serious setback in our very first game. The Saturday morning *Hopewell Enterprise* made excuses for our tie ballgame. The newspaper said that the new Benton

County School had combined the city and county school systems the previous year and should have been in the state's AA football division. Unfortunately, they were still in the Class A division, and they were our major competitor. Others blamed the loss on the muddy field.

In the article, Coach Humphrey said, "David Bourbon suffered a neck injury, a vertebrae at the top of his neck slipped out of place. I think it's called the atlas joint. The doctors are working on Bourbon this week, and the vertebrae are back in place. He's been given the okay to play. I'm going to use him only on defense though."

Our first game had taken its toll on our team. One of our starters had a pinched nerve in his shoulder, and another had suffered a groin pull. The next game was against Franklin on September 6. We won 14–0. My neck was sore for the rest of the season, but I played. We played hurt; that was part of American football culture.

On Saturday night, September 7, I had planned to go cruising with C. J. and Eddie Russell. We planned to drive the Circuit, stopping at Jerry's and Teen Circle. The Circuit was a eight-mile drive down Main Street past the Courthouse, and up High Street to Jerry's Restaurant. It was not unusual to drive this familiar route ten times a night. A gallon of gas was twenty-five to thirty cents. We knew everyone, of course, and the history of every business and shopkeeper along the route. It was our domain. We ruled it.

After a family dinner, I asked for the car, and my parents said okay. One of our neighbors also had dinner with us that evening. I helped Mom and Dad clean up the dishes and take out the trash, which was an everyday requirement in my household. I cleaned up and took the car keys off the hook by the door between the kitchen and garage. I hopped into the Rambler, put the keys in the ignition, and turned on the motor. I backed out of the garage quickly. *Crunch!*

I had forgotten to close the driver-side door. The open door smashed into the side of the garage. As I looked out the big opening to my left, the busted door was on the ground. The steel rail to the garage door and the wood framing were also smashed. I didn't move.

Mom and Dad were talking with our neighbor in the living room chairs when they heard the crunch. They rushed to the scene of the crime.

"What in the hell did you do, David?" my Dad yelled.

I didn't say anything.

"David, are you all right?" Mom asked.

"Yes, Mom. I'm okay."

"Ham, Dot, I think I'll leave." Our neighbor quickly left the garage.

Dad and I picked up the car door and put it in the trunk. We swept up the garage and tried to fix the garage door, but it would not go down. That night, our garage door stayed open.

"David, go to your room," Dad said. "You are grounded."

I called C. J. and told him what had happened. I would not be cruising that night.

Mom and Dad were reading the newspaper when I went into the living room. "Mom, Dad, I'm sorry. I was so excited that I forgot to close the door."

"Son, we are not going to ground you except for this one night, but you will pay to get this fixed," Dad said.

"Yes, sir," I said. I sat down to ponder my stupidity. My joint savings account with Mom had about $1,100 in it since I worked every summer. It cost me $480 to fix the car, the garage, and the garage door. The bill amounted to almost two hundred hours of hard work at my dad's business. But from that day on, I was always careful.

We won our next eight football games, ending the regular season 9–0–1, and we won the conference championship. We won one game by forty-six points. Our closest game was against AAA Mercer High School, which we won 7–6. We finally beat a bigger school. Coach Humphrey got to put a big, shiny conference trophy on his desk. The state Class A division playoffs were next, and we were in them. The playoffs began with eight Class A teams across the state. Therefore, we had to win three playoff games to win the state championship.

Glenda and I managed to see one another after football games and on the weekends—but seldom on weeknights. She was studious, captain of the cheerleading squad, and involved in many clubs and activities. We attended school parties and rode the Circuit most weekend nights. Glenda wore my varsity letter jacket. (Katie was the official owner of my junior-varsity letter jacket.) We wrote notes to one another during school and stuffed them through the grills of our lockers.

We had made our way to Taff Lane in the Rambler several times but stopped short of intercourse. I began to think Glenda might be the wrong girl at the wrong time for me in the Rambler. She was nice, but she was having trouble deciding if it was right for us to have sex. I never had such questions, but I was the one with the bed on wheels. I never pushed Glenda too far, and when she said stop, I always did. My classmates assumed we made great use of the Rambler, but in fact, we had not utilized its full capabilities.

On November 8, Glenda and I went to Teen Circle's Sadie Hawkins Dance. We had the week off before the state football playoffs, and it was a weekend to have fun and escape. Teen Circle was the heart and soul of our high school dances.

Before the Sadie Hawkins Dance, we worked on decorating Teen Circle's walls and ceiling with drawings depicting the town of Dogpatch, the imaginary hillbilly town supposedly in Arkansas between two uninteresting hills, with roads to nowhere and the hideouts of Hairless Joe and Lonesome Polecat. Al Capp began the cartoon strip in 1937.

Using poster boards and big rolls of white paper taped to the walls, each team could decorate a section. We created crop fields, hogs, hillbilly bar scenes, outhouses, and whisky stills, and we reproduced scenes from the *Li'l Abner* cartoon. We placed our classmate's names on the walls in the characters and drawings about Dogpatch. It was a decorated, colorful, and funny room that escaped the realities of Hopewell and the world around it.

Everyone was excited the night of the dance. I went as Daisy Mae, wearing a white mop wig, one of Mom's one-piece mostly white bathing suits, white panties over the bathing suit, and a half slip over my lower half. I stuffed newspapers in the bathing suit to enlarge my supersize breasts. I was hot!

Glenda dressed up as Li'l Abner with a ragged men's red shirt, patched up blue jeans, and big heavy men's working boots. Other classmates came as famous Dogpatch characters such as Pappy Yokum, Mammy Yokum, Lonesome Polecat, Hairless Joe, Evil Eye Fleegle, Fearless Fosdick, and Joe Btfsplk. Some carried around big whisky bottles filled with brown-colored sodas to mimic the Kickapoo Joy Juice that Lonesome Polecat and Hairless Joe produced in their still. Alcohol was not allowed in Teen Circle, and everyone was carefully checked at the door, but small amounts got in.

To top it off, the DJ played our favorite songs such as "All My Loving," "Yakety Yak," "I'm Sorry," and "Witch Doctor." We danced and danced and danced. The Teen Circle's inlaid wood floor had withstood this workout many times. We were exhausted by night's end, and the floor always won. It could endure a herd of cattle—or teenagers.

"Whew! Let's sit down. I'm so hot," I said to Glenda after our sixth dance in a row. Sturdy wooden and well-painted pastel-green booths lined both sides of the room, and we sat down in one of them.

C. J. came over with his date, Vicki Newman, and they sat down too.

"What a hell of a party," C. J. said.

We nodded in agreement.

"Did you see that Peggy Sander came with Danny Ingels?" Glenda said.

"I thought Peggy was dating Frank Davenger," Vicki replied. "Did you hear the rumor that Danny is queer?"

"Who cares?" I took Glenda's hand to return to the dance floor.

High school gossip was alive and well that evening, as usual. Multitudes of side conversations went on about who was dating whom, who liked whom, who got drunk, who was hitting the sack, and the silly incidents that happen in the high school classrooms, hallways, and parking lots.

The only time we sat down the entire evening was when the DJ took breaks and during the evening skit. Kevin Castillo, our starting quarterback, began the skit by reading from a big poster-board-sized book titled *The Diary of Sadie Hawkins.* "In this *Diary of Sadie Hawkins,* we have the goings-on in Dogpatch. I'm going to read you some of the things that were written down for the ages," Kevin said as the crowd laughed and joked around. "Here we go!"

Eddie: I hear you beat the side of your car up drinking that Kickapoo Joy Juice.

Each time Kevin read an episode, the crowd laughed and acted crazy.

Someone yelled, "Eddie did a forearm shiv on his fender several times and bent it up. He can't hold his liquor!" The crowd laughed and continued to do so with every reading.

Warren: Did Wolf Gal give you those awful scratches on your face?

Jerry and Betty: What were you two doing in the lounge at the Dogpatch Church?

Helen: What was going on in the parking lot behind the Dogpatch Funeral Home last Friday night?

David: Li'l Abner wants to use your Rambler.

Bonnie: You better watch out for Stupefyin' Jones—she's about to take your man.

Donnie: How did you end up in the women's outhouse at our high school?

Janet: I hear you had a date with Earthquake McGoon Saturday night, and you barely got out of there with your pants on.

Donnie and Benna: You say you went possum hunting in Dogpatch, but you didn't bring back any possums?

David: We hear you are looking for Dogpatch Cave to park your Rambler.

Marvin and Sarah: Where were you parked in Dogpatch last Saturday night when you had an unexpected guest—Police Detective Fearless Fosdick?

Kevin's skit continued for about thirty minutes, and it was fun.

When it was over, Kevin said, "Thanks to everyone for working hard on the party. Now, let's rock and roll!"

With that, the DJ began to spin "Sherry" by the Four Seasons, and we were up dancing the night away. Teen Circle closed down on special nights like this at midnight, and we stayed to the very end. It was a night to remember.

Our first playoff game was against Clinton County Cougars, a Class A high school in southeastern Kentucky. Most people from the bituminous mountains of southeastern Kentucky thought the blue bloods of central Kentucky considered them second-class citizens, so there was more at stake than merely a football game. Towns and entire regions of the state decreed high school football and basketball to be the main sources of local pride and respect. Clinton County had tough football players. Most were the sons of miners, farmers, and loggers.

The *Hopewell Enterprise* wrote front-page articles on our football team, and it was difficult to walk down Main Street without shopkeepers coming out of their store to wish us well and ask questions about the upcoming playoff game. High school banners went up on Main Street. Pep rallies were held during school, and the mayor and members of the state legislature made speeches. At one pep rally, our classmates dressed up as Clinton County idiot football players and cheerleaders and acted out a skit in the school auditorium. We were small-town gods. Mom and Dad even seemed to be catering to me.

In an interview with the newspaper, Coach Humphrey said, "We figured we'd be in the playoffs. We used three teams—offense, defense, and kicking—and we specialized like the bigger schools. It paid off because the boys developed more quickly and gained confidence. We have more speed than earlier teams. This team has lots of character. There's not one selfish boy. No one gets upset when another gets the publicity."

On Friday, November 15, 1963, we rode two school buses to Clinton County's field about a hundred miles away. The drive passed through small towns with names like Flint, Willow, and

Chet, framed by rolling hills of tobacco, corn, wheat, and soybean fields. We stayed that Friday night in a one-story motel that had a gaudy neon sign out front proclaiming the "Frontier Mountain Motel." The entire experience was unsettling to us. We were away from home, sleeping on hard mattresses in starchy sheets, without family meals and support. We had no fear or experience with such long-distance trips.

The game was at two o'clock, and we stayed off our feet since the coaches demanded that we rest. We ate breakfast and sat around the rooms on Saturday morning, watching TV reruns of *The Adventures of Rin Tin Tin* and *Lassie*.

Most players on both teams weighed between 140 and 220 pounds. The tallest player on either team was six foot two. Donnie Dorin was our fullback, and Dennis Eads was the halfback. Both were fast and strong, and both went on to play college football on scholarships. I had spent my football life trying to tackle these guys in practice, so I knew how good they were.

The Clinton County field was on the edge of the Appalachian Mountains and encircled by hills five hundred to a thousand feet tall. I thought we were playing in a fishbowl. The sky seemed smaller on this field.

We arrived at the stadium at noon and began to get taped and dressed. We were putting on our orange and black armor, I thought, much like the Roman gladiators. By one o'clock these thoughts had vanished, as we were on the field warming up and practicing our plays. The crowd seemed more hostile than in central Kentucky. They were chanting something strange that sounded like:

> Humphrey Dumpty sat on a wall,
> Humphrey Dumpty had a great fall,
> All the king's horses,
> And all the king's men,
> Couldn't put Humphrey together again.

By game time, we figured out what they were singing. It was a direct reference to our short and plump Coach Humphrey. Cougar fans dressed up like crude Humpty Dumptys. We didn't take kindly to the message that our coach was short, dumpy, and clumsy.

The Cougars wore black and gold uniforms. They marched down the field using a methodical mix of runs and passes. They scored on their first possession, and it was 7–0. I was playing defense, and we were upset.

"What's wrong with you guys?" Coach Humphrey said as the defense stood together on the sideline. "Now get it together and *stop* these guys!" We said nothing as we walked to the water cooler and bench.

We were shocked. No one had blocked us that well. Damn it, they were good.

Fortunately, our offense was very good, and we tied the score at 7–7 at the end of the first quarter. Rick got us together at the quarter break and said, "Fellows, we are the key to winning the game. It's defense, stupid. We've got to slow them down."

We did better in the second quarter and began to understand their blocking schemes, which were very different from what we had faced before. The strangeness of the trip down, stadium, motel, and chanting was becoming a thing of the past. We began to focus; we began to play defense the way we knew we could. We led at halftime 20–7.

Coach Humphrey gave his halftime speech, pointing out a few things we could do better. He finished by saying, "Men, this is what you have dreamed about for four years. Don't give it up!"

The third quarter was a good football game, but we had two turnovers. We were evenly matched Class A teams. Over five hundred of our fans drove down for the game with another two thousand or so from the hometown Cougars. All seats were taken, and hundreds of fans stood for the entire game. We ended the third quarter ahead 20–14.

In the fourth quarter, the Cougars marched down to our twelve-yard line, but we stopped them. They kicked a field goal, and now it was 20–17. We received the kickoff and made it to their thirty-six-yard line before we had to punt. A Cougar caught our punt, bobbled the ball, and was promptly tackled on their nine-yard line.

Our defense huddled, and Rick said, "Kick it up a level. Give it all you have."

On first down, we stopped them for a one-yard gain. On second down, their quarterback dropped back to pass, and one of our blitz schemes was on. Both defensive ends were to blitz, and the linebackers were to cover the offensive ends. Joe Wickens and I were the defensive ends. I ran inside their offensive end untouched, and Joe took the outside route. We hit the quarterback simultaneously and tackled him in the end zone. It was a safety. Our defense had scored two points. The score was now 22–17 with less than two minutes to go.

Clinton County kicked off to us from their twenty-yard line, and we returned it to the fifty-yard line. Time was running out. It was now up to our offense to hold the ball, get a first down, and win the game.

On first and ten, Kevin Castillo threw an incomplete pass. On second down, Donnie Dorin ran for eight yards off tackle. It was now third down and two yards to go on the Cougars' forty-two-yard line.

I stood by the coaches and listened to them debating whether to pass or pitch to Dennis Eads. The coaches called for the latter play, and guard Eddie Russell ran in the play. The pitch out went well, and Dennis turned the corner—and that was it. He raced by everyone and scored a touchdown. We made the extra point and won 29–17.

Our fans crowded the field, and we chanted, "Coach Humphrey! Coach Humphrey!" The Cougar fans silently walked away. We yelled and screamed in the locker room as we took off our armor. We had won the first and only high school state playoff game for Hopewell High School. No more snickers from Clinton County fans. We had beaten them on their hometown field. The trip home in the yellow school bus was fun. Fans had decorated our buses with toilet paper and soap and followed us home. About two hundred fans met us at our field in Hopewell at ten o'clock that night.

On Saturday morning, I read the newspaper article about our playoff win. I felt good. I learned we would play the Thor High School Spartans who also won their quarterfinal playoff game. I had the weekend for a much-needed rest before school Monday and preparation for the semifinal playoff game.

Glenda and I decided to go to the Hopewell Drive-In to see *Lolita,* directed by Stanley Kubrick, starring James Mason, Sue Lyon, Peter Sellers, and Shelly Winters. The poster for the movie was sexy. Lolita wore red "Love" sunglasses and lipstick and sucked on a red lollipop. The movie looked interesting, and I wanted a place were Glenda and I could relax and have privacy.

"Do you mind if I park in the back?" I asked Glenda as we drove through rows of drive-in speakers. "I don't want to horse around with my classmates tonight. I want to be with you." I found a parking spot on the back row with a tall fence behind us. I rolled the window down, hung the speaker over the window, and rolled it back up. In the middle of November, the temperature was in the forties.

"What do you want to eat?" I asked.

"Let's do popcorn, one Coke, and one 7Up," Glenda replied.

I walked the long distance to the refreshment stand and bought these items. Once back in the Rambler, I pulled out a pint of Early Times whisky and poured some into the two sodas. We ate, drank, and talked, paying a little bit of attention to the start of the movie.

I had accomplished my objective by being with Glenda and away from the chaos of the high school crowds. Glenda was thrilled we'd won our state playoff game and the chance to win a state football title. I put both seats down on my moving bed, and we lay on our backs and talked while holding hands.

I managed to roll over on my right side and begin to kiss and fondle her. She also rolled over to her left side and raised her right leg. It was the first time I had been intimate with Glenda. Her black hair surrounded me. I thought she was sensual, and now

I knew. We took off most of our clothes and proceeded to have intercourse. My previous sexual experience with Sally was paying off. At the end, we lay flat on our backs and hold hands.

Slowly we separated and began to put the pieces back together. The windows were steamed shut; no one could see us. Once we got dressed, I raised my two front reclining seats to their upright positions. *Lolita* was ending, and obviously we hadn't seen it, but our time was hotter. The Rambler's airliner reclining seats had finally been christened. It was a great time for both of us.

Once dressed, I turned on the engine and the windshield wipers so we could see out. As I drove out of the drive-in theater in a line of cars, she said, "When can we do that again?"

"Well, let's get you home on time. I'll call you tomorrow."

Once I got home, I collapsed in my bed with a smile on my face. I couldn't do this and play championship football at the same time. It was too exhausting.

CHAPTER 10

Friday Nights

"How are we going to play this superstar?" I asked Rick as we left Monday's film session.

Rick replied, "David, I have no idea, but you can bet they plan to run behind him all night."

Our opponent for the state Class A semifinal playoff game, the Thor High School Spartans, was a good football team. They had beaten two AA teams during the regular season and were ranked higher in the state football poll than we were. If we could beat them, we would go to Louisville to play for the state Class A title.

The Spartans were also a southeastern Kentucky high school, but they were located deep in the Appalachians Mountains. They were the sons of rugged and proud eastern Kentucky mountain people. Their families often worked in the coal mines.

I reluctantly had to face one of their sons—a six-three, 235-pound offensive tackle—who had already accepted a scholarship to Nebraska. On film, he looked agile and quick. I was no match for him in terms of size, speed, or strength. But I was not alone. Rick and C. J. had the same problem. Depending on our defensive and their offensive schemes, this superior athlete would be blocking us during the game. C. J. would most often line up head-on with him. I could get hurt, but you couldn't hurt C. J.

During Tuesday's practice, we walked through defensive and offensive plays. Everyone was injured in some way, but our small school didn't have the luxury of good and healthy backup players. Many of us would have never gotten on the field if today's doctors had to approve our game worthiness. We enjoyed the week because we were the gods of Hopewell. On my frequent stops to Mildred's Drug Store with other teammates, the owner gave us free milkshakes and fountain drinks.

On Wednesday during lunch at the school cafeteria, I sat with center and linebacker Rick Shaffer, fullback Donnie Dorin, C. J. Moxley, our defensive and offensive tackle, Eddie Russell, our offensive guard, and offensive end, Warren Stow. The six of us wore our orange and black football jerseys and filled the small table.

"Rick, do you remember when we played Castle County last year?" I asked.

"That's the last time I want to play a AAA school," Rick responded as everyone at the table laughed.

"Do you remember how I bloodied their big tackle's nose, and he went after you thinking it was me?"

Rick laughed. "Bourbon, you did a number on me during that game. And then you hit him in the groin with your helmet—and he left the field for a while. You're lucky he went out of the game. Otherwise, he would have crucified you."

My table of teammates nodded in agreement as they were laughing and horsing around.

Nothing is totally ethical on a football field, regardless of what nonplayers believe. In the sixties, a standard referee crew for a high school football game was three referees: one behind the defensive team, one behind the offensive team, and one line referee on the sideline. We didn't have game film, a multitude of television cameras recording our every move, six or more referees, slow motion, or instant replay. Offensive or defensive holding happened on every play. Fights for fumbles and loose punts were just that—fights. And cheap shots were often taken when the referees weren't looking. A painful injury was documented by memory, not slow-motion replays. If you could get an advantage, you took it.

"Let's do the same thing again. Let's try to get this big tackle mad, and maybe he'll forget he needs to block," I continued.

"Bourbon, sooner or later your antics are going to catch up with you," C. J. said in a prophetic way.

On Wednesday, I decided how I was going to play this superstar. Somehow I had to get him mad—really mad. Maybe we could get him kicked out of the game. I wasn't quite sure how to do this, but I had two days to figure it out.

Thor High School was 160 miles from Hopewell. We rode the school buses to Thor on Thursday, November 21. Originally the game was supposed to be Friday evening at seven o'clock, but it was rescheduled to start at two in the afternoon on Friday. The ratty field lights were not good at Thor High School, and they wanted the game finished before dark.

This time, we had experience with the long bus ride, being away from home, sleeping on cheap motel beds, and enduring a hostile crowd. As expected, we did not sleep well on Thursday evening. On Friday, we rested until about nine, had a good breakfast, and went back to the motel for some last-minute discussions with the coaches.

We loaded up the bus at noon and drove to the field. As we drove into the parking lot, the principal hurriedly came in and said, "President Kennedy has been shot in Dallas, Texas, and he's in critical condition," he said.

A dull wave of sadness filled my head. I had tried to be strong in the face of past upheavals, but this travesty got to me. Panic shuddered through the bus.

"Can we get out? Can we get out?" one of my teammates yelled to Coach Humphrey.

Coach opened the doors, and we quickly got out of the confined space. The band bus next to us emptied, followed by the cheerleaders, including Glenda, who joined us.

I hugged Glenda and rejoined my teammates. Soon a huddled mass of people stood crying, bewildered by this tragic announcement. Parents joined the huddle as they arrived.

"What else could possibly go wrong?" a teacher said as she cried and hugged several kids. Questions arose as we stood there in disarray. *How this could happen?*

"The Cubans did this," Eddie said. "Those bastards."

"I bet the Russians were behind it," Glenda said.

I thought about the recent Cuban Missile Crisis, the failed Bay of Pigs invasion, and Nikita Khrushchev banging his shoe on the table at the United Nations. Television had imprinted these images in our minds and created a level of daily stress. And the Class of 1965 had to cope with other turbulence, such as the Pill, the emerging Vietnam War, the women's liberation movement, racial hatred and discord, *Sputnik*, fallout shelters, Ernest Hemingway and Marylyn Monroe's suicides, and the Berlin Wall. It was too much. And now President Kennedy had been shot.

This final event shook me to the core. The world seemed to be falling apart. Was there no order left? My eyes were watering, but I tried to hide it. How could I be a football hero and cry on game day?

The team grieved for about thirty minutes in a huddle of humanity, and then the coaches moved us into the locker room. The locker room was like an old concrete barn with several three hundred-watt light bulbs hanging from the ceiling.

Moments after we got into the locker room, the Thor principal came in and said, "President Kennedy died about 2:00 p.m. EST today. Vice President Lyndon B. Johnson is our new president."

"Will we play the game?" Coach Humphrey asked the principal.

"Coach, I called the state high school athletic association, and they recommended we play," the principal reported. "But, Coach, if you agree, could we set the kickoff for 3:30 instead of 2:00, given the events of the day?"

"Yes, that's fine," Coach replied.

For the next hour, we tried to cope with the tragic news. It was not easy. I had forgotten about football. But we taped up and put on our armor. We went out on the field to warm up and practice. We were dressed in black pants and orange jerseys. At the other end of the field, the Spartans team was dressed in white pants and red jerseys. Nothing matched. The mix of colors seemed as awkward and surreal as the day's events.

To top it off, we were playing another playoff game in a weird fishbowl. The mountains, which were several thousand feet high, defined the sides of the bowl, and the dark and low rainclouds provided the lid of the bowl. In contrast, the terrain of central Kentucky was rolling hills of only a few hundred feet. And I had no idea how to play their superstar tackle. I wanted to go home.

"Eddie, everything seems off today—everything," I said as we were doing calisthenics.

"Yeah, I'd rather play another day," he replied.

We kicked off to the Spartans, and they worked their way down the field. Rick, C. J., and I avoided giving up any huge chunks of yardage, but they did run play after play right behind their all-state tackle. They would mix in a pass play and a run away from us occasionally, but they clearly wanted to run behind their big tackle. They were chewing up five to six yards per run, and we didn't seem to be capable of stopping them. The ball was on our twenty-five-yard line, and we were desperate. We couldn't stop their grind-it-out power football.

"C. J., we have to take the big tackle out," I said when they were in the huddle.

"How, in the hell are you going to do that?" C. J. asked as they ran to the line of scrimmage.

We didn't get to finish our conversation. They quick-hiked the ball and threw a short pass to their tight end over the middle for a twelve-yard pickup. The ball was on our thirteen-yard line, and there was no time to discuss things. The steamroller was coming straight at us, crushing our will.

On the next play, a first down and ten play, I told C. J. and Rick that I was going to try to hit him with a forearm shiver, my specialty, to see if I could get him mad at me. I figured if he chased me all over the field, then he wouldn't do a good job blocking. As they snapped the ball, the big tackle ran right at me. I tried to land my forearm squarely in the long horizontal slot in his two-bar facemask.

However, the Nebraska-bound tackle had similar ideas, and he cocked back his massive arm like a catapult. He released his forearm with the force of his entire body, and it slammed into the side of my helmet like a sledgehammer striking a railroad tie. Wham! My helmet stayed on, but my head snapped back like a whip. I was immediately knocked out.

The next thing I remembered was Clifton Porter standing over me. "Bourbon, are you okay?"

The coaches and trainers ran onto the field and began to examine me. After two more minutes, I was able to stand up and wobble off the field with the help of an assistant coach and a trainer. Dazed, I sat down on the bench on our sideline and contemplated my fate. I imagined the big tackle standing over me for a second and laughing at my lifeless body. He won that battle, and I would not play the rest of the game. Once I sat down on the bench, I realized my neck was sore, my vision was blurred, and I had a severe headache.

Eddie came by the bench and said, "Bourbon, are you alive?"

"Yes," I mumbled with an orange towel over my head as I wiped snot bubbles from my nose. Was the bench moving—or was it me? Privately, I was worried about my head, since my brain had taken a hard knock.

"*Well*, that big tackle sure cleaned your clock," Eddie said as he sat down beside me. Eddie was right. I had just received my own medicine. That tackle was too athletic and big for me to win the battle in the trenches. Before the night was over, several of my teammates joined me on the unable-to-perform injury list. American football is a brutal game. Human bodies, especially young ones, are not designed for such games. It is a game of attrition, and smaller high schools seldom win this game.

My teammates gave it a valiant try, but the Spartans were too good. We lost the game 21–7.

As I walked to the locker room with a pounding headache, I heard Eddie Russell talking to Kevin Castillo. "They were tough. That's why they're the highest-ranked Class A team in the state."

We didn't win the state Class A division title, but we did make it to the Class A final four. We won our conference, Coach Humphrey won the state's Class A Coach of the Year, and we ended up with a 10–1–1 record. It was the school's first ten-win season and the first conference championship since football began in 1909 at Hopewell High School. During our football banquet, Coach Bob Humphrey was given the key to the city, the school had a special pep rally on school time, and many players received all-conference or all-state honors, but not me. My career as a good high school football player was coming to an end. Football smarts only went so far. Besides, I had the Rambler.

I didn't go out for the basketball team my junior year and found myself, for the first time, not playing year-round sports. During the previous year, I faced the reality that Joe Wickens and other basketball players were simply better than I was. Without a sport to play, I had my first chance to be like other students. It was a new world. I would watch the basketball games as Glenda led cheers, and I hopped around the bleachers, gossiping about everything. This newfound freedom allowed me to get to know more classmates. Since my summers included long hours of work, there had been little time to get to know some of my classmates.

As in past years, I took my schoolwork seriously during my junior year. I focused on chemistry, physics, biology, trigonometry, and plane and solid geometry. I would help America win the space race. I was smart—but not so smart I didn't have to work at it. My favorite teacher was a single, skinny, thirty-five-year-old woman named Anita Zeiger. She often wore small-print and high-collar blouses that matched her conservative beliefs and manner. Her caring smile always captivated me. And oh could she teach!

Miss Zeiger spent hours helping students understand the intricacies of imaginary numbers and cosines. She believed that practice made perfect, so she required us to work hundreds—yes, hundreds—of homework problems. It paid off for me. After a while, I built up a sense of how to approach each problem and solve it. Once or twice, Mom and Dad even paid her to tutor me. I took four courses from her: algebra II, plane geometry, solid geometry, and trigonometry—and wished I could have taken more. Our small school did not offer a calculus course. She was very demanding, and that was good. I was awarded our high school's solid geometry and trigonometry award my senior year because of her mentoring. We don't thank teachers enough, and if I ever see her, I shall bow down to her in gratitude for her influence on my life.

After the football season ended in the crushing defeat to Thor High School, Thor went on to win the state championship. The Christmas holidays were coming, and I was recovering from a brutal football season and a demanding academic year. That winter, everyone was still coping with the assassination of President Kennedy and Lee Harvey Oswald.

Glenda and I watched as the Beatles arrived in New York among much fanfare on February 7, 1964. The four English rock and pop stars formed a band in Liverpool, England, in 1960. Ringo Starr, my favorite, played the drums; John Lennon played the rhythm guitar; George Harrison played the lead guitar; and Paul McCartney played the bass guitar. Beatlemania was born when they launched their American tour. Their 1963 song, "I Want to Hold Your Hand," was number one in England and the US. Before *The Ed Sullivan Show*, this song alone had sold 2.6 million records in the previous two weeks. We bought forty-fives and thirty-three LPs. The arrival of The Beatles officially marked the end of the Elvis Presley rock 'n' roll era. The four wore stylish clothing with skinny ties. They experimented with drugs, mainly marijuana, and talked about it publicly, which was not well received by Hopewell parents—including mine.

On February 9, 1964, I watched the Beatles on *The Ed Sullivan Show* with my family on our black-and-white television. Dad and Mom enjoyed the show, but Mom looked worried.

"Mom, did you like them?" I asked.

"Oh. Ah. Yes, they were great," Mom said. Dad rubbed his forehead. Katie had just turned five years old and was listening but didn't enter the conversation. She had been destroying the springs in our sofa by bouncing around on it to the tunes of the Beatles.

"You don't seem too convinced, Mom." I couldn't wait for school to hear what my classmates thought of the Beatles.

"I think things are changing too fast for you kids, too fast," Mom said and walked into the kitchen.

About half of the US population watched the Beatles that night, and the show broke previous television ratings. Their songs suddenly were playing constantly on the radio. The Beatles were different from American bands. Their music seemed to be structured differently and used new sounds and instruments. Their British mop-top hairstyles and pop-culture attitudes and behaviors were refreshing for a generation that grew up with Elvis Presley and Chubby Checker. The British invasion had begun.

On a Friday evening in March, Glenda and I were driving the Circuit and listening to "All My Loving" by the Beatles. We didn't seem to be talking much. We had been through good and bad days together for eight months, and she was beginning to talk about going to college in August.

As we rounded the courthouse square, I asked, "Are you excited about going to college? Coastal is a good school."

"Yes, I'm excited. Hopewell has little to offer us. It's too small." After we passed Webster's Radio & TV Repair Shop, Glenda said, "David, are you tiring of me?"

"No. Why do you say that?" I turned off the car radio and reached for her hand.

"I think I'm holding you back. Besides, I'm going to be seven hundred miles away when I go to college." We passed Nora's Cut & Curl shop, which had been there since I was born.

At the next stoplight, with Emmitt's Coin Laundry on the corner, the red light glared at us in the silence of the car. Two millennia seemed to pass before the traffic signal turned green.

I pressed on the accelerator. "Glenda, you're a wonderful girl, and I have thought about you leaving for college. The college boys will be after you, and I'm not going to be able to visit you." I had considered the cost of visiting her in college. And I wondered—if I ventured into her college world, would I be welcome?

That night Glenda and I broke up in as gentle a way as possible. There was no remorse. We had shared good times together, and it was time to close the chapter. I was sad, restless, and definitely confused.

I was upset about breaking up with Glenda—and the lost chance to win a state championship. Maybe I should call Sally? But how could we date one thousand miles apart? My dreams of finding true love and winning a championship were right in front of me, but they were unreachable. I couldn't sleep. I got out of bed—standing in my white underwear—my frailties revealed.

I picked up my plastic model of an aircraft carrier. I had spent many hours gluing and painting every detail of it. I threw my beloved *US Forrestal* straight down on the linoleum-covered concrete floor and smashed it to pieces. I regret destroying it to this day.

"David, are you okay?" Mom called down.

"Yes, Mom. I'm fine."

"Breakfast in the morning at seven, if you want it."

The pace of life goes on—even when you think it has stopped for you.

On Monday, the word of our breakup sliced through the high school like a surgeon's scalpel. By noon, everyone knew. We learned to say hi to each other in the hallways. Glenda would graduate in June 1964, but I had one more year. In another time and place, we would have been a good match, but not now.

Later that week, I was standing alone in the parking lot next to my Rambler when Glenda walked up to me with her glistening brown eyes and handed me my orange and black varsity letter jacket with the conference championship and state playoff patches on it. Glenda said nothing, gave me a hug, and walked away.

"Thanks." That was all I could think to say. As I watched her body sway away from me with her glossy black hair bouncing off her round shoulders, my thoughts turned to the many good times we had. We had grown up together and were better off for it. And Glenda had christened my Rambler.

With no girlfriend and only some spring track meets, I had time to scour a three-county area for the ideal parking spot. I did this meticulous search of the countryside by myself—trying to find "My Place" to park the Rambler. The ideal specifications for My Place would be a parking spot hidden by trees and bushes, not an entrance to a house or horse barn where people would be driving in during the evening.

One day as I was on patrol for the perfect parking spot, I rounded a corner of a curvy and dangerous single-lane, black-topped country road that descended about fifty feet around the creek. About halfway around the curve, I noticed a road that cut across a creek. I passed it, turned around at the next farm gate, and drove into the drive to find a small and gorgeous concrete-and-stone bridge that crossed the creek. The bridge was built for farm vehicles and had no railings or sidewalls.

I stopped, got out, and surveyed the site like a coach surveys a football field. Could I back down this drive and on top of the bridge at night without driving my Rambler off the narrow bridge? The steep downward curve of the road hid the site. I continued my drive across the bridge and found the small gravel road led to a barn. The way it was fenced off, livestock had no access to the gravel road or bridge. It was perfect.

I pulled out to the main road and began practicing backing into the gravel road and bridge. I did it six times, and only once did I have my back wheel half off the bridge. The desire to find My Place was so strong that I was willing to risk the Rambler and me falling six feet into the small creek.

My more immediate problem was that I had no girlfriend to try out My Place! As I drove home, I thought that maybe Glenda and I had broken up too early. But I was too young to circle back in time to pick up where I'd left off, and Glenda probably wanted to pursue her new life path, college, without me.

One day in solid geometry class, I sat beside Edna White. After talking with her, I asked, "Edna, are you dating anyone?" When I was in the tenth grade, I'd had a few dates with Edna, including when we dressed up as Davy Crockett and Annie Oakley for the Halloween sock hop. Then Edna was a studious and bashful girl without much of a figure. But over the past year or so, her body had blossomed. Her breasts were bigger now, and her waist seemed to be slimmer.

"No," Edna replied with a surprised look.

"Uh. Want to go ride the Circuit with me on Friday night?"

"Sure."

Off we went on the well-rehearsed trip to Jerry's, cruising the Circuit. I could drive the Circuit blindfolded. Edna was a senior and had dated Roger Yuger, who was now in college, but they had broken up. Edna had long blonde hair that fell below her shoulders, and she was tall. She played clarinet in the band. She was in my math classes and sometimes wore black-rimmed reading glasses. I liked her glasses. I knew Edna was a smart girl because we worked on math homework problems together in the library.

We were already friends and knew each other well. She had learned the route of the Circuit while dating Roger, so we drove it and talked incessantly about the events of the day.

One Friday evening in April, I headed out to My Place.

"Where are we going?" Edna asked.

"I found a new place to park. You'll like it," I replied.

As I approached My Place, my heart began to race. It was very dark with no moonlight. I privately wondered if I would be able to back the car onto that small bridge without falling off. I carefully pulled past the gravel road and began backing up slowly. I made it halfway onto the bridge before stopping. I opened the door to check my position. All four tires were on the bridge, and everything seemed okay. We left the radio on as it played one of our favorite songs, "If I Had a Hammer" by Peter, Paul, and Mary.

"Wow! David, this is a neat spot," Edna said. She had no idea how dangerous it was to back onto that bridge at night.

"Yes, it is a great spot." I turned the radio lower, and we began to hug and kiss. My blue eyes searched her green eyes. We knew one another well and were comfortable together. I was dying to explore Edna's upright breasts. My addiction to breasts overwhelmed other, more carnal, thoughts. We paused to listen to my favorite song, "The Book of Love," by the Monotones.

After listening to two more songs, I reclined both Rambler seats. I moved toward her and began to unbutton her blouse. We remained sitting up. We kissed as I held her tight. I put my hand under her blouse and unhooked her bra. Edna pulled away from me but did not tell me to stop.

"David," she murmured. "I don't think I can do this."

"Why?" A cool burst of wind rushed through a half-closed window as I waited for an answer.

"I'm still in love with Roger."

"Oh." We separated, and I stared nowhere. After moments of silence, I said, "But you were enjoying things?"

"Yes, I know." She began to button up her blouse. "I'm sorry. I just can't go all the way tonight."

I went out with Edna on and off the next month, but we knew we were friends, not lovers. At sixteen, love and sex were multidimensional ideas that baffled me.

I didn't tell my football buddies and friends exactly what we were doing or not doing. That was absolutely private. Of course, my classmates were constantly teasing me about the Rambler and wanted to know if they could rent it.

In June 1964 school ended, and I immediately began working for my dad. My first few days back, I rode around with the Boss, doing service calls and small air-conditioning and electrical jobs.

Dad was working in a clothing factory in Tennessee with a crew of six men. He came home on Saturdays and slept most Sundays. The long-distance work exhausted him and annoyed Mom. I overheard several arguments between them about Dad being on the road.

One Sunday after missing church, Mom said, "Ham, are you going to tonight's church social?"

"No, I have to make a materials list tonight."

"You haven't been to church or a Sunday night social for six months," Mom said in a strong and loud voice.

"I don't have time for that crap with this Tennessee job," Dad declared.

"Hamlet, you better make time. You don't even know Katie. I'm going alone." Mom called Dad "Hamlet" when she was mad at him.

"Fine, go on and go. I have to make a living."

The conflicts of being a family man and being the sole wage earner surfaced at odd times. In 1964, two-income families were not the norm in Hopewell, and I saw my family struggle with this dilemma. Mom cooked, cleaned, managed the household, and made our home a "home." Katie was five years old and kept Mom busy. Both parents anchored this family with very different roles.

On Saturday afternoons, I swam for the Hopewell Country Club swim team, but since I seldom had time to practice, I normally placed second to fourth in the backstroke and freestyle. The swim coach knew of my work situation, and he let me swim and pick up a few extra points for the swim team. One benefit of being on the swim team was that I got to see the best country clubs in the state and meet a lot of people I would later see in college.

After dinner, Dad sat down in his chair and said, "David, do you think you can run a new job?"

"Yes. What kind of job?"

"I got the contract on Jerry's Restaurant. I'm tied up in Tennessee," Dad replied.

"What do you want me to do?"

"Well, I'll give you the blueprints. You figure out what materials we need, get them, and run the job. You start tomorrow."

Monday morning at seven, Dad and I went over the blueprints. He checked on the status of other jobs and loaded up materials for the Tennessee job. Dad left about noon for the long drive with his crew.

I spent the rest of the day building the materials list based on the blueprints. I needed to visit the jobsite on Tuesday morning since they were beginning to pour the concrete footers for the building.

On Tuesday morning at seven, I drove to the jobsite in the Rambler—since all the shop trucks were busy—and laid the blueprint out on the hood of my car. The general contractor, who was next to me in his big truck, came over and said, "Hi, son, I'm Herbert." Herbert was taller than his truck cab and wore a full but uneven beard. His truck bed was packed with stakes, ropes, heavy rubber boots, two-by fours, a ladder, and a random assortment of hand tools.

"Hi. I'm David Bourbon, Ham's son," I said.

"Is your dad going to be here?" Herbert replied.

"No, I'm running this job. Dad's in Tennessee doing a job."

"Son, how old are you?" Herbert asked with a puzzled look.

"I'm sixteen. I'll be seventeen in August," I said. I sensed his apprehension, so I added, "Sir, I can do this job."

"Okay, I'm pouring the concrete floor on Friday morning. Get your conduit in there by Thursday evening. You only get one chance with concrete—so get it right."

"Yes, sir. I'll have my men here tomorrow morning." A rush of adrenaline surged through my body. The pressure was on, and I felt it.

We laid our conduits and boxes the next day with a crew of two. I measured and remeasured everything to make sure I had it right. I had to make many decisions that week, and I began to understand the pressure my dad experienced. Sometimes the blueprints were vague about what size conduit to use for the electrical panel's incoming power cables, so I decided to use a slightly oversized three-inch-diameter conduit to make sure it could handle the cables. The men did what I said. We took our breaks, just like on any job, and they didn't seem to take advantage of a young kid being the boss.

On Friday morning, I supervised the job and watched a continuous flow of concrete trucks rumble to the site and drop their loads. I made sure no conduits or electrical boxes were damaged, moved, or poured over. Herbert was too busy to talk, but he knew I was watching things.

On Saturday morning, instead of going to the swimming meet, I stopped by the jobsite to check the measurements on the monolith of concrete that defined the restaurant floor. Everything was correct. I had done it.

Later in life, I realized those construction experiences were a foundation for developing my logic and behavior. Construction work needs to be organized. Attention to detail is paramount to success. You have to talk to bankers and engineers one minute and a roughneck laborer the next minute. If you can't adapt quickly to new information or people, you fail. I found that what you said—and how you said it—was very different, depending on whether your audience was at school, at the country club, on a football field, or at a construction site.

One summer day, I was driving around in a shop truck with two of our men when I stopped at a light on a slight hill. The truck was full of tools and a load of ten-foot-long electrical conduit. The truck was a stick shift, and as I let my foot off the brake, the truck rolled backward, and we heard a crunching sound. We looked back and realized the conduit sticking out of the back of our truck had speared the front of a Rainbow Bread truck.

I got out of the truck and walked back to the driver. "Sir, I'm sorry, but I speared your truck." We stood there in the street and saw that the two trucks were now joined by a single piece of conduit.

"Well, son, you sure did a good job of spearing me," he said with a laugh.

"Yeah, David, you sure as hell mated these suckers," one of our employees blurted out.

They stood around laughing at the situation. Traffic stopped, and drivers honked their horns at us. However, I wasn't amused. We traded driver and insurance information and pulled the conduit out of the truck. It had cut a perfectly circular hole. I figured correctly that I'd have to pay cash to get the truck fixed because I didn't want my car insurance rates to go up.

From that day forward, my name at the shop was "Rainbow Man." The guys would laugh and say, "Let Rainbow Man drive." "Watch out, don't fuck that truck." "David! Pull over! Here comes a bread truck."

The summer work at the shop included finishing a seafood restaurant, riding around with the Boss doing odd jobs, and some weeks in Tennessee helping Dad hang more than three hundred eight-foot-long fluorescent lights in the clothing factory. I made a lot of money for a soon-to-be seventeen-year-old, and the funds were accumulating. I had over $3,000 in my savings account and $500 in my checking account.

One hot Thursday afternoon in late July, the Boss and I were called to Emmitt's Coin Laundry on Main Street. Their air conditioner had gone out, and the place was a furnace. It could not dissipate the heat from the machines, much less from the sunlight. We pulled up in front of the laundry in the Boss's new 1960 F-100 truck, and I unloaded our toolbox and Freon gas gauges.

As I set the artifacts of blue-collar work down on the blazing sidewalk, I saw a green 1961 Chevy coming down Main Street. Roger Yuger recognized me and smiled as Edna, seated in the passenger seat, ducked down slightly. Edna's college boyfriend had returned home for the summer. I was working so hard that summer that I didn't even think to ask Edna about Roger.

The Boss and I entered the laundry to find out why the air conditioner didn't work, but my mind was far away, coping with an empty love life.

CHAPTER 11

Auburn Hair

"Hard to believe we're seniors," I said to a group of football players at Peggy's house. Peggy Sander was hosting another before-school party in August 1964. We were drinking sodas at a picnic table. Kevin Castillo, Warren Stow, Marvin Jacobs, C. J. Moxley, Donnie Dorin, Joe Wickens, and Rick Shaffer defined the group.

Our senior year would soon begin, and expectations in Hopewell were high for the class of 1965. Townspeople were abuzz again about Hopewell winning the state Class A football championship. We had twenty-two returning seniors and sixteen starters from the previous year's team.

"Man, time is moving fast! I hate to see us break up," Rick replied.

"Are you guys ready to play Ballard High School in the Bluegrass Bowl next week?" Marvin, our 125-pound junior class president, asked. He played football, but he did not start and seldom played.

"Sure, we know the routine." Donnie put his hands on his hips in a gesture of confidence.

"I don't know, Marvin. It's too early a game," Kevin added.

I hung around with the guys that evening playing badminton, horsing around as only high school kids can, and didn't talk to many girls. I didn't have a girlfriend. As I drove home that evening, I thought about past girls in my life—Mary Hallman, Beth DeMoss, Sally Leonard, Glenda Woodbury, and Edna White. It began with an innocent crush on Mary when I was five years old. Beth left town for boarding school, Sally moved to another state after two wonderful junior high years, Glenda graduated last year and went off to college, and Edna was fun, but she probably was in love with Roger Yuger. I had yet to find the right gal.

Our team was invited to kick off the season with an appearance in the Bluegrass Bowl against a Class AA team. We were excited, but we didn't have much time to prepare. The first game kicked off at two o'clock with the Hopewell Thoroughbreds playing the Ballard Knights. We were picked in preseason media polls to win the state Class A championship. The Ballard Knights were favorites to win their big-city conference. The second game began at seven with the Hickory County Lions playing Marysville High School. These two teams were also expected to win their conferences and compete in the state playoffs.

All week, the Hopewell newspaper ran stories on our team and the upcoming Bluegrass Bowl. Coach Humphrey was quoted in the paper. He said, "The Bluegrass Bowl is a prominent event. The teams selected are preseason favorites in their conferences." State newspapers followed with similar articles about the games and matchups.

In one newspaper interview, Coach Humphrey provided descriptions of our starters:

Warren Stow: A fine pass receiver with great open-field running after he catches the pass. He must work on blocking the big men at the line of scrimmage. He needs to keep his feet and square up on them.

Rick Shaffer: Truly an all-conference player—maybe all-state. Must work on blocking at center position but is outstanding at linebacker.

Donnie Dorin: Our answer to Jim Brown. He could develop into the best back in the state. He does it all—strong and fast.

C. J. Moxley: Big and strong but must work on his speed. C. J. has a powerful initial lick. C. J. must battle his tendency to let up once he has whipped his man. You can't hurt him.

David Bourbon: Tough and experienced. He will whip anyone in front of him but must work on stamina. A smart football player with no weakness when not tired.

Eddie Russell: He'll go to war and has improved steadily. There are better players but none that can whip him. He needs more confidence in his ability to play.

Kevin Castillo: Could be the best quarterback in Class A football. You don't need to take an inventory—he has it all.

In a pep rally at the football field on the Friday evening before the game, the mayor of Hopewell gave Coach Humphrey the key to the city. The city council also made Coach an honorary fire chief. Our team, as well as about one thousand fans, cheered as each player was introduced, and Coach repeated much of what he had said in the newspaper. I was excited, and I slept less than four hours that night.

The morning of the game, a parade in downtown Marion— the host city of the Bluegrass Bowl—highlighted the high school bands, cheerleaders, floats, mayors, and dignitaries. Even my mom rode in the school board parade car. All eyes were on our Hopewell football team.

On August 29, 1964, the day of the Bluegrass Bowl, we rode the school buses over in the morning and entered the locker rooms around eleven. The kickoff was scheduled for two, and most of us ate breakfast at home and skipped lunch. It was partly cloudy and in the eighties, which was more humane than normal for August.

In the gray concrete-block locker room, Coach Humphrey said, "Men, this is our Rose Bowl. We can beat them. Stay on your blocks and think about what you are doing."

We left the locker room in a stampede of youthful exuberance and went through our pregame drills. I felt we were not ready to play—it was just too early to play a big game, and the state media was watching our every move. In retrospect, I also think we were not prepared for the growing media interest we faced as players. The media's focus was supposed to be on big local, state, and national events—not a high school preseason football bowl game. And we were playing the top-ranked preseason Class AA team in the state.

We won the coin toss and elected to receive the ball. They kicked off, and Calvin O'Conner ran the ball back to our thirty-one-yard line. Kevin Castillo called 231X, and we broke the huddle. Donnie Dorin took the hand-off and ran through the gap between our left guard, Eddie Russell, and center, Rick Shaffer. Donnie ran for four yards, and the game was on. We made it to their forty-five-yard line before we had to punt.

I lined up as a defensive end, and we awaited their first play. The Ballard quarterback did a quick pitch out to my side of the field, and they ran for eleven yards.

"Rick, they're fast," I said as we jogged back to the new line of scrimmage. Ballard continued to march down the field and scored a touchdown. It soon became evident on both sides of the ball that we were bigger than Ballard, but they were much faster. Kevin threw an interception. We fumbled the ball once and missed an extra point. Nothing seemed to be going our way. The halftime score was 27–6.

"What the hell is wrong with you guys?" Coach yelled in the locker room. "You seem to be asleep! Our timing is off!"

We said nothing. Our heads were down. We were embarrassed. Whatever the reason, we were flat or simply outmanned. And to our fans, our play seemed uninspired. This was the wrong game at the wrong time.

We kicked off to Ballard to begin the second half and managed to stop them at midfield. This gave us a boost as our offense trotted out onto the field, and we managed to move down the field. Donnie made some good runs, and Kevin hit a few critical short passes.

"Bourbon, get in there at left end and block down on that tackle," Coach Humphrey said. Coach used me on offense when he needed a critical block. I would quickly know if I needed to block their linebacker or tackle—and the best way to do it.

With the ball on Ballard's sixteen-yard line, I came onto the field and told Kevin the play. Kevin called 225X, and we broke the huddle. As I set up, I realized their linebacker was lined up on his defensive tackle's right hip. I was hoping the linebacker would play back off the line of scrimmage, but I was not so lucky. Rick hiked the ball to Kevin, and he handed it off to Donnie. Ballard's defensive tackle and linebacker moved to the outside together, and I quickly decided my only chance to block them was to throw a horizontal body block. I managed to cut the legs out from under the linebacker. And as he fell to the ground, he temporarily blocked his own defensive tackle.

With his power and speed, Donnie ran through that hole and into the end zone. The score was 27–12. We went for two points after the touchdown, but we did not make it. We now had hope.

Ballard received the kickoff and methodically scored another touchdown. The game was spiraling out of our control. All I could do was endure. The score was 34–12 at the end of the third quarter. At 27–12, we had peaked. The Ballard Knights scored again in the beginning of the fourth quarter, missing the extra point, and led 40–12. Ballard began playing more of its second-string players. We lost 46–19, and the pride of Hopewell went down in a humiliating defeat.

Little was said in the locker room; even Coach Humphrey was quiet. Our fans cheered us as we got on the bus for the long ride home, but the taste of defeat was bitter.

Our first day of school after the loss to Ballard was tough. State media called it a mismatch, and we immediately went from a number one ranking to number nine in the state Class A polls. We couldn't dwell on the past because our next game was Friday, September 4, against Hillard High School.

During school, everyone met in the auditorium and listened to school officials define rules and regulations, provide course-schedule updates, and pass out advising schedules. The superintendent even made reference to "new laws that might impact how we do things around here" in his short speech. Many parents and teachers were tense because the Civil Rights Act of 1964 was signed into law on July 2, 1964. We had already integrated our Hopewell black and white school systems my tenth-grade year, but everyone wondered if the law required even more dramatic changes, such as combining the city and county school systems.

Mom worried about the impact of the Equal Pay Act of 1963, which prohibited salary differentials based on sex. She knew the teachers' salaries, and there were several big discrepancies between the male and female teachers. I had heard her talking about it with Dad at home. Dad loved Mom and admired her, but he didn't quite get this equal-pay-for-equal-work idea. As the only woman on the school board, Mom was going to study the law and be a champion for equal pay.

After our auditorium meeting, our senior class of about 110 students met in the library to elect class officers. The big library room had windows on three sides and bookracks at the windowless end. The librarian's desk and the checkout counter were beside the racks, and behind the desk, there was an entrance to a back room where the yearbook and school newspaper, *Goings-On*, were produced. Long tables with tan Formica tops occupied the rest of the library. The well-lit library was sometimes used for meetings and study hall. The library was stark, but the people were friendly. I saw this room as a haven for serious study with the social challenge of communicating with classmates without talking.

"We need to elect officers for your class," Ms. Judith Rose said. Ms. Rose taught English, and her take-charge attitude had been chiseled by more than twenty-five years of dealing with high school students. We were randomly seated around the big library tables and looked toward the bookracks and checkout desk.

"Do we have any nominations for treasurer?" she asked.

Two classmates were nominated and put on a paper ballot.

"Who do you want to nominate for secretary?"

Two more classmates were nominated and put on the same ballot.

I was kidding around with my football buddies, sort of half-listening to the nomination process. Ms. Rose gave us more than one dark stare. "Now who would you like to nominate for vice president of your class?"

Two classmates were nominated for VP. The final task was to nominate classmates for class president. We sort of knew who would be elected class president since he had been president our junior year.

"Who would you like to nominate for class president?" Ms. Rose began.

"I'd like to nominate Marvin Jacobs," someone said.

Many others nodded.

"Are there any other nominations?"

"I'd like to nominate David Bourbon," C. J. Moxley said.

All of a sudden, I quit kidding around. Me? They want to nominate me? I wanted to punch C. J. in the nose. For sophomore year, I had been elected treasurer of our class, but that was it.

I began to think about what was next. I had to give a short speech about why I wanted to be class president. Marvin Jacobs had been on the debate team for years, so I had no chance of winning a speech contest with him. My blood pressure began to rise, and I blushed. Fear swept through my body. The pressure was on.

One by one, the candidates for treasurer, secretary, and vice president made their short speeches and sat down. The class politely clapped for each with a constant murmur in the background of whispers and muted giggles. Twenty minutes had passed since I first heard my name nominated, so I had time to try to think of something to say. What could I say?

"Let's have Marvin and David say a few words, and then we will vote by paper ballot," Ms. Rose said.

Marvin confidently got up first. "Class, I have been your president this past year, and I think we did a good job. We accomplished our goals, and if elected this year, I'll try to do the same as last year. We'll raise money for a class trip, do some charity work, and get everyone involved. Our class officers last year worked well with school administrators, clubs, and parents. I do hope I can count on your vote. I have the experience. Thank you!"

The class applauded, and Marvin sat down.

Marvin pronounced every word perfectly, with no pauses. *Now that was a perfect speech.* His posture was perfect, and his hands didn't wave in the air. I stood up with a red face. Some of the class hooted. I thought, as I got up to speak, that my nomination could have been a joke, and I was speaking to simply entertain my classmates. Public speaking was not my strong suit, and I was nervous.

"Ah, I'm surprised at my nomination—thank you—please be patient with my rambling words." Some in the class laughed. I paused and looked down at my feet and then out the window. I tried not to look at C. J. and Eddie. I could hear them giggling as I stood there. "I'm organized, and I'll get things done. You know that. We need to pay for things, and with your help, we'll have sock hops in the gym and at Teen Circle," I said. I awkwardly put my hands in my pockets. "We'll get local businesses and charities to sponsor our events by going door-to-door. We'll raise money for the Bob Hardy Foundation. The more money we have, the more good we can do, and the more fun we can have." I paused again, not really knowing how to end my speech. "Thank you for nominating me—it is an honor. I won't let you down."

The class applauded, and at Ms. Rose's direction, the candidates left the library. We waited in the hallway, talking and trying to act calm, but my heart was beating fast. Being nominated for class president and making a speech in front of my teachers and peers was stressful. When making a speech, you are alone—and all eyes are on you. It was more stressful than a football game, and you can't hide under a helmet among buddies on a large field. It was also more stressful than asking a girl for a date, since that was private and not a public-speaking event.

As we reentered the library, Ms. Rose said, "Class, we have counted the ballots, and your class of 1965 officers are Sylvia Copeman, secretary; Marvin Jacobs, treasurer; Danny Ingels, vice president; and David Bourbon, president. Congratulations to the new officers. I wish you the best this year. Our meeting is adjourned. Now, please be quiet in the hallway and get ready for your next class."

I stood up in a slight state of shock. Classmates came up to offer me congratulations. One said, "Try to get the Righteous Band for a sock hop."

Another said, "Cool, dude, now you have all the cooties." He slapped my back and gave me a slight push.

C. J. gave me a bear hug and lifted me off the floor like a toy. The rest of the school day, I tried to act normal, but I was surprised they'd elected me. I was nothing but an electrician's son.

During our first week in school, a junior caught my eye. Anna Brooke had been elected a cheerleader, mainly due to her good looks and perky personality. Her clothes were classier than her peers' clothes. Anna's large breasts and hourglass figure got everyone's attention. She had auburn hair that almost met her shoulders and flipped up in beautiful big curls. Her liquid green eyes were penetrating, and she reminded me of Ann-Margret.

Her dad drove around town in a 1963 Lincoln Continental, which impressed everyone in Hopewell. This was the same type of car President Kennedy rode in on that fateful day in Dallas. The two of them lived in a nice brick house on a hill. Her mom died when Anna was six, and her hardworking dad was seldom home before six. Anna came home after school for years to an empty house.

After the game with the Hillard Bears, which we won, I walked out of the locker room to find Hopewell parents and cheerleaders, including Anna, standing outside. With sweat still running down my face and my letter jacket on, I said, "Anna, what did you think of the game?"

"You guys looked great tonight."

"We weren't ready to play last week," I replied as I realigned my letter jacket and tried to button it up. "Are you busy Saturday night?" I mumbled. Whether she said yes or no, I worried I would turn red with embarrassment.

"No, I don't have anything going on tomorrow night," she said.

"Would you like to go drive around … maybe see a movie?" I still did not look into her eyes.

"Sure. What time?" Anna asked.

"How about seven? We'll ride around and get something to eat at Jerry's."

On Saturday evening, we rode out to Jerry's Restaurant in the Rambler and circled the drive-in parking area several times, hoping to pounce upon a spot. On weekend nights, the restaurant area was packed with cars looking for a highly valued drive-in parking spot. After I circled the lot like an eagle seeking prey, a parking spot opened up. With some aggressive driving, we got it. Weekend nights were always exciting at Jerry's. We listened to songs on the radio like "Where Did Our Love Go" by the Supremes, "Oh, Pretty Woman," by Roy Orbison, and "Louie, Louie" by the Kingsmen. We knew everyone's cars and the people in them.

"Do you want to go inside?" I asked.

"Let's eat out here so we can see who's cruising."

"What should I order?" I said as I watched a 1955 Chevy Bel Air Coupe drive by.

"How about a J-Burger with no mayonnaise, fries, and a 7Up," Anna responded.

I pressed the speaker button, and a young voice said, "Hi. Welcome to Jerry's. What can I get you?"

"One J-Burger with no mayonnaise, fries, and a 7Up, and one Classic Club with everything on it, onion rings, and a Cherry Coke."

"That will be two dollars and eighteen cents with tax," the voice from the speaker box said.

We ate in the car, talking about everything from classmate romances to current events. I tipped the delivery guy thirty-five cents.

"What do you think of the Rolling Stones?" I asked Anna.

"Mick Jagger looks like the devil. He scares me. My dad didn't like them when they appeared on *The Hollywood Palace*."

About that time, "House of the Rising Sun" by the Animals came on the radio, and we stopped talking and listened intently to it, singing every word.

C. J. and Vicki pulled his 1960 Chevrolet Impala into the parking spot next to us. We put the windows down and gossiped between the two cars.

"Why is Rick with Sandra?" Vicki asked. "I thought Kevin was dating Sandra."

"No, I think they broke up, but I heard Kevin can't get his letter jacket back."

We didn't get out of the cars and stand around because the restaurant managers would ask us to leave. Or they'd call the police—and they were never far away. After sitting there for two hours, I ordered two more sodas and a strawberry pie to keep the management from asking us to leave. It was actually a cheap date night if you hung around Jerry's restaurant all night. It was the social happening in Hopewell. By ten o'clock, 90 percent of the restaurant patrons were high school kids. I took Anna home about eleven, walked her to her door, and kissed her good night on the cheek.

"I had a good time. See you Monday," I said.

Anna and I continued to date. We were young, carefree, and exploring each other. We often went to the drive-in movie and made out, each time becoming a little more intense.

We saw movies such as *Kissin' Cousins* starring Elvis Presley, *Dr. No* starring Sean Connery and Ursula Andress, *A Hard Day's Night* starring the Beatles, and *Bye Bye Birdie* starring Dick van Dyke, Janet Leigh, and Ann-Margret. I placed a *Bye Bye Birdie* movie poster of Ann-Margret on my bedroom wall to remind me of Anna. Anna's auburn hair was as radiant as Ann-Margret's. I was told Ann-Margret was a natural brunette, but I didn't want to believe it. Ann-Margret was my fantasy girl. She went on to fame and fortune with five Golden Globe awards and one Emmy, and she was nominated for two Grammys and two Oscars.

We parked at My Place and did just about everything young kids do except go all the way.

On a Saturday night in October, Anna and I went cruising around Hopewell. We had won our away football game against Class A opponent Bellville the previous night, and we both were tired. Anna had been cheerleading, and I was trying to help the team win. We beat Bellville 19–7 and were now 6–2.

"Let's head out to My Place and just listen to music and talk. Let's get away from the crowd," I said.

"Sounds good to me," Anna replied.

I had become an expert at backing the car down the gravel driveway and onto that narrow bridge in the dark. The air was cool, and a half-moon shone through partly cloudy skies. We talked about the game and who had gone with whom. We began to hug and kiss, as we had done many times the past six weeks. "She Loves You" by the Beatles was playing on the radio.

Anna's sexual behavior was as intense as her brilliant auburn hair. All of our senses were focused on completing the consummation. I slipped off her skirt and panties and my pants in record speed. The Rambler seats were laid back in a willing position.

Anna opened up her legs slowly. I spread them apart like a book, and her delicate pages were revealed. Gently caressing all, I thrust myself into her. We were finally one. It was a perfect first encounter, maybe too fast for Anna, but addictive for me. The fragrance of our lovemaking was intoxicating. We lay there for a while, holding hands.

"Listen. Do you hear the water?" I said.

"Yes, it's a great night," Anna replied.

"I used to listen to the water with my grandpa, Clarence Burk, on Duncan River," I replied.

"I'm getting cold," Anna said, as we quickly put our clothes back on.

"Let's turn the heater on."

We sat in the car with the radio off, got warm, and held hands with an occasional kiss.

"Are you okay?" I asked.

"I'm fine." She leaned over and hugged me.

On the drive home, we said little. We were happy.

Anna and I dated my entire senior year and visited My Place often. Eventually, Anna got a prescription for birth-control pills from her family doctor. I never asked her how she managed to do this, but I suspect her dad never knew. The Federal Drug Administration approved the birth-control pill in June 1960, and by 1964, we assumed it was safe. It allowed us to enjoy each other without fear of pregnancy, and of course, for many sixties kids, it ignited a sexual revolution.

During football season, I had practice every afternoon. We didn't take advantage of Anna's empty house. But once football season was over, since I did not play varsity basketball, we had a new venue for our sexual escapades.

"How's this afternoon look for me stopping by your house?" I asked Anna on Wednesday at my locker.

"Today would be good," Anna said. She grinned and did a quick sassy turnaround toward her next class. I watched her walk down the hallway with braided pigtails and a cute green skirt and white sweater. *Wow. Am I in love?*

After school, I drove my Rambler into her driveway, and she opened the garage door. My Rambler would be off duty today. As soon as I walked through the kitchen door, we began kissing. We took off each other's clothes as we made our way slowly toward her bedroom. Our bodies were hot almost immediately. The risks were high in doing this in Anna's own house—and in her own bed. It made things even more exciting. But what if her dad came home unexpectedly?

By the time I got to her bedroom door, I was naked. Anna only had her panties on. We ended our erotic time as a twisted pile of naked youthfulness.

"You're a devil," I said. Anna flipped her red-hot hair, glanced at me with her wicked green eyes, and rolled over me on her way to getting up as if to say, "Yes, I am."

Afterward, I put on my underwear and T-shirt. Anna put on some gym shorts but left her top bare. She knew I couldn't resist watching her absolutely beautiful breasts as she wandered around the house.

"Do you want some iced tea?" she said as she opened the refrigerator door and pulled out a pitcher of iced tea. I wasn't watching the pitcher since Anna still had no top on.

"Sure." I sat down at the kitchen table and watched her every move. I was exhausted and needed some recovery time. I was still huffing and puffing while Anna was only lightly breathing. She was torturing me, and it was working. I loved it.

As we drank iced tea and ate snacks at the kitchen table, I asked, "Anna, do you think we're in love?"

"I think we are. It's fun, isn't it?"

"But how do we know this is love?" I replied as I poured myself more iced tea.

"Well, I think about you every day. Can't wait to see you," she responded, holding her glass with both hands. Her breasts were pushed up between her arms, and my glass almost slipped out of my hand.

"Yes, I do the same—I mean, I daydream about you in class too," I said as I tried to collect my thoughts and not be a one-act comedy. "I think Ms. Zeiger noticed my lack of attention." I tried to regain my composure. "My parents say there is puppy love and real love, but I don't know the difference, do you?"

Anna turned her penetrating green eyes toward me. "I don't know the difference either, but I think we have the real thing."

"Yeah, I think you're right," I replied.

We got up from the kitchen table and went into the living room. We turned on the television to look for a good show. I fumbled with the TV remote. It was getting late, and I wondered if Anna would hold me to my promise of more lovemaking. I worried her dad would come home. Besides, I needed time to recharge.

"Anna, when's your dad coming home?" I asked.

"He's in Marion at a meeting and won't be home until seven or eight o'clock tonight," she said with a grin. I scooted next to her on the sofa. We began kissing and slid onto the floor between the coffee table and the sofa. I pushed the coffee table slightly out of the way, and Anna put one leg upon the sofa and the other leg leaned against the coffee table. We worked together to create a love making frenzy, and the room showed it. Magazines, empty ashtrays, and books all came crashing to the floor.

Afterward, I lay back with my head under the coffee table. We didn't talk, but I was hoping we were finished for the day. After a couple minutes, we began to survey the damage and had to laugh at the destruction. But our joy didn't last.

Anna glanced at the clock. "David, it's 6:10. We've got to straighten up. Hurry!"

We both jumped up and quickly put everything, including us, back the way it should be.

"Anna, the rug in the living room has a little mess on it. I'll get a kitchen towel and get it up," I said.

By 6:30, Anna was opening the garage door—and I was backing out of the drive. I was very good at backing the Rambler into and out of tight places.

The next day at school, I saw Anna at the break between the second and third periods and asked, "Everything okay?"

"It worked out fine. Dad got home at seven," she said with her Ann-Margret smile.

We never got caught at her house, but I'm sure the neighbors were aware of my visits. Anna and I repeated our lovemaking rendezvous in her house and in my Rambler whenever the opportunities arose.

C. J. saw me drive into Anna's garage once, so he knew what was going on, but to his credit, I don't think he told anyone. My Place and the Rambler were always our first choice, but especially in bad weather, Anna's house was the scene of some wild sexual encounters.

We decided by November 1964 that we were in love—and those days would last forever. I honored Anna. She was a beautiful young woman of merit. I was convinced it was the real thing. Anna was gentle, but she possessed a youthful wickedness that pulled me into her like Earth's gravity pulls an apple off a tree. It was futile to resist.

Like many teenagers, I was unsure how Anna fit into my future plans, even if it was true love. I was a seventeen-year-old high school senior, and she was sixteen. Understandably, neither of us had yet to find our way in life, and based on my past experience, college tended to separate high schoolers.

We were at the apex of youth—a very special moment in our lives—but we could not recognize it then. We had no experience to tell us whether what we had was true love or not. And if we were in love at such a young age, what should we do—get married, date, break up, or what? Later in life, I realized that I should have left the communication lines open, but I didn't.

I could not go back then or now. My barge of life was moving downriver and gaining momentum. It could not stop.

The state playoffs would begin in a week, and we were in them. It was our last chance to win it all.

CHAPTER 12

Play by the Rules

It was time to win it all. Our first playoff game was against a familiar foe, the Clinton County Cougars. Our team still remembered the degrading "Humphrey Dumpty" cheer, although we won that playoff game 29–17. This year's playoff game would be played on our field. We won our last regular season football game on November 6, 1964, and we ended the regular season with seven wins and two losses. Both our losses were to Class AA schools: Ballard High School in the Bluegrass Bowl and Bracket County in a regular season game. But we were 7–0 against Class A schools, and we made the state playoffs for the second year in a row.

According to an article published in the Hopewell newspaper before the game:

Two of the eight Class A football teams will be battling it out in the state playoffs—the Hopewell Thoroughbreds and the Clinton County Cougars. The winner of this Third Regional will play the winner of the Fourth Regional. The Thoroughbreds have allowed only two touchdowns in the last four games and only three other penetrations by opponents past the fifty-yard line. That points to defensive power, which has kept Hopewell rolling through the season. Clinton County has speed and two top running backs. One thing about Hopewell is they have had a long season—longer than the Cougars. The Thoroughbreds opened in the Bluegrass Bowl and were soundly beaten by a bigger high school. The Thoroughbreds are a bit weary, as Coach Humphrey has admitted.

The newspaper concluded one article by saying that Bob Hardy was expected to arrive in an ambulance from a Baxter hospital to attend the game, but a change in his treatment schedule would prevent him from attending the game. Although the team and coaches didn't talk about it, we were looking for Bob on the sideline during pregame warm-up, only to learn he would not attend. This shadow hovered over us—we knew what had happened to Bob could happen to us.

The day before the game, our high school closed at noon. We had a pep rally in the auditorium. The mayor, our principal, the chairman of the Hopewell Chamber of Commerce, and Coach Humphrey gave brief salutations of encouragement and praise. A small portion of the band began by playing the national anthem, and we stood with our hands over our hearts.

The cheerleaders led us through several cheers, and I watched every move Anna made. The only skit included seven classmates dressed up as Clinton County goofballs who stumbled through offensive football plays. The principal ended the rally by saying, "Let's be good citizens at the game. Have fun!"

We played the game in the afternoon on Saturday, November 14. The temperature was thirty-six degrees. We traded summer sweat for watching our breath create a fog in front of our faces. The Hopewell and Clinton County Parents and Teacher's Clubs hosted a hospitality wagon for the fans. Hot chocolate and coffee were in high demand. The eighty-piece Hopewell Band played before the game and included our drill team, and the seventy-piece Clinton County Band played at halftime. Our band had won numerous awards, including representing Kentucky in the annual Cherry Blossom Festival in Washington, DC. Four college scouts attended the game to evaluate prospects.

We won the toss and elected to kick off to the Cougars. We stopped their sidesaddle T offense on our forty-five-yard line and took over on offense. Our backfield arsenal consisted of Donnie Dorin, Kevin Castillo, a speedy senior flanker named Calvin O'Conner, and a very good blocking fullback named Keith Youngdall. These skilled players were the strength of our team.

On our first offensive possession on second down and five yards to go, Kevin threw a long touchdown pass to Calvin. We led 7–0, and the local crowd of twenty-five hundred people screamed their lungs out. We slugged it out in the first half and led 14–6.

Coach gave his halftime pep talk in our locker room. "Men, we are playing well. We've been here before. No mistakes. No turnovers. They are a balanced team. There is no single weakness I can see. Just keep doing what you are doing."

We received the kickoff to begin the second half and had to punt. Kevin was also our punter, and he boomed a very high kick. Several of our players got downfield quickly and waited for the punt returner to catch the ball. The ball hit his chest and promptly bounced off, and we recovered. We had the ball on their nineteen-yard line.

On first and ten, we ran Donnie up the middle for a short gain. For our second play, Coach sent in a play 236Y around the right end. He sent me in to block as a left end.

As I went in, Coach said, "Bourbon, cut off the cornerbacks or safety."

We huddled, and Kevin called the play as his cold breath hung in the air. "Okay, 236Y," Kevin barked.

Dorin would take a pitch out from Kevin and run around our offensive right end. Most of us were supposed to block down to the left to clear a path. We broke the huddle in a simultaneous clap and jogged up to the line. My task was to run diagonally from my left end position across the field and try to block anyone ten or more yards down the field. Coach trusted me to block the right person at the right time.

"Hut one, hut two," Kevin called, and off we went.

As the play developed, Youngdall flattened a blitzing linebacker, and our line blocked down. We took out the first line of defense. Donnie was so good that if you gave him a crease, he would run for a touchdown. I screened a cornerback for just a few seconds and then watched Donnie score a touchdown.

I felt a player zooming up behind me about the same time Donnie crossed the goal line. Before I could turn and see my fate—wham! Immediately, I could feel a sharp pain and fell to the ground. I was clipped from behind by a late play and a cheap shot. I lay on the ground in acute pain and never saw who hit me.

C. J. came over to me and said, "Get up, Bourbon. It's not over." He realized this was not like past situations.

I held my knee in acute pain. The game was stopped, and Coach and the trainers came out. They called for a doctor on the stadium speakers, and one came out to me. He tried to move my leg from side to side, but it hurt so badly when I tried to move with him.

"Call an ambulance," the doctor said. "His knee is torn up bad."

I was loaded into the ambulance by stretcher. Mom rode with me. Dad followed in his truck. The pain was incredible. Tears were rolling down my face. I was nauseated from the pain and the thought of missing the remainder of the football season. I had worked for six years to win a state championship, and now I would not be on the field.

The ambulance medic frowned and said, "Son, hold on. We'll be at the emergency room in less than five minutes. I don't want to screw up the doctor's diagnosis by giving you a sedative. Just hold on." He put several ice packs on my knee and wrapped them with an elastic bandage. I flinched as they touched my skin.

Mom put a second pillow behind my head and held my dirty hand. "David, it's okay. It may be a broken bone, you know. We're at the hospital," she said.

"Mom, it's not okay!" I yelled back at her. My dream was coming to an abrupt end.

They opened the ambulance door and shuttled me into the emergency room. They moved me from the stretcher to a bed with wheels. The doctor did a few physical tests and said, "Get him to X-ray now." He gave me a shot in the leg. Within thirty minutes, I was back in the emergency room with X-rays in hand.

The doctor examined the X-rays and said, "David, there are no fractured bones. You have torn your knee ligaments and cartilage. I'm going to put your leg in a brace and give you some pain medicine and these hospital ice packs. Use the ice packs for the first forty-eight hours and then stop. I recommend you go see a surgeon in Baxter as early as possible."

Mom and Dad took me home and tried to cheer me up.

Late that evening, C. J. and other teammates came by my house to check on me. I was in Dad's reclining chair with ice packs on top and under my knee and a big towel wrapped around it. My face was ashen, and my spirit was demoralized.

"Bourbon, we won the game 20–6. We're off to the semifinals," C. J. said.

"Good! Given the pain I'm in, I won't be with you," I replied in a tormented voice. "They didn't even call a penalty on that damned play! No one saw it—they were all watching Donnie score. Even my dad didn't see me get clipped from behind."

"It was a cheap shot. I am really sorry," Kevin said.

"Fellows, thanks so much for coming by, but it's late. We all need to go to bed," my dad said. My teammates left.

Saturday and Sunday were very painful days. I didn't sleep. I didn't think the sedative was strong enough. The surgeon called us from Baxter, and Mom set up an appointment for Monday. After I had endured three days of pain and swelling, Mom drove me to see the surgeon in Baxter. He looked at my X-rays, which we had carried from Hopewell Hospital, asked how the injury happened, and pushed and poked at my leg.

"David, you have an ACL tear. These ligaments are badly torn and probably some others. I may want to do surgery, but for the time being, let's give you some stronger pain medicine and get you in a different type of brace with crutches. I want to see you this Friday. I think you know you won't play any more football this year." As I heard those words, I knew my football career had vanished.

Mom went to the library and found some information on knee injuries and ACL tears. I learned the ACL, or anterior cruciate ligament, provided knee stability, especially with side-to-side and pivoting motions. When the ACL is damaged, the knee may buckle or give way. And surgery in 1964 didn't guarantee the problem would be fixed. Through major strength training, other leg muscles may partially compensate for a damaged ACL. Recovery from ACL surgery takes months and requires physical therapy and strength training.

My teammates were getting ready to play the Tolbert Raiders the next week in the semifinals of the state Class A playoffs. I limped around the high school hallways in pain. My schoolmates offered their condolences. I would kid around with them and smile, but I was depressed. Our dream was coming true. We had worked so hard to get to that point, and now that we were there, they would play, and I would not.

On Wednesday afternoon after school, I asked Anna if she would drive out to Jackson Creek and the Thoroughbred Meadows Farm. It was a special and peaceful place to me, as I had many happy memories of BB gun battles and magnificent horses running in the fields. Anna accepted my invitation.

I picked her up after school, and we went to Jerry's Restaurant to get a bite to eat. We ordered take-out hamburgers, fries, and Cherry Cokes. We were eating and listening to music as we drove, and we said little.

Anna was my pal as I tried to cope with my current struggle. I only wanted to be with her. It was forty-five degrees that November afternoon. The Rambler's heater and radio were on. Anna was wearing my varsity letter jacket. I wore my white V-neck sweater with a varsity H. I wore the sweater all week to show my support for my teammates and the upcoming semifinal playoff game. The sky was vivid blue with a few clouds. The sun was brilliant and low on the horizon. It would be dark by six o'clock. About half the autumn leaves, in their bountiful rainbow colors, remained on the trees, despite the wind's effort to take them. The bluegrass was still slightly green but was readying itself for hibernation.

We drove through the farm's iron entrance gate. The gate was almost always left open for farmhands and tourists. I parked in a pullover spot alongside the main road, which was parallel to Jackson Creek. Many of the roads in the area had blacktop pullover parking spots for tourist vehicles, including buses. Tourists would get out of their vehicles, take pictures, and watch the thoroughbred horses. I knew every inch of that farm.

Anna walked and I hobbled on crutches up to the white fence. We leaned over the wooden rail to gaze at Jackson Creek, the limestone dams, and the horses in the fields. Fields in the area had double fences to keep the tourists away from the horses. Horses had bitten tourists who tried to feed them, and the solution was double fences. We just looked at the picturesque scene and didn't talk. People came from all over the world to see that iconic scene where I grew up.

I watched a small branch fight its fate as it hung on the edge of one of the four small dams on Jackson Creek. Each dam was a masterpiece and had been constructed slightly differently. Each dam had a concrete foundation but was covered by Kentucky limestone. Some were gently terraced, and others abruptly let the water fall down two feet or so. This small branch put up a good fight, but it finally succumbed to the power of the water and fell gracefully over the dam.

"Anna, did you see that small branch fall over the dam?"

"No, but I see it floating down the creek. It will find another dam shortly."

I put my arms around her as the winter sun was falling from the sky. "Life is like that branch—much of its fate is determined by chance. Ultimately, we all face dams and fall over," I said.

Anna smiled at me and looked back at the creek.

"Anna, for a while, I was the master of this space. We had some great BB gun battles on Jackson Creek in the middle of the winter."

"Yes, I've heard those stories from Emmett and you." Anna began to shiver in the cold air. "Everyone knows you were the guys up on the water tower too."

"Can I tell you a story?" The Hopewell water tower oversaw our conversation. "When I was really young, Dad would cover me with the Sunday newspapers, and I would play dead. It became a Sunday family ritual. Then I would burst out of the papers and go after my dad. We would wrestle on the living room floor, and he would let me win. I would sit on top of him and celebrate my victory." I stopped holding Anna and moved back to lean my chin and hands on the top rail of the fence.

"But I can't win with this injury. I can't even be on the field."

As I hung my head, Anna gingerly moved behind me and held me with both arms.

"When I was little, I thought I could be the next Johnny Unitas. Winning the state championship was my dream. Now, I can't help them. It hurts more than I let on."

"David, I know," Anna said. I turned around, and we kissed lightly. We stayed there another fifteen minutes watching nature play its games with twigs and leaves on Jackson Creek. Then we walked back to the Rambler and began our drive back. I thought about the good times I'd had at Jackson Creek and the order of the place. Life was simpler when I was ten years old in these meadows. The creek worked perfectly. It did its job—day in and day out. It was the lifeblood of the farm and the creatures that lived on it. It was my sanctuary too.

"Can we beat Tolbert High School?" Anna asked as we passed the water tower.

"Yes, I hope so." I took Anna home and walked her to the door. After a kiss, I said, "Thanks for going with me. I needed you."

I was tearful on the drive home, and I thought of the unseen scars the ACL injury had caused me. I thought about the anxiety of going to the playoff game and standing helplessly on the sideline. *Where should I stand? Should I even be on the sideline?* I didn't want to do anything to take my classmates' focus off executing every block, tackle, and pass. *Maybe I should sit in the stands.*

On Friday, I returned to the surgeon's office with Mom. The doctor's office was next to a hospital. It was a new building, and the big aquarium in the front lobby created a relaxing atmosphere. The admissions people checked us in, and a nurse escorted us to an exam room.

"David, are you willing to do significant weight and strength training on that knee?" the doctor began after entering the room.

"Yes, sir," I replied.

"Well, let's try this first and see where we are in three months. I'll set up the physical therapy. We'll go slowly at first. Follow the training carefully. You can further damage your knee if you overdo it."

"Why not surgery?" I asked.

"David, Mrs. Bourbon, as we speak, the surgical methods are radically changing for this type of operation. Although many surgeries are successful, many are not. Even with X-rays, you never know exactly what you're going to find in there. Physical therapy and weightlifting may work well enough for you. With surgery, we could make things worse, and you might not have the range of motion you have now."

As I limped out of the doctor's office, I was not to have to face the knife.

Meanwhile, my teammates were preparing for the playoff game with the Tolbert Raiders the next weekend. The newspaper made a big deal of me and another injured starter not playing in the game. Coach Humphrey was quoted in the paper as saying, "Bourbon is a good player. He's one of the best in the state, but we've had some good practices, and we'll be ready." He also talked about the loss of fellow senior Bruce Applegate. "Bruce's neck injury is a pinched nerve, and that takes time to heal. He won't play because we don't want to risk permanent injury. He was one of our best tacklers, so we will miss him. No more playing for him in high school."

Bruce and I rode down on the team bus to Tolbert. I was still in pain a week later. I wore my leg brace, took pain medicine, and used crutches. Bruce wore a neck brace. Sitting on the sideline as wounded warriors was a new experience for us. We did not like it. We would miss the final battles of our football careers.

We did not want to influence our teammates in a negative way, and we stayed at one end of the bench and back from the field as much as we could. Bruce and I talked to each other about the game, but we didn't talk much to our teammates. They needed their space. The battle was on, and we knew it. If we won the game, we would play for the state Class A championship. They had worked for years to get to that point, and we wanted them to win it all.

The Raiders were another central Kentucky Class A team. They also suffered from being too small a high school, but every few years, they were in the state playoffs. They were similar to us in many respects except for their two big tackles and their speedy all-state halfback.

C. J. and Rick would have to protect our side of the defense without me. Joe Wickens, my friend and past basketball foe, would replace me. Joe was as good as I was, but now he had to play both offense and defense. With Bruce and me hurt, our team had even less depth. Too many of our players had to play offense and defense.

The lack of depth normally showed up in the fourth quarter. American football is a game of intense violence in short, dramatic wind sprints. As the game continues, some players lose their quick first step or the strength to battle continuously for minutes at a time. This is especially true for the bigger guys. How long, for example, can you push with all your strength against a moving wall? That's what it's like to block a defensive player or rush the passer.

The Raiders won the toss and elected to receive. The manicured bluegrass field was wet from the rain before the game. They drove down the field and scored, but they had three critical third down plays to get their first downs. We received the kickoff and worked our way down the field to score. Our offensive skill players showed why they were all-conference and Donnie Dorin was all-state. The score was tied at seven at halftime.

Coach was upset at halftime and said, "We had three chances to stop them on third down and didn't! That is the key to the first-half score. Defense, fellows! Defense!"

The locker room was stone quiet.

Coach paused and looked up at the ceiling. The glaring fluorescent lights were too bright and revealed every blemish of people and equipment in the locker room. He slowly lowered his head and yelled, "Someone needs to make a play. Go out and do it!"

The team stood up and ran out onto the field for the second half.

Bruce and I sat in the back of the locker room and watched. From my new vantage point, I gained a different perspective on what we were doing. I saw the youthful but serious faces of my teammates. I saw that the locker room was awash with the remnants of human toil: mud, blood, sweat, water, damp towels, and athletic tape. It all converged to create a musty smell. I saw that a football game is just that: a game created by humans. It's not life or death. I saw Coach Humphrey as the plump family man who was a super motivator. He did not push weightlifting and wasn't the best analyst of the game, but he got the big picture. He was absolutely right—the score should be 7–0. We had three chances to stop them, which is all you get in life.

For the second half, we received the kickoff, but we were stopped on their thirty-eight-yard line. Since it was too far to kick a field goal, we did a short punt, hoping to pin them deep in their territory. Kevin's punt hit the fourteen-yard line and rolled dead at the two-yard line. The short punt worked. Our defense held them, and after a Raiders punt, we took over on offense. The third quarter was almost over.

We marched down the field with a good combination of runs and passes. The field was muddy and chopped up like thick oatmeal. The third quarter ended with us on their twenty-two-yard line.

To start the fourth quarter, Coach Humphrey ran Donnie off tackle for a six-yard gain. On second and four yards to go, Coach called a rollout pass to the right to Joe Wickens, with the option to go deep to Calvin, our speedy flanker. Rick hiked the ball on Kevin's count and rolled out to the right. Joe was covered, so Kevin threw it to Calvin in the end zone. The wet ball glided through the air to land squarely in Calvin's arms—only to slip through. On the next play, they stopped us for a one-yard gain. When it was fourth down and three yards to go, Coach called time-out.

The team huddled on the sideline, and the coaches discussed whether to go for it.

"Let's go for it," Donnie said.

Coach paused, turned to his assistant coach, and said, "Go for it or try a field goal?" We did not have a good field-goal kicker.

"Go for it!"

"Okay, let's run 234X. We had success with that play tonight," Coach said.

My teammates left the sideline huddle and broke directly to the ball to run the play.

Kevin called out the signals and handed the ball off to Donnie. He was met at the line of scrimmage by two Raider players and stopped short of the first down.

Our sideline was silent. Coach hung his head. Our fans shrugged helplessly. The Raiders took the ball over on downs on their fourteen-yard line.

Bruce and I looked at one another with deliberate faces.

"Bruce, we had another chance and blew it," I said.

Bruce kicked a clump of mud. People work their whole lives to win a championship. Our time was now, and it seemed to be slowly slipping away. And we weren't in the fight.

The Raiders marched down the field with time running out. It was late in the afternoon, and the sun was beginning to set. They were on our fifteen-yard line with a fourth down and two yards to go. They called time-out and elected to kick a field goal.

"Watch out for the trick play," Coach warned the defense. "Stay back, linebackers. Don't blitz."

The wiry Raider kicker trotted out on the field and set up his kick. As he called out their signals, Coach called our last time-out. He was trying to ice the kicker. During the time-out, little was said except when our assistant coach yelled, "Don't jump offside!"

The referees blew the whistle, and we lined up for the kick. The ball was hiked and placed down correctly, but the kicker slipped a little as he kicked the football. It sliced to the right of the goal and did not go through the uprights. We jumped in joy! The game was tied 7–7 with twelve seconds to play. We had one more chance.

We took the ball over on our fourteen-yard line. Coach didn't have any time-outs, so he called one play during the previous field-goal time-out. The play was for our ends to cross over the middle, while our flanker went deep. Kevin called the play, and we broke the huddle. The ball was snapped, and two defensive players covered our flanker. Kevin threw the ball to Joe Wickens, and he ran down to the Raiders forty-eight-yard line before time ran out. The game was still a tie.

"Bruce, we're going to overtime," I declared.

Each team walked to its respective sideline and waited. After a long pause and huddle by the referees in the middle of the field, Coach went over to talk to them. The Raiders coach also joined the group.

"Coach, one of our referees is calling the Kentucky High School Athletic Association. To protect the players' health, we think if a playoff game ends in a tie, we follow the Alabama System rules," the referee stated.

Both coaches were upset, but I think they knew the rules. Finally the referee who went to the locker room to make the telephone call came back and said, "The game is over. Whoever has the most points based on the Alabama System wins the game."

As we huddled, Coach explained on the sideline what the Alabama System rules were as he remembered them. As we listened to the rules, we were dumbfounded. The teams and fans waited as the statisticians compiled the final game statistics. Everyone sat around in amazement since most of us were finding out about this Alabama System for the first time. We kicked the ground and slapped our hip pads as we waited. No one talked; we just stared helplessly at one another or into the stands.

After ten minutes, the announcer came on the stadium speaker system. "Ladies and Gentlemen, in Kentucky state playoff games, we follow the Alabama System. We do not play an overtime quarter. The primary objective is to protect our players from injury. In the Alabama System, a tie ballgame is settled based on three game statistics. They are as follows: one point for the most first downs, one point for the most offensive yardage, and one point for the most offensive penetrations inside the opponent's twenty-yard line. Based on the game statistics and this system, the Tolbert Raiders have two points, and the Hopewell Thoroughbreds have one point, so the Raiders win. The Raiders advance to the state Class A finals next weekend. Please leave the ballpark in an orderly fashion. We have extra police on duty, and they will arrest you if you cause trouble. Thank you for your cooperation, and have a safe trip home."

We stood in stunned silence as the Raiders yelled and celebrated.

"How can this be?" yelled one of my teammates.

Coach was visibly upset, but he seemed to be most worried about someone throwing something or starting a fight. He hurried us into our locker room and locked the door. We walked slowly, thinking it had to be a mistake.

Our fans let out agonized moans, and some began yelling insults at the referees. We worked so hard to get here, and a set of arbitrary rules determined who advanced—what a disappointment. Many of us were mad or crying. Some smashed their helmets on the floor. Others kicked the locker room benches. Bruce and I found a corner to watch a dream unravel.

"Men, sit down," Coach said as C. J. threw his shoe into the shower. "Please! Please, sit down," our coach yelled.

Many of us refused to sit down.

"I knew the rules. In a regular season game, we would just record a tie and move on. But in playoff games, they adopted the Alabama System to protect you. When players get hurt in overtime periods, many people—including parents and lawyers—get upset. We had a great season, and as far as I am concerned, you are champions. Get dressed. I'm going to keep the door locked until everyone is dressed. Then we walk out of here together as men who played by the rules. I recommend you get on the bus and don't talk to anyone," Coach said.

"Screw the rules, Coach," Rich yelled.

My teammates took off their uniforms for the last time and hopped in the shower. The leftovers of battle—blood, sweat, mud, grass, and broken hearts—slowly worked their way down the drain.

Bruce and I stood next to the door, and we could hear shouts from our upset fans. It wasn't a happy scene inside or outside.

Once the players were dressed, we left the locker room as a team. Our parents, cheerleaders, and band members formed a long line, shouting words of encouragement. We walked through the line of fans like honored gladiators.

"You never gave up!"

"Screw the rules! You are our state champions!"

"We are so proud of you!"

We were silent as we walked to the buses. Their kind words didn't negate the pain, although we could see the anguish on their faces. They were hurting because their sons were hurting.

On the bus, some of my teammates had more to say. "Those sons of bitches! How can they do this? It's not right," someone shouted.

Darkness cloaked our misery. Very little was said on the long ride back home. I said nothing. I thought about the legitimacy of the Alabama System. I thought about our chances to win the game and the missed opportunities. By the time the yellow school bus pulled up to our field, I had concluded it was all very unfair. We would never win the state Class A championship.

Mom and Dad were there to pick me up. They didn't want me to drive or go with other kids. I piled into the Rambler. My Rambler was witness to many ups and downs in my life, including this one.

"Dad, can you believe this? We were so close. So close."

"Yes. I'm not happy, but I've been a high school football referee, and I knew about the Alabama System. I didn't know they applied it to playoff games though."

I went straight to my basement room and shut the door. I tried to make sense of my day and eventually fell asleep. The solitude of sleep is a way to escape the realities of the day. The whole week, I had eaten little. In the morning, I ate a dozen donuts Mom had bought at the Foodtown store for eighteen cents. Mom hugged me and said nothing; she knew I was in pain.

The Hopewell newspaper and the *Goings-On* newsletter wrote many follow-up comments on the game. A few examples are as follows:

> I was sick for four days after the Tolbert Raiders playoff game. All you can do is hold your head up high and act like the true southern gentleman you are. You don't have a thing to be ashamed of because you worked hard and achieved a lot. The City of Hopewell is forever proud of you and grateful for what you have done for our small town.
>
> —Mayor Stanley Tubbs

> These twenty-two senior boys built great Hopewell football teams over the last four years. We raised our status in the state for our town, community, and high school. We won like champions and lost like champions. I will be forever grateful for the fun and experiences we shared over the last few years.
>
> —Coach Humphrey

> I was very proud of our football team, fans, cheerleaders, and band during the Tolbert Raiders game and afterward. I was disappointed that the boys didn't win, but they played a good and clean game. We'll have fond memories of your games and all the things going on around your efforts. Congratulations on a fine season. We'll miss you.
>
> —Hopewell High School Teacher

The Thanksgiving holidays were a difficult time for everyone in Hopewell. The next week, the Tolbert Raiders easily won the Class A state football championship 27–7.

CHAPTER 13

Our Town

Hopewell was alive with idyllic Christmas decorations and a cheerful approach to life. Our family was happy. Katie would be six years old in January 1965. She was beginning to understand the world around her. We began to act somewhat like brother and sister, although the age difference was eleven years. Katie had mastered kindergarten and would begin the first grade soon, and I was planning to graduate in June. We decorated the house with Christmas lights and had time to attend the First Christian Church.

The sting of not fulfilling our dream of winning the state Class A football championship was still with all the people of Hopewell, but we were healing from the defeat of our dream. My damaged knee and leg had responded well to weight training. Dad and I had fixed a pulley system on his basement workbench where I worked out with both legs. My legs had always been the strongest part of my body, and now they were super strong. I watched a new television show named *Hullabaloo* to pass time and heal from my mental and physical injuries.

And, of course, there was Anna. In a section titled "Through the Porthole," *Goings-On* made references to what they guessed we were doing my senior year. Typical school newspaper one-liners went like this:

- *Anna, David was with Ann-Margret last night? Where were you?*

- *David B. resolves that he will stop talking to Anna at least thirty seconds before the bell.*
- *Anna, what's so interesting on Jacobs Mill Road?*
- *We heard Bourbon rents out My Place and the Rambler to Anna free.*

In the past, classmate gossip about the Rambler and My Place exceeded what actually was happening. I had lost one year of dating with the silver teeth. My lovemaking began with Sally, often stumbling, but learning along the way. But with Anna, I was fulfilling my dreams, and the Rambler was doing a superb job. Besides, we were in love.

Anna and I spent Christmas at both houses and enjoyed home-cooked meals, family, and relatives. My mom cooked apple pies and corn bread from scratch just like her mother. Heaven was a slice of homemade apple pie with a scoop of vanilla ice cream on top or corn bread with a dash of real butter. Other dishes I liked included baked-oyster casserole and steamed cauliflower or broccoli. Dad always cooked a big country ham or turkey. Natural-grown food was the norm in Hopewell then. Much of our food came right from local farms and gardens.

In January, Mom said, "David, there's a letter here for you. I think it's important. It could be your college test scores."

My anxiety level was high because I knew I was good in math, but I had blown off language courses. Somehow I got it into my head that all that mattered was math and science. Mentors, including my parents, tried to tell me differently, but I didn't listen.

The immaculate white envelope was on the kitchen table. I noticed the return address, which confirmed it was not junk mail. I decided to pour myself a glass of cold milk. The envelope seemed to stare at me; it was the keystone to my future. I finally sat down at the table, put my empty glass on the table, took a deep breath, and picked up the envelope. I used my index finger to carefully open the letter. Such private and stressful events were happening thousands of times across America.

Sure enough, it was my standardized national test scores, my gateway to the next stage of my life: college. Vietnam, of course, could interrupt my plans. I looked at the raw scores at first and didn't understand them, but finally I found something I did understand—my national test score percentile: math 96 percent, verbal 74 percent, and overall 87 percent. I stared at the results, immune to all else.

Mom was preparing dinner, giving me privacy. Her head was down as she focused on cooking tasks. Mom didn't ask me how I did, but she understood the stress of opening that envelope.

"Mom, I did okay," I said. I repeated the national percentile scores to her.

"David, that is wonderful! Your math percentile is super—a tribute to the hard work you and Ms. Zeiger did."

"I read too slowly. I never finished the verbal exercises and questions. They hurt me, Mom. Hopefully this will get me in college." I got up from the table and headed to my room. I was disappointed in my verbal scores, but I had no one to blame but myself.

Applying to college was an easy decision for me. My decision hinged on going to the best school I could within Kentucky since tuition and expenses were low. I only applied to the University of Kentucky and was accepted. I was going to major in architecture or engineering. I thought these majors would fit my profile and skills—and help America win the space race.

My high school days would end soon, and that meant the yearbook had to be finished. Two of our most talented classmates, Carol Barron and Jake Payne, were the editors of the 1965 yearbook. They made every effort to capture the memories of our senior year. In the yearbook, they wrote:

As the years go by and memories grow fainter, we hope this annual will help you recall the events of this wonderful year; a year we will not forget—for there will never be another like it.

Many things had converged at the right time and place to create a set of transcendent life experiences in our small town. I worked hard on the yearbook because I wanted to capture the moments that could not be repeated.

Carol Barron had a study period the same time I did, and we worked in the back room of the library on yearbook pictures, text, and layout. Carol and I had fun, but I kept her from accomplishing much. Since I knew something about football, Carol and Jake asked me to do a tentative layout of the varsity football pages. They wanted to know how the seniors and Coach Humphrey should be presented. Three pages were allocated to this task. The librarian gave me a key to the school and library so I could work on it on Sunday afternoon, March 7.

I told Mom I could not go to church because I needed to work on the yearbook. The rest of my family went off to church for the eight o'clock service. I arrived at Hopewell High School around 8:30 and began to work on the yearbook. I wanted to truly highlight each senior player. Since we had twenty-two of them, it wasn't easy to fit them in three pages. I put Coach Humphrey in a coaching drill stance in the center of the page.

I also wanted to try to capture the action of the game that we loved so much. To do this, I had to shrink the twenty-two player pictures so I could insert two action shots—one with a pass in the air and the other of us making a tackle. I tried to use action pictures with as many players as I could. The results were two action pictures that included ten players. My spatial skills were being put to good use.

I had a draft layout completed by 11:30. There were two more pictures I would have liked to include, but everyone wanted space. People, clubs, and teams were competing for space—teachers and administrators, class pictures of four grades, the prom, cheerleaders, the art club, the band and drill teams, Future Homemakers of America, the Latin, French, and Spanish clubs, and the debate team. The challenge for Carol and Jake was to make everything fit together in a cohesive manner with a limited number of pages.

I kept looking at Anna's cheerleading picture, trying to decipher every freckle and strand of auburn hair.

At 11:45, I used the library phone to call Anna.

"Anna, hi! What are you doing?"

"Nothing. Dad's at church, but I didn't go," Anna replied.

"I'm working on the yearbook in the school library. You can see all the pictures we won't be able to use. Some are really cool. Why don't you come over here?"

"I'm on my way."

Within fifteen minutes, Anna was knocking on the high school's front door. I opened it, and we kissed. Holding hands, we walked down the long, dark hallway to the back room of the library. Anna wore a pair of tight blue shorts and a white T-shirt carefully tucked in. Everything had to match that blazing auburn hair! And it worked. Even at sixteen, Anna was used to guys chasing her. She knew no other life.

"Look at these pictures." I handed her a set.

"Wow. These are great. I've got a year before we do a yearbook, but it's interesting to see." Anna brushed back that hair. For about thirty minutes, we sat at a worktable and discussed each picture. We were having fun, but I kept looking at her breasts. When Anna got up and walked toward another set of pictures, I knew it was futile to resist. My heart and other things were resonating in that stark library workroom.

Anna took a group of pictures and jumped up on the waist-high counter that surrounded the library workroom. I went over to her, inserted myself between her legs, and we began to hug and kiss. At that moment, I knew we were in trouble. Anna probably had been planning what would happen since she left her house.

I took her blouse and bra off and threw them on the linoleum floor. Anna was sitting straight up with her arms arched back. She knew I could not resist. In the daylight of the library yearbook room, I could see her breasts slowly flush red. I cradled them in my two hands and kissed them senseless.

We always began this way, and it really turned her on. Anna would twist away, wanting me to forcefully pull her back into my grasp. She was so beautiful with her hourglass figure, blue shorts, radiant red hair, and miraculous breasts. And, of course, I was trying to bust out of my pants. I pulled her blue shorts off and saw how her purple panties apologetically guarded her tunnel of love. I took my fingers and slowly pulled her panties down and off her legs. Now she was naked on the counter. Oh! What a perfect sight! We both were unbearably excited now as we began panting. We were about to make love, and we were doing it in a forbidden place—the high school library. It never crossed our mind that a janitor or the librarian might interrupt our escapade.

I took off my pants, grabbed her back and pressed hard, and lifted her onto me. We didn't move much. I carried her to the worktable in the center of the room, and gently laid her down on it. My strong legs finally came in handy, including my reconditioned knee. Yearbook pictures and papers scattered on the floor, but we completed our selfish act on the workroom table. We shouted incoherently for a moment, and then all was silent and still.

We are happy. I rolled off the inhospitable table and leaned against the counter. Anna smiles at me and rests on the table. Our life in pictures surrounded us.

Eventually Anna said, "David, we christened the library!"

"Yes, and we have a mess. Wet papers and scattered pictures." At that point, the realization hit us that we better get moving to correct the disarray of the room. We got dressed and began to clean up. A couple of pictures and a few papers were wet and smelled like lovemaking. We stacked the pictures the way I thought they were supposed to be and wiped down everything.

"This is much better than going to church," I said as we walked down the hallway holding hands.

Anna giggled but said nothing. Our hallways were full of pictures from the past, including one of the graduating class of 1920. As I passed that picture, I thought that I was not the first to have sex in the high school, and I doubted I'd be the last. We both drove home.

The next day during my study period, I went to the library workroom to evaluate things. If only rooms could talk.

Carol said, "David, does it smell funny in here?"

"No. It's a little stuffy after the weekend. I think they turn off the fans," I replied with a smile.

In April, we began to rehearse for the senior class play, *Our Town* by Thornton Wilder. The play would be on Friday evening at eight o'clock on May 14, 1965. Several teachers with experience in the English, debate, and art clubs championed the play, which had won a Pulitzer Prize and had been a hit on Broadway. The play required a large cast; in fact, forty-five of our 110 seniors were in the play.

Russell Jordan played the lead part as the stage manager. Russell was selected as the best high school actor at Kentucky's state drama festival. Several other classmates accompanied Russell to the festival and were also learning acting. Overall, the play was in capable hands, but it became obvious in the first rehearsal that acting was definitely not a strength of mine. Somehow I got the part of Mr. Webb, another key character in the play. My only strength was that I could memorize my lines, hit my cues, and speak loudly. I didn't see a future in football or acting. In fact, the only places I seemed to excel were in the classroom and my Rambler.

Fortunately for me, Mr. Webb doesn't enter the play until the end of act 1. When the curtain went up, I looked at my playbook and my lines, but I froze. I drank a gallon of water and tried to relax. I was ready to jump out of my skin. I needed to go to the bathroom, but I couldn't. I pranced around backstage in total agony, awaiting my trip to the guillotine—the stage. What was I supposed to do if I forgot my lines in front of the audience? Football was much easier than this—much easier.

When my time came, I walked through a trellis, found my stage position, and began my lines.

"Well, I don't have to tell you that we're run here by a board of selectmen. All males vote at the age of twenty-one. Women vote indirect. We're lower middle-class: sprinklin' of professional men—10 percent illiterate laborers. Politically, we're 6 percent Republicans; 80 percent democrats; 4 percent Socialists; rest, indifferent. Religiously, we're 85 percent Protestants; 12 percent Catholics; rest, indifferent."

Stage Manager: "Have you any comments, Mr. Webb?"

And with this shaky introduction and my throat in my stomach, I moved methodically through my lines in front of more than three hundred people. At least my first lines had many numbers—I was good at numbers. I made it through my seventy-one lines in act 1 with no major errors, but I was still so nervous I didn't really listen to any of my fellow actors. Whenever they finished their lines, I began mine with a tractor-beam focus. I knew my family—and Anna and her dad—were in the audience, but I couldn't see much because of the glaring stage lights.

In act 2, I had about sixty-seven lines, and the play seemed infinitely longer than a football game. I was mentally and physically exhausted after act 1, yet the play wasn't over. Backstage, I studied my twelve lines in act 3.

I ended my acting career with my final lines, "Where's my girl? Where's my birthday girl?" I walked off the stage and wanted to collapse. I had used 100 percent of my adrenaline to complete my one and only acting job. The execution of the play and the curtain call procedure impressed me. It reminded me that precision is required in all things: fishing, science, math, football, English, and acting. I could relax. We walked out onto the stage to a standing ovation.

After the play ended, my family and Anna's were waiting in the gym. Janitors and volunteers began to fold the chairs for storage.

"David, good job," my dad said.

I grabbed Anna's hand.

"Yes, I don't think you missed any lines," Anna said.

"No. I got through it, but that is my last acting job," I replied. "It was way too stressful."

To conclude our senior year, the next big event was the prom.

Our "Ladies and Knights of Camelot" prom was a gala Friday night affair in the high school gymnasium on May 21. It began at eight and ended at eleven. Clusters of balloons hung from the ceiling, and steel chairs and card tables provided places to sit and talk. Most girls wore white prom dresses, and the guys wore white dinner jackets with black pants. Anna wore a tiered white dress with white high-heel shoes and the wrist corsage I gave her. The dress provided the background for her stunning auburn hair. Anna was beautiful, and she knew it.

The five-piece orchestra played low-key, slow-dancing music in a planned effort to tone things down. One benefit of the gentle music is that we could talk to each other. We danced to songs like "Walk on By" by Dionne Warwick and "Love Me Tender" by Elvis Presley. A week before, we had performed *Our Town* on that same stage. My acting and basketball career ended in that little gym in the middle of nowhere. My football career was over. We were close to the end of our high school days.

"Let's dance." I reached for Anna's hand as the band began to play "All I Have to Do is Dream" by the Everly Brothers.

"Do you like Vicki's dress?" Anna asked as we danced.

"I haven't looked at it. Where is she?"

Anna frowned; we had talked to Vicki and C. J. twice already.

"Vicki's mom made that dress from a picture in *Glamour* magazine," Anna said in an annoyed tone.

"Ah yes, I see her now. That dress would look better on you," I replied.

As the song ended, Anna said, "I'm going over to talk with the girls for a while."

"Okay, I'll be at our table." Soon, Eddie, C. J., Warren, and I were sitting at our table, talking and using our skills to clandestinely pour whisky into our paper cups under the table. Donnie and Rick walked up and said, "You guys got anything to drink? We're out."

The girls huddled at one table to talk about dresses, hairdos, makeup, and who knows what else. My buddies were focused on the after-prom party, sex, drinking, and football.

"Sandra is upset because the corsage I gave her is red, and her dress is lavender," Rick said. "I don't see that it matters."

"You dumb-ass potato head," C. J. replied. "The girl has been preparing for the prom for a month. Did you ask her what color her dress was?"

"No." Rick hoisted his spiked drink to his mouth. "I don't even like her dress."

"Well, don't tell her that, you idiot," Eddie proclaimed.

A few minutes later, Vicki and Anna came over to our table.

Anna said, "You guys, go find your dates. This is a prom, not a drinking party."

The prom was fun, but the after party was special. Jill Lester, our classmate who was voted best looking, lived on a small farm about ten miles away on winding country roads.

During the drive, Anna and I listened to Bob Dylan's "The Times They Are a-Changin.'" We arrived at Jill's house—a big two-story white farmhouse with wide porches on three sides. Jill's brave parents allowed us to have our after-prom party at their house. Speakers were set up on the porch tied to a stereo that played thirty-three LPs and forty-five RPM vinyl records.

Parents brought food and snacks throughout the day so we would have plenty to eat late that Friday evening. Parents acted as chaperons until late in the evening. Everyone behaved, and the parents surely knew our drinks were spiked with liquor. Beer was allowed; even the parents were drinking beer. By one o'clock, all chaperons had left, some taking their sons and daughters home with them. Jill's parents were now our chaperons, but I only saw them once in the kitchen.

After the prom, most of us changed clothes in the gym, our cars, or at home before heading to Jill's house. I parked my legendary Rambler in the yard about one hundred feet from the front porch. Anna and I smooched in the car and drank bourbon mixed with Coca-Cola in paper cups. Drug use had not yet invaded Hopewell High School.

"Bourbon, are you going to get out of that moving bed," Eddie Russell shouted as others on the porch laughed.

"Yes, eventually!" I yelled back. Reluctantly, Anna and I left the car and joined the party. Everyone danced to the tunes of the day in the grass and on the porch, some kissing, holding hands, and being silly.

By two, most of the class had left, but a group of us sat on the wraparound porch, drinking and talking. Anna sat in a sturdy white rocking chair, and I sat on a short white stool. C. J. and Vicki Newman were to the right of us in a white two-seat swing hung from the ceiling with rusty chains. We were looking out at the yard. Rick Shaffer and his girlfriend, Sandra Pelfrey, were to our left sitting on a hardwood bench. Carol Barron had gone to the prom with Eddie Russell, and they leaned against the wall near a corner of the house. Donnie Dorin and his date, Estill Fisher, had taken two chairs from the kitchen and faced Anna and me about eight feet away. Warren Stow, Jill Lester, and Kevin Castillo were leaning against the porch railing on the very outside corner of the porch about twenty feet away. Their dates had gone home.

Jill's parents, who had been hiding that evening, came out on the porch and said, "You kids ought to be going home. It's time to shut down. If you can't drive, you can sleep on our sofas for a while."

Everyone thanked them for hosting us, and we promised we'd come back the next day to clean up.

The cool air had begun to surround us, and I began to feel an emptiness inside. The thirteen of us didn't want the night to end. We were hanging on to the old life. I thought it might be one of the last times we'd be together, and I'm sure others had similar feelings.

"We had a great senior year," Rick said as he raised his cup in an informal toast.

We all raised our drinks.

"Yes, we are a tight group," Eddie declared.

"Why do you think we get along so well?" Rick asked.

"I think it's the small town. We all know life on Main Street," Carol responded.

"Who hasn't been to Mildred's Drug Store or Teen Circle?" Jill laughed.

"What fun it is to drive the Circuit and hit Jerry's!" Sandra said as she hugged Rick.

"Yes, we'll never get those good times back," Carol remarked.

"I'll always remember that Sadie Hawkins dance," Vicki said.

"I think the football games tied us together, too." Donnie raised his beer.

"Yes, we've been through some great times together. I can't believe we were cheated out of a state championship," Warren said.

"Wow, what a crazy way to end a playoff game," Rick, our all-conference linebacker and center, said.

"Yeah. It looks like we either go to college or Vietnam," C. J. said. He squeezed Vicki's hand.

Kevin, our all-conference quarterback, had been leaning against the porch railing and listening. He took one step toward the group and said, "What do you think, David?"

"It's coming to an end, isn't it? These could be our best years," I said. I took a drink of bourbon and Coke, and Anna leaned over and hugged me.

Everyone nodded in agreement as I looked up at the last remnants of the class of 1965.

CHAPTER 14

Stone Fences

"Bourbon, let's have one shot before we go," C. J. said as we stood by the Rambler.

"Okay, as long as you can drive," I replied. I thought it was fitting that C. J. and I were the last to leave. I found my bottle of bourbon in the backseat of the Rambler. Anna, Vicki, C. J., and I stood by the Rambler, and I poured one last drink.

"Best of luck," I said.

C. J. and I raised our paper cups and downed our drinks. Anna and Vicki raised their cups but only took reluctant sips. We thanked Jill, who was standing on her parents' porch, and got into our cars.

"C. J., drive slowly," I said and closed my car door.

"Yes, and put on your lap belts," Anna shouted.

C. J. and Vicki left in his 1960 Chevrolet Impala, and Anna and I followed.

"David, should you guys be driving?" Anna asked as I took a right turn out of Lester's driveway.

"Yep. I'm good. I ate at midnight," I replied.

As I followed C. J.'s car at about twenty-five mph, it became obvious that C. J. was going faster.

About two miles from Jill's house, C. J. rounded a sharp curve going about forty-five. Twenty would have been a safe speed in the dark at that late hour.

C. J. didn't even try to brake or make the turn. His car wheels barely squeaked. He drove as straight as an arrow through a four-foot-high stone fence.

Anna and I heard a huge boom as C. J.'s car lights went out.
"Oh, my God! C. J. had a wreck!" I yelled.

Anna began to cry as I drove toward C. J.'s hissing car. Its back wheels were deep in the dirt. The full moon, covered intermittently by clouds, provided light. I parked the Rambler on the road behind C. J.'s car, opened my door, and rushed over to C. J.'s car.

About half the car had burst through the stone fence and straddled the pile of stones. The limestone fences had been built by Irish and Mexican laborers long ago, and fortunately for C.J. and Vicki, without cement or mortar. They had endured the tests of time, but this one succumbed to C. J.'s assault.

Steam from the radiator was pouring out of the front of the car, and the hood had been torn completely off. The crushed doors were forced toward the backseat. The front two feet of the car was totally annihilated.

"C. J., Vicki, are you all right?" I asked.

There was no response. It was as silent as the devil's pit. I approached the driver's side window and saw C. J.'s chest against the steering wheel. His head was against the smashed front window. His head had not gone through the window, but his forehead had split open, and blood covered his face. I tried to open his door, but it imprisoned him. C. J. was unconscious. Vicki was dazed and moving.

"Anna, take my car and go back to Jill's house. Call the ambulance *now*," I shouted. "Wake up Jill's parents—and get them over here. Hurry!"

I ran to the other side of the car. Vicki was slumped over. Her lap belt was on. Her door partially opened, and I released the lap belt, carefully got under her arms, and dragged her out of the car onto the grassy field. I could smell gasoline and was afraid the car might explode. I dragged her far away from the wreck.

I ran back over to C. J.'s side and thought about how to help him. I tried to open his door, but it would not open. I went to Vicki's side of the car, crawled into the front seat, and sat there for a few seconds, trying to decide if I should move him or not. What if he'd broken his neck?

I decided to get C. J. out of the car. I unbuckled his lap belt, put my hands under his big arms, and dragged him out of the car with intermittent tugs.

C. J. was a heavy guy, but I got him about twenty feet from the car. I rested a few seconds and then moved him farther away from the wreck. I put C. J. down gently in the thick bluegrass. He was unconscious but breathing. I ran to the wrecked car and collected his letter jacket and a pair of cotton pants from in the backseat. As I ran back to C. J. and Vicki, the engine caught fire. I dragged Vicki closer to C. J. The engine fire was small, but I had no way to put it out.

We were about forty feet from the wrecked vehicle when it exploded and burned. I felt a ball of heat move past my body. I ducked my head down and knelt between C. J. and Vicki. Fortunately, the main force of the explosion went upward. The smell of burning oil, gas, and plastic upholstery was sickening. I covered Vicki with the letter jacket and used the cotton pants to gently wipe the matted blood from C. J.'s forehead and face. He had an ugly blue bump on his forehead, a two-inch gash in the middle of it, and a dark-purple bruise underneath one eye socket.

Jill, Anna, and Jill's parents arrived. Jill, Anna, and Mrs. Lester attended to Vicki, while Mr. Lester and I discussed what to do with C. J.

"David, let me see how bad his head is cut. Is any blood coming out of his nose or ears?" Mr. Lester tried to examine C. J.'s head and arms with a flashlight. "I only see one big cut on his forehead." The fire from the explosion weakened and provided us with flickering light. "I don't see any other breaks or cuts."

"Vicki's waking up," Mrs. Lester called from about fifteen feet away. Vicki was too dazed to understand what was going on.

"If you can help her get to our car, take her to the hospital," Mr. Lester replied.

It had been a full fifteen minutes since the wreck, and there was no sign of the ambulance yet. We were out in farm country on a narrow country road at three o'clock in the morning.

Anna, Jill, and Mrs. Lester took Vicki to their car and drove to the emergency room.

Mr. Lester and I were attending to C. J.

The breeze felt stronger and colder as night dominated day. We were trying to decide what else to do to help C. J. when his eyelids began to flutter. He finally opened his eyes.

"C. J. can you hear me?" Mr. Lester asked.

C. J. paused, moved his head to one side, and mumbled, "Yes."

Minutes passed. We began to see the flashing lights of the ambulance making its way down the curvy country road.

"David, I'm going to leave you and flag the ambulance down. I'm sure they see the burning car," Mr. Lester said.

"Okay," I said. I held C. J.'s head with one hand and applied light pressure to his forehead with the cotton pants. "C. J., don't move. The ambulance is here."

C. J. had lost consciousness for about twenty minutes. "Where's Vicki?" he mumbled.

"Mrs. Lester, Jill, and Anna took her to the hospital. She's not hurt badly," I replied, not knowing if this was true or not. "Relax. Help is one minute away." I watched the ambulance and fire truck stop in the road. Three men ran over with a stretcher and a big first aid toolbox. The fire truck used its floodlights to illuminate the area.

"Son, was anyone else in that car?" a fireman asked me.

"Yes, Mr. Lester's wife took the passenger, Vicki Newman, to the emergency room."

Two other men used big commercial fire extinguishers to put out the fire. They used the hoses to wet the area around the wreck.

The three men switched places with me and checked C. J.'s vital signs. "Son, don't move. We are going to move you to the stretcher and get you to the emergency room. Can you breathe?"

C. J. nodded.

They wiped C. J.'s wound and face with water and carefully moved him onto the stretcher.

A fireman put a heavy ointment on his cut and wrapped his head in white antiseptic gauze and tape. They strapped his head and body into the stretcher. The five of us, including Mr. Lester and me, helped carry the stretcher to the ambulance. One of my shoes got stuck in the mud and came off as I was carrying the heavy stretcher.

"David, let's go to my house to clean up. Are you okay?" Mr. Lester said as we watched the ambulance lights and siren sounds diminish.

"Yes, I'm fine, just rattled," I replied.

As we walked back to my Rambler, one of the firemen asked, "Son, what are the names of the two people in the wrecked car? What are your names?" He wrote our names down. He also wrote down our license plate numbers. "We'll call a tow truck in the morning once it's light."

I went to Mr. Lester's house, washed up, and called my mom and dad at 3:45.

"Hello," my dad said in a sleepy, troubled voice.

"Dad, it's me. I'm fine, but C. J. had a wreck leaving the after-prom party," I said.

"Is C. J. hurt? Who was he with?" Dad asked.

"He was with Vicki. They both went to the emergency room. C. J. could be really hurt. I don't know about Vicki. I'm at Mr. Lester's house and will drive to the emergency room now."

"I'll meet you there. And, you are not hurt, right?"

"Right. Dad, can you call Anna's dad, explain what happened, and tell him that she is absolutely okay? Tell him we'll bring her home."

"Yes. I'll do that. Drive carefully."

I hung up the phone. My energy was dwindling. I thanked Mr. Lester for what he had done and drove methodically through the country roads to the hospital.

Mr. Lester followed me in his car so he could pick up Jill. At the emergency room, I saw Jill and Anna talking with Dad.

I parked my Rambler and entered the bright emergency room waiting area. In my bloody, muddy clothes with one shoe missing, I hugged Dad and Anna. They both immediately inspected me to see if I was all right. Mr. Lester hugged his daughter. The five of us sat in the waiting room and discussed what had happened. Vicki's parents and C. J.'s parents were inside the emergency room.

At five o'clock, two doctors came through the big swinging doors of the emergency room and asked us to sit down in the waiting area. Their white jackets were smeared with blood and dirt.

"Vicki is going to be okay. She broke two ribs, and breathing is painful. She probably has a mild concussion," the doctor said as we sat on the edge of our seats and listened. "C. J. is in more trouble. He suffered a severe concussion and possibly some traumatic brain injury. We treated and stitched up the cut on his forehead. X-rays show he did not fracture his skull, but his brain may swell. We might have to take out part of his skull to relieve pressure."

"David, did Vicki and C. J. have their lap belts on?" the doctor asked.

"Sir, I know Vicki did, but I can't quite remember if C. J. did," I replied with a puzzled look. "Yes—yes, I think he did. I remember unhooking it to pull him from the car."

"Well, that's what saved them from more serious injury."

"What happens next?" my dad asked.

"Vicki and C. J. will be in intensive care tonight and tomorrow, at least. Vicki may be able to go home soon. C. J. could be here all week. We need to continue to check for internal injuries. Our job is not done yet."

The doctors stood up and walked back through the big black doors.

We were about to leave when Vicki's parents came out to greet us. "David, I want to hear what happened," Mr. Newman said. "Was C. J. drunk?"

"Mr. Newman, I don't think C. J. was drunk, but he took that curve too fast. He lost control of the car."

Mr. Newman hugged me and said, "Thank you for pulling them out of that car. It caught fire, didn't it?"

"Yes, sir, it did," I said as Anna and Dad smiled.

Dad and I drove Anna home, and her dad greeted her on the porch. Mr. Lester and Jill also drove home.

Vicki was discharged from the hospital the next night with broken ribs, a mild concussion, and a few bruises and cuts. I called the hospital daily, and on Wednesday, they told me they did not have to remove any of C. J.'s skull. He was conscious and doing better, but the areas around his eyes were black and blue, his vision was blurred, and he had a constant and severe headache. The intensive care nurse told me these were symptoms of a moderate to severe concussion. Only his immediate family was allowed to see him.

On Friday, May 28, one week after the accident, someone from the hospital called my house and told me I could visit C. J.

Anna and I arrived during evening visiting hours. When we first walked in C. J.'s room, Anna grabbed his hand and squeezed it. I went over and patted him on the arm. His forehead was covered in a bandage. The areas around his eyes were black and purple.

"How are you feeling, big man?" I asked.

"Better," C. J. replied with a half-smile on his face. "I can't get rid of this damn headache. They have to put me to sleep each night."

"It could have been worse, buddy," I said.

Anna and I sat down on steel chairs.

"I agree," C. J. said. "Thanks for pulling me out of that car, man. You are a hero. I don't remember any of that. Was it a big explosion and fire?"

"Yes, it was big, but not that big. I don't think you had much gasoline in your tank," I replied. "It was scary."

"I was talking to Vicki and didn't realize how fast I was going. When I looked up, I had no chance of making the turn. I figured the hell with it and drove the car straight into the fence. I did have time to tell Vicki to brace herself."

Anna and I smiled; this was classic C. J. thinking. He was always the risk taker in our class. And on the football field, he was invincible. But a historical stone fence, immune to human folly, leveled the playing field.

My parents, Anna, and I visited C. J. every other day. Slowly C. J. got better. In retrospect, an isolated farmhouse on a country road was not the ideal place to have an after-prom party. C. J.'s car was the only one of about sixty cars that had an accident. We should have set up designated drivers or slept at the Lesters' farmhouse, but no one thought about that in 1965. Back then, our parents naively trusted us to do the right thing. And Mr. Lester had told us, at the end of the night, that if we couldn't drive, we were welcome to sleep on his sofas and chairs.

C. J.'s accident was an abrupt change of focus from graduation. It made us reflect on our good health and fortune. The alumni banquet was our next major graduation event. Given the rich history of our high school, I looked forward to this end-of-an-era event.

The banquet was held in the gymnasium where I played basketball and attempted to be Mr. Webb in *Our Town*. The banquet was held on Thursday evening, June 3, 1965, and 125 people attended. Our entire class was invited, but graduation was the next day, so only about half of our class attended.

C. J. was home and did not attend, but Vicki was there. Anna did not attend because she was a junior. Assembly music provided the background as the invocation began the banquet. The president of the Hopewell Alumni Association welcomed the class of 1965.

It was my turn as class president to accept the invitation to join the alumni association. I stood up, went to the podium with my talk on an index card, and said, "On behalf of the graduating class of 1965, I wish to thank everyone who helped in planning this banquet. This banquet is something that seniors look forward to because it ends our high school days. It is an honor to become members of one of the oldest alumni clubs in the state.

"This past year has been an exciting and beneficial year for us. The friendship and events experienced will always be remembered. We have had some good and troubled times. We almost won the state Class A football championship. We witnessed a wonderful young man named Bob Hardy fight a terrible injury. Now we shall seek separate roads in life. In the years ahead, it will be a pleasure to come to this banquet and renew old acquaintances and traditions."

After a long pause, while I moved to the next index card of my speech, I broke from my prepared speech and said, "With graduation tomorrow, many of my classmates did not attend tonight. But thank God we are all healthy. C. J.'s recent accident shows us how fleeting every second is. We should make the most of every day." I choked up. With a big sigh, I continued my prepared remarks. "We, the class of 1965, will participate and support the activities of the Hopewell High School Alumni Association. My classmates and I will see you next year. Thank you so much!"

To my surprise, the audience began clapping, and I received a standing ovation. Several awards were given that evening. I received the Hopewell High School Alumni Cup. A business meeting was held, and we ended by singing "Auld Lang Syne." The proud history of our alumni association had been preserved for another year.

Mom, Dad, Katie, and I drove home that night in the Rambler and had a cheerful family discussion about the glorious evening for our family. My parents were proud, and even six-year-old Katie seemed impressed by the evening's festivities.

At home, I called Anna and described the alumni banquet events. "Anna, after my speech, they gave me a standing ovation. I couldn't believe it."

"Why does that surprise you?" Anna asked.

"I've never seen that before. I didn't know what to do."

"Maybe the audience was proud of you," Anna said.

"Yes, you could be right, but the more I think about it, I think they were proud of the Class of 1965."

"What time will you be at graduation?" I asked.

"Dad and I plan on being there before seven o'clock."

"And are we going out after graduation to My Place?" I sheepishly asked.

"Sure, I want to give you your graduation present. I have a surprise for you," Anna purred.

"I'm looking forward to it. Good night!" I hung up the telephone while Anna giggled in the background.

The graduation ceremony was held in the gymnasium at seven o'clock in the evening. The senior class had 110 students. The gym was packed with classmates and their families, teachers, school administrators, and other civic leaders. In the assembly area, we hugged and gave each other high-fives.

C. J. attended graduation. It was two weeks after the wreck, but he was not yet himself. Mentally, he was still foggy and did not joke around as he used to do. His forehead and left forearm were still bandaged.

Vicki, C. J., and I shared a group hug before we lined up in alphabetical order. I tried to watch C. J. so I could help him out if he got confused. I don't think most classmates understood how off C. J. was.

As the class of 1965 entered the gym to "Pomp and Circumstance," I pondered our future. *How many of my classmates will actually graduate from college? How many will raise families and live in Hopewell? How many will die or be injured in the Vietnam War?* I wanted to slow everything down. It was all going too fast. The minister began the invocation and stopped my reflections.

Our commencement speaker, Mr. Buck Emerson, had graduated from Hopewell High School in the twenties. He was an executive at International Business Machines. "Today, you receive your diploma as recognition of your hard work and academic achievement. Our country needs your capabilities to solve our problems and improve things. Be smart. Be persistent. Protect our freedoms. Help society. Build great companies. And have fun along the way!

"I think I did these things at IBM. Let me tell you our story. I worked for the electric typewriter division. In 1957, we moved to Baxter, Kentucky. There, I helped develop and implement the most advanced typewriter assembly line in the world. Our teamwork, quality control, and advanced manufacturing and warehouse technologies were the best in the world. We produced our millionth typewriter in 1958. The typewriters, carbon paper, and ribbons proudly display the IBM trademark.

"In 1961, we announced a new technological breakthrough that revolutionized the industry—the IBM Selectric typewriter. Its sphere-shaped typing element contained eighty-eight alphabetic, numeric, and punctuation characters. Because the writing element moved and not the paper-carrying unit, it had no movable carriage. Our product design and manufacturing team designed the next-generation typing element and built the most advanced assembly line in the world to produce it. We used less material and space to do the same functions, reduced costs and vibration, and there was no carriage-return jolt. By simply changing the spherical typing element, a typist could change fonts and styles. We recently announced a magnetic tape to store the typed information as another example of innovation. And we changed our name to IBM's Office Product Division to reflect our goal of developing totally integrated office systems.

"How did this happen? The answer is what I mentioned at the beginning of my speech. We worked hard to accomplish our objective. We hired smart, innovative people. We helped society communicate and enhanced worldwide democracy and freedoms through the written word. We built a great company that raised our standard of living and supports our families. We fulfilled the American dream. And we had a lot of fun along the way.

"You will make the transition to the real world of work and find many obstacles and opportunities. Work hard to learn new things. Work hard to support your family. Try to please yourself, your company, and your country. And most of all, work hard to protect and support the American Dream. Thank you—and best wishes."

We gave our commencement speaker a standing ovation.

As I stood up, I thought things seemed to be aligned. The commencement speech was what my family, Hopewell, and America strived for. Had these goals been achieved? No, but Americans were working on them. Mr. Emerson gave a very good speech that added a dose of civility to our graduation. I was young and naïve, yet his speech inspired me to tackle the next era of my life.

We sat down, and the principal came to the podium to introduce the school board. The chairman of the school board and my mom began to call our names and hand out diplomas. The cover for the diploma was black with "Hopewell High School" in orange letters. Since I had worn the school colors in letter jackets and athletic jerseys my entire life, I thought the colors were beautiful. The diplomas were given out in alphabetical order, and Bourbon was early in the list. We lined up on the side of the stage, and when the chairman called my name, I walked up the stage steps toward my mother.

Mrs. Dorothy Bourbon was dressed in a light blue chiffon dress that hung below her knees. Her brown curly hair lay on her shoulders, and her eyes matched her hair. The dress had a scalloped neckline with dark blue linen trim and a somewhat indented waistline. I thought Mom looked slightly sexy, but professional. She was the only woman on the stage.

Mom was beautiful when I was five years old—when we defeated the devil's pit—and she was even more beautiful at my high school graduation. Dad was sitting in the audience with Katie, and I'm sure they were proud of us. When I took those last steps toward Mom, memories raced through my mind. I thought about my first seventeen years of life and its ups and downs.

My family and classmates were the only ones who really knew me and what it was like to grow up in Hopewell, Kentucky, amid the upheavals of the fifties and the hostile sixties. These experiences would bind us together for life. Others would never understand. Like so many graduates, I was happy and sad at the same time.

Graduation is a marker in life, a ceremony that simultaneously defines an end and a beginning. Even at my young age, I knew that life is about renewal, and I sort of had a premonition that I would go through many renewals. The Class of 1965 had come of age, and I was a very proud part of it.

As I approached Mom, we smiled at each other with a hint of tears in our eyes. Mom handed me my diploma. At that instant,

I honored my class and its place in time and space. I shook her hand, flipped my tassel to the other side, and embraced my mom in a long hug.

Our hug froze time, and for a moment, we were free of all earthly challenges. As I backed away from her, I said, "Mom, what's next?"

ABOUT THE AUTHOR

David A. Bourbon was born in Lexington, Kentucky and earned his first two academic degrees at the University of Kentucky. After working in corporate America, he enrolled in a PhD program at The Ohio State University. Upon earning his doctorate, he joined the faculty at Duke University, and later taught at other top business schools, including the University of Warwick in the United Kingdom. Dr. Bourbon has taught undergraduates, MBAs, PhDs, and numerous executive programs.

After decades of authoring research articles, business cases, and five college textbooks, he was up for a new challenge—writing novels. His debut novel, *Romance in My Rambler*, is the first in the Class President Series (www.theclasspresidentseries.com). It is the story about a US baby boomer coming of age amid the upheavals of the 1950s and 1960s. He has been working on this novel and others, in bits and pieces, for thirty years.

Dr. Bourbon and his wife, Cindy, live in South Florida and enjoy writing, boating, beaches, golf, and sunshine. He is an avid sports fan, and if time permits, he reads astronomy books.

Printed in the United States
By Bookmasters